A Convenient Escape

CONVENIENT RISK SERIES, BOOK 3

SARA R. TURNQUIST

MOUNTAIN
SUMMIT PRESS

If you would like to stay up-to-date on this and other series from Sara and receive a free ebook, sign up for her newsletter:

https://saraturnquist.com/list

CHAPTER 1

The Inevitable

Why should it be so bright and sunny on the day of a funeral? It didn't seem right. As if the world rejoiced with the sad soul's passing. Would the ground be so accepting of his remains? The thought was morbid. Even for one of Lily's darker moments.

She pushed it to the side. Not even her estranged grandfather deserved such tidings. Where was her respect for the dead? A shiver shook her body despite the sun's warmth bearing down upon her.

A quick glance at her father yielded no more certainty than she had received these last several days. The man's relationship with his own father had been a mystery. Why had she never known her grandfather? What kind of man was he? Her uncle spoke of the man rather well. But her father's features betrayed his feelings beyond a shadow of doubt— somewhat of a blessing, as he would not utter one word on the subject. At least, not to her.

Perhaps he had spoken to Joseph. Wouldn't her brother have told her? They shared everything. Or so she thought. Peering to her other side, she spied Joe. Though he was three years her junior, he stood a solid foot taller. Not that she minded. He had become her confidant

1

and protector over these last few years when Ma's antics had...had become more difficult to bear.

She would have been lost without Joe. Somehow, he kept on smiling through it all. How did he do that?

He shot her a look. His gaze deepened and his hand covered hers.

She squeezed it.

A cough to the other side of Joe drew his attention.

Ma.

It became a coughing fit.

No. Not today.

Lily closed her eyes. *Dear Lord in heaven, not today.*

Joe released Lily's hand and drew Ma closer to his side as he pulled out his handkerchief. Perhaps no one would think any more on it. And Joe would keep her contained.

At least Lily could hope.

She chanced a glance at Pa.

He glared across his small family, as if daring any of them to step out of line and embarrass him. Tarnish the great image of Sheriff McAllen.

Lily shook, unable to control her body's reaction. She pulled her arms around herself and sniffled.

Pa's handkerchief appeared before her.

Without turning in his direction, she slid out a shaking hand to retrieve it.

How much longer must they remain here—a spectacle before the whole town? On display? Every movement, every sound scrutinized? It became more than her nerves could manage. A familiar unease pierced her beneath her ribs.

She tasted bile.

It would not happen. She would not let it.

Clenching her teeth, she swallowed against the pressure in her throat.

At last, the preacher finished speaking and stepped to the side.

What remained? The prayer? Had he prayed?

Not yet.

What was he waiting for?

Reverend Jones looked to them expectantly. To her.

There was something she was meant to do.

She sensed Pa's eyes boring into her.

God, if You have any mercy, enlighten me.

Joe laid a hand on her shoulder, rubbing his fingers there and pressing her forward.

Forward?

She stepped out from the line. Toward the grave.

Oh, yes. Her flower. She was to place it upon the coffin. Ma, too.

Glancing back over her shoulder, she reached for Ma's hand. Threading her trembling fingers through Ma's, she led the unsteady woman toward the pine box.

Ma's footfalls were not even. Lily prayed others wouldn't notice.

As they drew up to the coffin, Lily gulped. She had never been so close to a dead body. Nor had she ever wished to be.

Thankfully, the box had been closed and sealed. Not that she would have even recognized the man within had he been lain out as if in sleep. She had not known him in life.

It seemed wrong to playact this way—this pretense of sorrow, of grief. She forced her guilt to the side...as usual. And laid the rose upon the pine box's lid.

Ma followed suit.

Lily turned to step back into line, but Ma would not budge. Lily's stomach sank. They were so close.

If only she could beseech Joe. He would help her. But if she peered at him, everyone would see.

What was she to do?

Her whole body seemed to shake. She leaned closer to Ma. "It's time for us to step back," she whispered.

Ma continued to glare at the casket. Her eyes glazed, uncomprehending.

Lily closed her eyes and licked her lips. Then she tugged at her mother's arm again.

The woman would not move.

And then Lily was being pressed. Ma was pushing her.

Lily held tightly to her arm.

"No, Ma," she pled. "Not here."

Pa was behind them in a second. His arm around Ma, pulling her away from Lily.

But that didn't deter her from continuing to reach for her daughter, intent on inflicting some sort of harm.

Lily froze, aware that she had become the object of everyone's attention as Pa led Ma into the anonymity of the crowd.

But Joe's calming presence was there a moment later. He took her arm and led her back to their place.

Lily's aunt and cousins placed their flowers without incident. Then Reverend Jones stepped forward and spoke some closing words that Lily didn't hear. The pounding of her heartbeat in her ears was too loud.

Everyone around her bowed their heads. But Lily could not. Would not. She did not wish to speak to God on this or any other day.

Joe tugged at her sleeve. Had he noticed? But she refused to oblige him, continuing to stare straight ahead.

The prayer ended and the crowd dispersed.

Time to find Ma and Pa. Or was it?

Must they?

For nothing good awaited her there.

A handful of well-wishers approached her uncle and aunt, and all but ignored her and Joseph.

It stung, but she tried not to let it. There truly wasn't a relationship lost between her and the man buried this day.

As the churchyard emptied and the preacher said his personal farewells to the family, Joseph offered an arm to Lily.

She took it and let him lead her toward the small town streets. Would they seek out Pa? He had most likely taken Ma to the jail—the best and quickest place to get her out of view.

Lily did not wish to face either of them.

But Joseph was more the dutiful child than she.

As they walked, she tried not to slow their steps too noticeably. Still, she needed some extra moments to still her racing heart. How could it be so erratic?

But as they neared the main stretch, Joseph turned them toward the school.

Relief released some of the tension in her shoulders. And she fell into an easier pace with him.

Only then could she concentrate on his words.

He spoke of nothing of consequence—the weather, the happenings of the town. Benign topics that any passer-by would be able to overhear without concern.

As they neared the big tree beyond the school, he stopped. "Want to swing?"

She furrowed her brows. Swing? A woman her age didn't partake in such a girlish pastime.

"I'll push." He smiled.

She crossed her arms. "I don't know if that's entirely appropriate."

He laughed. "For a brother to push his sister?"

"For a grown woman to swing," she countered. Was he crazy?

Turning his head this way and that, he leaned toward her and lowered his voice. "Who's gonna know?"

She rolled her eyes.

"Come on, Lil. I know how much you used to love it." He grasped the rope on one side of the swing. "You know you want to."

He was right. She did. And there wasn't anyone around to wag their tongues about it. Maybe she could...

"All right." She threw up her hands.

His lips spread across his face. He maneuvered behind the wooden seat and held the ropes.

She turned and sat, clasping the ropes just above his handholds.

He lowered his hold and pulled the swing back. Then released it and sent her soaring.

And she left the earth. Everything...her troubles, her problems...all of it fell away, and it was just her. In the sky, the gentle breeze surrounding her as she moved back and forth in a steady rhythm.

She wasn't sure how long Joseph indulged her, but when she slowed, it was too soon. As he allowed her momentum to still, she was breathless from laughter.

"You don't smile enough." He held out a hand to help her up.

Grinning, she held onto the moment for every last sweet piece of joy it could give her. "I could say the same for you."

He ducked his head, looking to the ground.

"What?"

Shaking his head, he avoided her gaze.

"Joe." She pushed at his shoulder. "What are you hiding?" Though the mood was playful, dread crowded at the edge of her mind.

His smile fell. Things became more serious.

"Joseph?" What was wrong? Couldn't they share everything? Since they were young they'd often only had each other to lean on. What was this?

"It's probably time we head back." He tugged her hand onto his arm as he moved off in the direction they had come.

She pulled her hand from him. "Something's not right. Tell me."

He paused, looking at the ground and then at the horizon. Then at her. His one brow pressed down and the other lifted. Almost as if he were pained.

The trepidation from earlier returned. Her heartbeat thudded in her ears.

"I...um...took a job as a ranch hand at the Miller ranch."

The ground disappeared from beneath her. Or at least her knees wouldn't hold her anymore.

She gripped for his arms.

He steadied her.

They had always been there for one another. And now he was leaving her? To face them alone?

"What...?" The word sounded weak to her ears. Had it even been audible?

He eased her back onto the swing. And pushed a hand through his hair. "I'm sorry, Lil. I just...I can't do it anymore. I gotta get out and live my life."

Why couldn't she feel anything? Sad? Angry? Anything? All that existed was this numbness.

"I need you to understand that. Please, understand that."

"W-When will you go?" Somehow, she had made a full thought and formed a cogent question. Somehow.

"Monday." He let out a breath.

"Three days?" That wasn't much time. No time at all for her to get used to the idea. Much less prepare. Or...find a way out. No, that was impossible.

She was stuck in this nightmare.

And he was leaving her to face them...alone.

Dan Hayworth settled into a chair. He fought down a grumble that rose in his throat. Why had he been sent on this errand? It seemed much more suited to Slim. But Brandon decided it would be Dan. So, he had come to fetch the new ranch hand.

But he'd arrived earlier than expected. No one could begrudge him a cup of coffee in the café before collecting Joseph and his things.

Watching his hands clasped on the table, Dan almost missed the woman who stopped by.

Her skirt was the first thing he spotted; the floral pattern set against a tan background could not be described as interesting. But it had a gentle flow to it.

His gaze drifted to her face.

Lily.

What was she doing here? Why wasn't she at home, helping Joseph pack? Bidding him farewell?

He mentally kicked himself. Such was none of his business. It just always seemed that those two were close.

She pressed an accommodating smile onto her features, but he could tell it was put on. Her eyes did not reflect any such levity.

"What'll you have?" She brushed red-blonde hair out of her face. Some must have fallen out of her pinned up design. Most of the thickness had been gathered and secured off her neck.

But he remembered many years ago...back in their school days... when her tresses flowed free, only partly held back by a lone ribbon.

The movement of her hand drew him back to the present. She held her pencil just above her notepad. And with it, her focus.

Had she even looked at him? Did she ever?

For all the years they had known each other?

Or was he always just the carpenter's son? And now nothing more than a ranch hand himself?

As if that wasn't good enough. But it had been when she had pursued Cutie.

He fought the urge to cross his arms.

Averting his gaze, he looked off toward the door. "Coffee, please." His words were tight.

She sighed and lowered the notepad. "Coming right up." That same plastered-on smile touched her lips and she turned. Without so much as a glance.

Typical.

He shook his head. No more of those thoughts. They would not serve him.

A quick scan of the room left him much more relaxed. Only two others dined—a couple across the room by the window. It was past the breakfast hour and not quite time for lunch. He might not have long for his coffee before he would need to head out. If it wasn't here soon.

A scream pierced the air.

Dan was on his feet before he fully registered what was happening.

Where had it come from?

He jerked his head this way and that.

The kitchen.

A second later he found himself beside the stove.

Lily, pale, jerked at her skirt, the hem of which was drenched.

The floor was covered in dark liquid, and Mrs. Jackson righted a pot.

Had Lily upended it and spilled the hot brew on herself?

He grabbed for her hand and led her to a stool. Falling to a knee, he lifted the fabric away from her leg. Indeed, it was still rather warm to the touch.

Lily seethed through clenched teeth. Her hands formed fists that jerked between curling to her chest and grabbing at her leg.

Dan pushed at them. They were obstacles. He turned to Mrs. Jackson. "A cloth. As cold as you can make it."

The woman nodded and turned to fetch it.

He lifted Lily's skirt to examine her shins.

Lily pushed out a breath but didn't fight.

Catching her features, he sought her eyes. But they wouldn't find his. Sealed. Clenched shut. A futile effort to block her tears?

"I need to get these stockings off. We must cool the skin." He tugged at the laces of her boots.

Shifting his focus back to his work, he eased off her boots and then her stockings.

Her bared skin was red and angry but not damaged.

He breathed out a sigh, and his shoulders relaxed.

Looking up toward her features again, he once more sought her eyes. "Nothing permanent."

She opened her lids, tentatively, at last meeting his gaze. "Truly?"

Her voice seemed so small. A pang caught in his chest at the stirring in her green eyes.

He tipped his head forward, a small movement.

It must have assured her, for she released her tight fists.

Mrs. Jackson returned with the dripping cloth.

Dan took it, pressing it first to one shin and then to the other.

Lily's eyes shut again; her features twisted. From pain? Or more from discomfort? He hoped the latter.

Some moments of silence passed.

"Shall I fetch the doctor?" Mrs. Jackson interjected.

"I don't think he will be needed." Dan glance at her, removing the cloth and indicating the skin which had started returning to its normal color. "There does not appear to be any deeper injury."

Mrs. Jackson nodded.

He looked to Lily again.

Her eyes were no longer shut, but she stared at him. A faint pink colored her cheeks.

"Are you feeling all right?" Dan furrowed his brows. Perhaps they should send for the doctor.

"Yes. It's just that…" Her voice trailed as her regard shifted from Mrs. Jackson to Dan's hands and back.

Only then did he realize how unseemly this was—so much of her legs bared, and he…

"Oh." Rising, he then handed the cloth to Mrs. Jackson. "My apologies. I didn't mean to...that is, I only..."

"It's all right, Dan." Lily dropped her skirt over her legs and ankles.

He peered at her. Her lips had lifted at the corners. This time, the smile brightened her eyes as well.

"I...thank you for your quick assistance."

"Of course." Everything about him felt shaken. His insides seemed ready to crawl out of his skin.

He offered a nod to the two women and turned to step out of the kitchen. Then swung back around. "I...um...could see you home if you'd like. I happen to be headed that way."

Lily's eyebrows rose. "Oh?"

He tilted his head. "Yes, ma'am."

She looked at Mrs. Jackson.

"Please, go home. Rest." Mrs. Jackson offered her a kind smile. "You won't do me any good like this."

Lily lowered her features. Then she peered up at Dan through long, dark lashes. Did she know how endearing that was?

"If I can have a moment to gather myself, I'd like that."

Dan nodded. And a moment later, he still stood there, staring. He flinched at the awkwardness and sidestepped out of the kitchen.

He stepped to his table and settled back into his seat, praying no one paid any mind to his features, which had likely reddened. As he sat and considered the exchange, he realized that she had called him by name.

The ride to her family's humble home passed without much conversation. Even though Lily's father often boasted she could engage a fence post.

But this was different. Somehow.

Daniel Hayworth was not a man whose company she had frequented. Nor, necessarily, avoided. He'd always seemed quiet. Always thoughtful. And that intimidated her.

Even now, he stared after the horse, his attention rapt on its movement. But what went on in his mind? Where were his thoughts?

She fared better with men she was more accustomed to. Like Cutie. Men whose eyes had been fixed on her. Whose thoughts had been easier to read. Their intentions laid bare.

Only...

Things had not worked out with Cutie as she'd hoped.

Dan shifted beside her, pulling the reins and slowing the horse.

She looked up. The smallish house stood before them. Her features warmed despite her determined lack of consideration for Dan.

When she glanced over, he was halfway out of the cart.

What? Why?

He came around and lifted his arms to her.

What could she do? She swallowed.

Perhaps he only meant to be a gentleman. So, she placed her hands on his shoulders and let him help her down. But she would not meet his eyes. Though that found her staring at his rather broad chest.

Now with her feet firm on the earth, they stood in silence.

Her mouth was dry all of a sudden.

Say something. She commanded her tongue. "I thank you. For seeing me home." It was weak. But it was something.

She dipped her head and turned, stepping out of his space. In a few moments she would be inside the house and away from this strange encounter.

The dirt crunched behind her.

Was he following her? She dared not look.

Why would he? Did he think she was incapable of walking to her own door without him? A bit chivalrous? Or perhaps a bit presumptuous?

As she approached the door, she spun, laying a hand to the latch. "Thank you, again. I appreciate your quick assistance and your care in ferrying me home." She put more firmness in her tone.

He nodded but remained where he was.

What was he thinking? Was he so bold?

She made a half-way decent curtsy and opened the door, prepared to escape within. As she closed it behind herself, grateful for the barrier, he reached forth and halted the door's progress inches short of the frame.

Then she found his eyes. Surely, he would not think to take advantage of her here. Her brother and her mother were both within. All she had to do was call out.

He seemed determined. Did he think her alone?

"Might I come in?" He stepped closer, now towering over her, his body closer than it needed to be.

Her heart thudded. She could hear the pounding in her ears. As much as she told herself to cry out for Joseph, her mouth would not obey. Why? Did she fear Dan would hurt her? Or was it something else? Something about the sensations threading through her at his proximity? Something she didn't dislike.

So, she remained, neither giving more room for the door's opening nor pressing for its closing.

"Lily?" a voice called from within.

Thank goodness! Joseph would rescue her. She let out a breath. Her fingers ached from holding the door so tightly.

Dan tried to look around her. Was he nervous? Discouraged? She couldn't discern.

But she couldn't tear her eyes away from him.

"Lily, is that you?" Joseph's voice neared. He must have entered the small great room behind her. "Why are you home so earl...?"

She jerked around when his question trailed.

His eyes had cut to the door. And set on the man just outside.

There. Now all would be well. Her body slackened. While she gripped the door to maintain her balance, she forced herself to keep her gaze on Joseph.

"Dan! Good to see you. Won't you come in?"

What? Lily shook her head. She must have misheard.

Joseph covered the space between them in a second and laid a hand on her shoulder. "Lily, you know Dan."

Lily furrowed her brows. This didn't make sense.

Putting a hand over hers on the latch, Joseph pulled the door open.

Dan arched a brow at Lily before turning his attention to Joseph. "I hope I'm not too early."

"Not at all." Joseph smiled. "I'm ready as I'll ever be."

Dan nodded.

What was happening here? Lily couldn't decide. Her brain hurt.

"Shall we?" Dan gave Lily a sideways glance but turned his focus to Joseph.

"I'll get my things." Joe turned.

He would not leave her alone with Dan, would he? She couldn't... wouldn't be alone with him.

"Can I help?" Dan stepped forward.

Lily held up a hand. "I would like to speak to my brother. Alone."

Joseph quirked a brow. Then looked to Dan and said, "We'll just be a moment."

Lily's face burned. She grabbed Joseph's sleeve and led him to the back hall.

"My things are in the barn," Joseph protested. "Why are we—?"

Pinning him with a glare, she halted his question.

He followed her into the back partitioned off area that served as her room, small as it was.

Once the blanket dropped behind Joseph, she spun on him. "What is going on here?" She pressed the words out.

Joe's eyes widened. Was her tone so harsh? "W-w-what do you mean?"

"Why is Dan here? In our home?"

Joseph looked at the floor for a few seconds before meeting her eyes again. "He...ah...has come to take me to the Miller ranch."

Everything fell into place at once. And Lily's face heated several more degrees. She pressed her hands to her cheeks. How could she not have realized?

That's why Dan said he was headed this way. It was *he* who was coming to collect Joseph. *He* worked at the Miller ranch.

"Did you..." Joseph seemed to choose his words carefully. "Did you not remember?" It was impossible to miss the hurt in his eyes.

Or the pricking behind her own. "No. I knew it was today. I just... didn't know Dan would... that he ended up at the Miller ranch."

Joseph's brows met. "Didn't know? He's been there for several years."

She waved a hand between them. "Let's not quarrel over that."

He nodded, letting out a breath.

Silence fell between them.

"Why didn't you say anything before you left for work?" Joseph's voice was quiet.

Lily crossed her arms over her midsection, raising a hand to pinch the bridge of her nose. "I don't know."

Joseph mirrored her stance, only he seemed to be hugging himself. "I see."

What did that mean? She jerked her head up, meeting his glare with her own. Her features were hard and set, but that didn't keep her tears from falling. "See what?"

"This doesn't have to be so difficult, Lil." His gaze had softened.

"That's easy for you to say. You're the one who is leaving." She wiped at her face. Stupid, stubborn tears.

Joseph's eyes locked on hers. "But I'm not leaving you. I'm always there for you."

She shifted her focus to the ceiling. He might speak such fine words, but they were hollow. How could he help her the next time Ma went on a rant and...

There was no point thinking on it now. He was leaving, and that was that.

"Please, just go." Her voice shook.

"Don't make it be like this." Joseph stepped closer to her.

She moved away. "Just go," she pushed out through clenched teeth.

Joseph dropped his hand and slinked out of the space, pausing as he held up the blanket partition. "But I *do* care."

The quilt fell into place, and he was gone.

Dan pushed back from the dining table, nodding at Cook as she took his breakfast plate.

"That was fantastic," Joseph announced, patting his stomach. "I'll have to be careful. I don't want to get thick."

"Oh, shoo." Cook's cheeks tinted.

Dan wanted to roll his eyes.

"We'll make sure to work you hard enough." Brandon Miller offered the young man a smile as he raised his coffee cup.

Brandon's wife laid a hand on his shoulder as she stood and relieved him of his plate.

She tilted, slightly off balance with her growing midsection. How much longer would it be before the ranch was graced with another little one?

Brandon gripped her arm as she righted herself. The look that passed between them was for them alone.

But Dan couldn't turn away. The ache filling his chest deepened more every day. When had it started? When Brandon and Amanda found each other? When Cutie and Mariena married? The happiness surrounding him seemed a bit too much. It wasn't meant for everyone, though.

"What's the plan for today?" Joseph sought Brandon's attention.

Was he so eager?

As Dan's regard fell to him, he saw just that—Joseph was quite jittery with nervous energy. His legs bounced as he ran his hands over his knees.

That had to stop.

Brandon cut his glance from Amanda to Joseph. He paused, thoughtful, as if caught off-guard by the question. Had he not considered what would happen with the young man that day?

The boss's eyes met Dan's then landed back on Joseph. "It'd be best if you got a proper introduction to the place."

Joseph nodded, still shifting his limbs as if he needed to relieve himself.

Dan took a swig of his coffee, letting the warm brew soothe him and take his mind off the man several years his junior. He did not envy Brandon's task, playing guide to the newcomer.

"But I thought we had to—" Slim started.

Brandon cut him off with a hand held up. "We do. And we will."

Slim's brows furrowed. What had they been tasked with? Oh, yes, the calves. Branding day. The boss preferred to be a part of that. Would Brandon delay it in order to show Joseph around?

"I thought Dan would be able to take care of orienting Joseph to the ranch." Brandon glanced at Dan once more.

Dan swallowed hard. That was the only thing keeping him from spitting the coffee out.

Him? Spend the day with Joseph?

The young man beamed at him.

Dan offered what felt like a crooked smile.

"When do we go?" Were Joseph's hands on his knees the only thing holding him down?

Glancing once more at Brandon, Dan saw what could only be described as 'glee' in the man's eyes. But he couldn't be sure. No matter. "I'm ready when you are."

Perhaps the sooner they started, the quicker it would be over.

Joseph jumped up so fast his chair knocked into the wall.

All the men stared at him.

He offered a sheepish grin. "Sorry. I...get a little excited sometimes."

"You don't say." Slim shot Dan a look.

A look that made Dan want to punch him in the face.

"It's all right," Dan said as he rose, eyeing Slim. "We understand. Happens to the best of us. Slim here about lost his breakfast when we heard the General Store was carrying scented soap."

"I...what?" Slim thrust out.

Brandon let out a laugh.

Dan walked to the door, not bothering to look back. He left the voices of his fellow ranchers behind him as he stepped onto the porch.

Joseph joined him moments later, adjusting his hat. "Where do we start?"

"I think a ride around the property."

Dan didn't wait for a response but led Joseph to the barn where they went about saddling a couple of mares.

Slim and Brandon approached the stalls soon after, as Dan urged his steed to move out. He was sure he didn't imagine the scowl on Slim's face though.

It did give him a brief moment of pleasure before he pushed the horse into a trot. Hoofbeats behind assured him that Joseph had accomplished the same.

Dan led him around the perimeter of Brandon's land. It took them farther away from the homestead and barn than he usually gave credit.

The grazing area was on the bigger portion of the land, but did not encompass the whole of it.

Before mid-morning, they stopped by Uncle Owen's favorite fishing spot to water the horses.

Dan rubbed his horse's neck and wished he could just enjoy the quiet of this peaceful place. But that was not possible. Just had been the case everywhere they went today, Joseph would want to talk...and ask questions. Too bad it was Dan's job to answer.

Perhaps if Dan started off, he could forego a lot of the mindless questions. He turned toward his pupil and watched as Joseph brought his horse nearer to Dan's.

The younger man seemed to consider something beyond the stream. Dan could almost see the questions forming.

Sure enough, Joseph opened his mouth.

Dan broke in, "This is the farthest south the Miller land runs. And this stream is one of Uncle Owen's favorite spots."

Joseph nodded. Then opened his mouth again.

But Dan continued, "We don't bring the cattle this far. We just don't need to. Perhaps one day the herd will be so large. But that wouldn't be for some time."

Again, Joseph seemed to consider his words, peer off into the distance. And then open his mouth.

"It is a fine prospect though," Dan managed to jump in again. "And a great fishin' spot."

Joseph's forehead creased. Was he frustrated? Perhaps Dan did him a disservice. So, he quieted, focusing on his mare grazing.

Joseph shifted his feet. All was silent for a few moments. Maybe Joseph's questions had been answered. Dan sighed.

"What do you suppose that is?" Joseph blurted out, pointing into the distance.

There, among the shrubs, lay a colorfully clothed lump. Dan narrowed his eyes to get a better look. "I think someone dropped a bedroll."

Joseph pointed to the sky. "Then why are those vultures so interested?"

Silence.

Dan shifted his focus. Joseph spoke true—buzzards circled above. Most often, Dan would dismiss it as some sort of animal. But no wild creature would wear cloth of such vibrancy.

"Let's check it out." Dan wasn't sure about taking Joseph into an uncertain situation, but he didn't want to risk leaving him back here alone either.

"Shall we tie up the horses?"

"No." Dan pressed out firmly. Would he be able communicate the need for strict obedience? "We keep them with us."

Moving toward what appeared to be nothing more than a blanket dropped beside the wilderness shrubbery, Dan remained cautious. And, as they neared, the shape belied that something...most likely a person, lay underneath.

Without a second thought, Dan drew his revolver and handed his horse's reins to Joseph. He slowed his steps all the more while indicating for Joseph to get behind him. They continued to close in.

Even standing over the intruder, all they could see beyond the blanket was a spill of dark hair and shoed feet. Dan guessed by the proportions that the person could not be an adult. Why would an adolescent—a child—be out here in the desert alone?

Dan reached for the edge of the blanket-like covering. Gripping it, he jerked the cloth off.

And uncovered an Indian brave—no more than ten years old. By the war markings on his face, he was Apache.

CHAPTER 2

The Shattering

Dan jerked back and leveled his revolver at the Apache brave. "Stand back."

The scuffle of hooves on the hard dirt behind was the only response.

His eyes did not shift from the motionless form for any reason. He dared not. Not for even a moment.

Bringing his other hand around to steady the gun, he cocked the hammer. Best be ready to fire. It could be a trick.

"What are you doing?" Joseph called, louder than he should. If the brave only slept, he would wake the boy, stir him to action.

"Quiet," Dan hissed.

Joseph appeared at Dan's elbow. "You're not going to shoot this... this child, are you?"

Dan continued to glare at the dark hair splayed on the ground. Joseph didn't understand. How could he? He hadn't lived out here on the range. Hadn't seen what these natives could do. *Had* done. To Mariena.

"You aren't serious." Joseph's protests continued.

"Get behind me," Dan ground out, not wavering, nor removing his steely gaze from the lax body. The Apache were a warring nation. He must not take any chances.

Joseph jumped in front of him, the muzzle of Dan's gun now pointed at his chest. "I won't."

"You don't know what you are doing." Dan side stepped, trying to move around Joseph.

The younger man shifted to the right as well, continuing to insert himself between Dan's weapon and the Apache youth.

"You don't need to do this. The boy is unarmed. He's near death, if not dead already. He needs our help, not our animosity."

Dan had no more time for Joseph's pleas. "I'm going to tell you one more time, step away."

Joseph's eyes hardened. He did back away, but only to spread his body in front of the limp form.

Gritting his teeth, Dan burned. Why wouldn't the younger man just listen to him? How could he make Joseph understand?

But as long as the man barred his efforts, Dan was stymied. He released his gun's hammer and lowered it. This was hopeless.

A flash of movement. And a yelp.

Joseph cried out.

His eyes widened.

He fell forward.

A knife protruded from his back.

The brave had come to life.

And taken Joseph's.

Lily burst through the front door and into the field beyond. Her vision blurred with unshed tears. Hot. Overflowing.

Why?

Would this nightmare ever end? The day Joseph moved out had left her empty. It seemed the cabin had shrunk by half. There was no room. Nowhere to go.

Ma's rants had become more difficult to avoid. And, the worst of it...she no longer had a buffer to soften the heaviest blows. No one to calm the storm.

And no one to fall on when everything came down around her.

Her legs continued to move, to where she didn't know. Or care.

How many times? How many more?

A part of her wanted to stay. To ensure Ma wouldn't hurt herself. But the bigger piece of her didn't care. Not anymore.

For her own wounds cried out for tending. Those within. And those on her body. How could anyone endure such and press on? How much longer could she?

The ground became more uneven. She wiped a hand across her eyes. Her vision cleared...for a few moments...before more tears clouded her way.

What did it matter? If she should stumble and fall? One more wound added to the others. A lifetime of pain. And so, she pressed on.

The grass beneath her feet crunched as if she offended. Did anything in this world invite her existence? Perhaps not.

She stopped. Her chest heaved and her legs tired. Deflating, she fell to her knees and her body crumpled forward.

And found that no more tears were forthcoming. Only this raw sadness. She had become hollow. And heavy. Weak. Nothing more left.

She knew this place well.

Why couldn't she be more? Be stronger? Or at least less needy?

The cavernous ache in her chest had to be filled. Somehow. She would surely cease to exist if not. How had she not already crumbled and lost all that remained? What would supply this gaping pit, she did not know. Perhaps someone to be strong for her? To rescue her? To take her away from this?

But who? How?

She had made herself more than available to potential suiters. Well, to the eligible men in the town.

Had such hopes for some...especially Cutie. But every time...she had been discarded, tossed aside.

What was wrong with her? Was there something about her? Something men did not wish to saddle themselves to? What?

A lump in her throat pressed upward. Perhaps it would choke her and relieve her of this misery. At least then she might escape this meager existence.

The wind whipped around her. It was pleasant. She lifted her face and let it dry every trace of her tears. At some point she would have to return to the house and see to Ma. Would she be roving about, mindlessly ranting, or passed out somewhere?

With any luck, the woman would have forgotten whatever angered her. And they could start the cycle all over again.

Lily released a breath.

All over again.

As if she had a choice.

Dan's chest had been emptied of all but this open wound. Though by now he'd numbed to some extent. What was this?

That moment...the moment scarred forever into his mind...repeated every time he closed his eyes. Though the movements of the Apache brave, the shock in Joseph's eyes, the way he fell...all of it...had happened as if time slowed—a waking nightmare. Would it end? Did he deserve for it to?

"Dan?"

He turned toward Brandon. The man's eyes had a depth to them, but a softness as well.

"Yes, boss?" Dan managed, though his voice was weaker than he'd like.

"You all right?" Brandon's words were gentle and spoken with a hint of firmness. How many times had his boss insisted he'd done nothing wrong? Even insisted Dan had done everything he should have in the situation?

It didn't matter. Joseph had trusted Dan. And he was in control. He should have...

Brandon cleared his throat.

"Yes, sir," Dan pushed out on a breath.

Brandon raised a brow but slightly.

Why did it matter if the man believed him? This was *his* weight to bear...and his alone. Brandon couldn't understand that.

And what else should he be thinking or feeling as they made their way to the McAllens' home? With such tidings as these.

Dan looked opposite Brandon at the Arizona landscape, but it was the faces of the McAllen family that filled his vision—the sheriff...his wife...and...Lily.

How would Lily receive the news?

A sickness filled Dan's gut. Those two siblings had always been close. Something Dan couldn't understand. His brother and sister were so much older. Neither cared much for a baby brother tagging along.

Lily and Joseph's relationship seemed more like a friendship. Perhaps like Dan's friendship with Cutie. Or Slim. Dan closed his eyes and tried to imagine how he'd react if something happened to one of them. All the breath seemed to rush from him. And he struggled to maintain some sense of calm.

Even so, it still couldn't be the same. Lily and Joseph had been with each other since they were small. Could she even remember a time without her brother?

Would it be for her like it was for him when his Ma...?

Why had Dan volunteered to do this with Brandon?

Because it was his duty. It was the right thing. He had been there when it happened, and he was responsible. No matter what Brandon said.

The horses slowed.

Dan turned.

Brandon pulled on the reins.

Shifting his focus to their surroundings, Dan found himself staring at the McAllen cabin. Had it only been a day ago that he had halted this wagon at this very spot? The day he collected Joseph.

A dagger of fresh pain sliced at his heart. It wasn't right. It just wasn't.

He sensed Brandon's gaze. "You ready?"

Though he wasn't, he nodded.

Brandon dropped down his side of the wagon.

Dan did the same.

They walked toward the front door. The rough, well-worn wood soon provided the only barrier between them and the family.

Brandon afforded Dan one more brief glance.

But Dan refused to look his way. He noted the sympathetic gesture in his periphery. And for the millionth time, he regretted his boss's forgiving attitude.

Dan drew in a deep breath as Brandon raised his hand and knocked. Deep down, he wanted to bolt. The urge overwhelmed him. But he suppressed it.

This was best. It was right. He deserved this.

The door creaked and Sheriff McAllen appeared on the other side. Recognition crossed his features and he opened his mouth.

"Good afternoon, Mr. Miller, Mr. Hayworth. What can I do for you boys?" McAllen stepped outside and closed the door behind himself.

Dan looked to Brandon, hoping his boss would speak. As much as he wished to take the lead, he couldn't utter a sound.

Brandon slid his hat off.

Dan did likewise.

"Sheriff, may we come in?" Brandon's simple request was gentle.

McAllen's brows furrowed. "My wife is…not feeling well. I don't think that's a good idea."

Brandon licked his lips. "Your daughter, Lily, is she at home?"

McAllen's features hardened and he crossed his arms. "If you must know, Mr. Miller. I haven't seen my daughter since I returned home. I found my wife unwell, in a rather…difficult state, and my daughter disappeared."

Lily? Missing? An uneasiness swept through Dan. He met McAllen's gaze. The man seemed less bothered with her well-being than Dan would have thought.

"Have you sent deputies looking for her?" Brandon's tone deepened.

"Gentlemen," McAllen said, glancing between them as he shuffled his feet. "I appreciate your concern. But this is not unlike Lily. She is prone to wandering off. She is probably on the property somewhere, just daydreaming."

"And you are certain she is safe?" Dan interjected.

McAllen peered at him, his gaze sharpened. "I assure you, Mr. Hayworth, if I had any inkling that my daughter was in danger, I would go looking for her myself." McAllen's tone eased. "As I said, she does this often."

He spoke the last sentence as if Lily were nothing more than a nuisance to him. It was rather curious to Dan. Why would she roam about? With her mother so unwell?

Still, it wasn't altogether unbelievable. After all, hadn't he himself been delayed the night Ma's sickness overtook her? Though he *knew* she was very ill. So very ill...

Brandon ran fingers across the rim of his hat. "Sheriff, we have come with news. It may be best if we found a place to sit."

McAllen's eyes widened. Did he only then consider that Joseph was not with them? "What do you mean? News?" His voice, though level, had a tremble underneath.

"As I said." Brandon's tone was firm. "I think it's best we sit and talk." He stepped forward.

McAllen shot a hand out. "Where is my son?" The shake in his voice had vanished, replaced by raw grit.

Brandon sighed. "We need to speak about this when—"

McAllen's face paled. "Tell me. Tell me now." The sheriff put his hands on Brandon's arms.

Dan's insides bottomed out. He had no words. An image of his Pa when the doctor told them there was nothing more to be done flashed before his eyes. Sadness filled him, but that old anger crept in, just under the surface.

Brandon gripped McAllen's forearms. "Sheriff, I need you to sit."

The man shook. "He's dead, isn't he? I know it. My son is dead." McAllen's head dropped and his body slackened.

Brandon held him up. His gaze cut to Dan, and he jerked his head toward the door.

Dan pushed the latch and held the door open as Brandon ushered the sheriff inside. But when Dan moved to follow, Brandon shook his head.

"Go find Lily. She should be here." Brandon then turned his attention back to the sheriff.

If it were possible, the weight in Dan's stomach sank even farther. But he determined he would do it. He deserved this chore. After all.

Lily rubbed a stone between her fingers. What a find. It sparkled and shone in the blazing sunlight—mesmerizing. And the brilliant brightness of the day lightened her spirit, if only just.

As if there were still hope within. After so much turmoil and heartache.

She drew the stone closer to her face. What made it glitter so? Something within the rock, inherent in its makeup? Or were there tiny pieces, shards of shimmering particles tucked into the crevices?

A sigh escaped. She had returned to a calmer place. A more settled place within herself. Perhaps now she could return...withstand the storm. Wrapping her hand around the stone, which seemed cooler than it should, she shifted her legs.

The stream, which should hardly be called that—for it was not much more than an arm's width of water trickling through the area, beckoned her. Its movement, slow as it was, called to her. Its coolness called to her. What adventure would it know?

Could she seep into the water and ride its lazy current away from this place? She closed her eyes and imagined the sweeping journey into the wilds of the wilderness, unafraid, unassuming.

Coolness fell over her back.

She opened her eyes. Had her daydream become more?

A shadow had fallen over her.

Jerking around, she pulled away from the intruder.

Dan's tall frame stood there.

Dan? What was he doing here? Coincidence? Or something a bit disconcerting?

She stumbled as she rose. "D-Dan?"

He did not move any closer. As she continued to watch him, she relaxed, more certain he had no thought to harm her.

His features remained stoic. Thoughtful as ever. Did he know how to be lighthearted and fun? He was not at all like Cutie.

Maybe that wasn't a bad thing. After all, Cutie hadn't followed through on his intentions to...

"I came to take you home." Dan stretched a hand in the direction of the path.

Her brows furrowed as she passed in front of him. "Why would my parents send you?"

He hesitated. "Just looking out for you, I guess."

That didn't seem right. Her parents worried after her? There must be some other reason. Why would he even be at the house? Unless...

She spun. "Did you bring Joseph for a visit?" Her heart filled and she quickened her step. How she longed to see her brother!

Turning, she became curious why Dan remained where he stood. He looked up, meeting her eyes. And he swallowed, something indistinguishable passing over his countenance.

"What is it?" She paused. Several paces lay between them. Not so much she couldn't catch the sadness in his eyes as he watched her.

Something was wrong. Terribly wrong.

She couldn't breathe for a moment. Her lungs wouldn't work, or her body wouldn't pull in the air. It was an eternity before, desperate, she finally drew in a ragged breath. "W-where...is my brother, Dan?"

He looked away. Would he deny her the truth? Refuse to speak the words?

Her hand trembled as it came to her chest. And her heart clenched, a vise squeezing it even as it beat furiously. How was that possible?

"It's...ah...probably best we wait until we return to—"

Her eyes pinned him. He *would* tell her. She would have it be so.

Stretching her legs, she rushed toward him. "Tell me," she screamed as tears pricked her eyes. "Tell me, you coward." She slammed her fists against Dan's chest.

He didn't move as she worked out her anger on him. Was he so unmoved by her pain?

"He's dead, isn't he?" Tears poured down her face as she thrust her hands against his chest again and again. "Why? How could you? I don't believe you! It's not possible."

Hands came to her elbows, lightly touching her.

"He's my brother. Don't you understand?" The words poured from her as she emptied of everything. "My brother!"

The warmth of the hands at her elbows moved to her arms. She wanted to shake him off but couldn't.

"Joseph," she wailed.

"Joseph," she cried for her sibling, her confidant, her best friend. But she knew he would not come. No matter how she railed against the truth, it would not change.

She fell against Dan's solid form, weeping.

His arms came around her back, enclosing her. Was he the only thing holding her upright?

"It's not fair," she whimpered. "It should have been me."

Dan's hand pressed the back of her head gently. "No." His words were broken. "It should have been me."

Why would he say such a thing? It didn't matter. Her world had been shattered. What would become of the pieces?

CHAPTER 3

The Problem

Heartbroken. The pieces of Lily's life lay crumbled about her. And men waited to bury them with her brother's body.

Her father had taken Ma away. Not that it mattered. Did Ma even notice? She was in a rare way today. They all were... hurting in their own way. But not together. And why would they? They never were.

Lily stood over the casket. The sky, overcast and gloomy, pervaded the scene with an eerie tone. Now this was more suited to a funeral. Much more.

Would she have accepted anything less? If the earth had welcomed this loss as it had that of her grandfather? No. That would not have been right.

At least, in this, she could respect God's compassion—a day that mourned her brother's passing. Marked it with a shroud of foreboding.

For everything in Lily's future had become as uncertain as her ability to remove herself from this place.

Had everyone else gone? She could not make herself turn and look. Instead, hunched over, she wished to throw herself into the hole dug for Joseph. Perhaps that would be a suitable end for her, too. For all that anyone cared, it might as well be.

Voices, male, exchanged words nearby. One was certainly the reverend's, the other was deeper. And more difficult to distinguish in its softness.

Still, she refused to give it credence. What did they care? Did she upset their timetable? She cared not...she would remain with her brother as long as possible.

Reaching a hand forth, she rubbed her gloved fingers along the pine. Why couldn't she have seen his face? Just once more?

Would it have been a salve to her heart? Or created a deeper wound? Seeing him still in death. But she longed for one last chance to glimpse her brother on this earth. If only she could pull off the lid. But it was not possible. For the casket had been sealed with nail and hammer.

Tears stung her eyes once more. Everything. Yes, everything had been taken from her. And she had not one piece of life left to hold to. What did it matter what became of her?

There was no life worth living.

She sensed more than saw movement off to the side. Someone stepped near. Who would dare...?

Whomever it was stood in silence for a handful of moments.

Lily held her breath. What did this figure want with her? Was this person sent to usher her away?

"Lily..."

The single word, spoken from that deeper male voice, was nearly her undoing. Her name came forth with tenderness and regret. Did someone—did he—truly have such a care? Or was it put on?

She wiped at her tears. Not that it staunched those forthcoming.

The man stepped closer. "Lily, I'm sorry, but the reverend says it's time." His words hitched. Did he care for her pain? Or was it evidence of his own?

He had spoken enough words to now give away his identity—Dan. She had witnessed so little interaction between her brother and Dan. Did he have such consideration?

Another step toward her and Dan stood an arm's length away. Would he remove her if she did not comply?

"I..." she started, preparing for him to lead her away. But her vision blurred at the thought of leaving her brother...forever. And the emptiness in her hollowed-out chest ached anew. "I can't."

He released a deep sigh.

She closed her eyes. Yes, he must have been charged with removing her. No matter what. Did he now simply decide how he must go about it?

Dan shifted to stand beside her, shoulder to shoulder, facing the pine box encasing Joseph. "Then I'll be here, too."

She looked up at him. His regard did not move from the casket, but a few muscles worked along his firm, square jawline. For whatever reason, he must care.

That offered a glimmer of hope. Perhaps where she should not. Still, she could not help but think...might there be someone who understood? Who may relate to her pain? Or at the very least try?

A soothing warmth as gentle as a loving touch fell around her heart, granting her a peace she thought long gone. She had the urge to set a hand on his arm, his shoulder, his elbow...something. But it didn't seem right. This place, this time was too solemn.

She turned back to the light-colored wooden box. How long could they tarry before the reverend intervened again?

Somehow, she knew Dan would not tolerate further intrusion. He would permit her this time, this moment for as long as she needed it.

For that, she was grateful.

And she shifted her mind and features toward the earth prepared for her brother and wept once more.

Dan reined in his horse as the small homestead came into view. His emotions were too many and too great within him to discern anything with clarity. Too many memories, too many emotions...

Lily had remained silent as they rode from town. What else could he expect? They had laid her brother to his eternal rest today. Did she know more about the events surrounding Joseph's death beyond what Brandon told?

Brandon had been the one to share the tale with the family. The man had been generous and vague about Dan's role. Though the sheriff did question Dan separately.

But did Lily know about Dan? About the true part Dan played in Joseph's final moments? If she did, he was surprised how calm and trusting she was with him.

He wouldn't blame her if she refused to be in his presence again. Much less accept a ride home from him. But she had been quite amiable.

She must not know.

"Dan," she said into the silence, interrupting his thoughts.

He turned toward her.

"I...thank you...for your help today. For letting me...take my time."

He nodded, looking at the wooden boards of the wagon beneath his feet. Any decent person would tell her what truly happened. But he just couldn't make himself. Her wounds were too fresh.

"It seems that friends are something I'm rather...short on right now." Her voice broke.

A pang shot through his chest at her sorrow. Lily? Short on friends? She had always been surrounded by friends in their schooldays. Always so many to adore her and want to be like her.

But where were they today? What had happened to them over the last few years? Had he been too absorbed in his own troubles to notice?

Her hand shook as she raised it to wipe away a tear.

He then realized he was staring at her.

When she met his gaze again, she had a question in her eyes. But what was it? What did she want from him? A gesture, a sign of friendship? Of care?

He wanted to make such a gesture. So much. Had wanted to. But what was appropriate?

Without further thought, he reached for her trembling fingers still in her lap and covered them with his larger hand.

She flipped her hand over and intertwined their fingers.

Why did that simple movement warm his core? It shouldn't. This was Joseph's *sister*. And they had just come from burying his body. This was not where his mind should be.

But as much as he fought against his feelings, he could not help the overwhelming desire to protect her washing over him. She was so delicate and small in this harsh world. Didn't she need someone to look after her?

That had been Joseph's job, and he was gone. Someone needed to step in and watch over her.

She leaned into Dan's arm, her head on his shoulder. "I just don't know what to do, you know?"

Dan turned his face toward hers, his lips nearly brushing her forehead.

"I can't believe he's gone. Really gone." Her voice cracked into a whimper.

More tears would come.

What did she need? What did *he* want when faced with death?

Consolation.

Dan slid an arm around her. Now she was drawn to his chest. And he embraced her from the side.

As much as she shook, she soon settled into his arms. Did she find some measure of comfort there? In the arms of the man responsible for her brother's death?

He closed his eyes. This wasn't right. But could he take away what peace she found there because of his selfish desire to share the truth?

No, he would be strong and let her pull from his strength. For now.

The truth would come later.

Dan glanced at the house. How might they appear to her father? It was not appropriate for him to be embracing a woman who was not his sister or his betrothed. Or for him to find such enjoyment having her in his arms.

As he shifted his focus back to her, he saw a curtain move. Had someone been watching?

Though he was loathed to do so, he pulled back from Lily. "Let me get you inside. It'll be dark soon."

Her wide green eyes gazed up at him. "Will you be safe going home?"

He couldn't help but smile. Was she so concerned after his well-being? "Yes, but I'd best not tarry."

Hopping down from the cart, he then walked to her side and

assisted her from the high seat. Was it his imagination or did her hands linger on his forearms longer than necessary?

When she released her touch, he led her to the door. But as he raised a hand to knock, she held up a hand.

"Ma is probably sleeping. I don't want to wake her."

Dan nodded.

"I'll just slip inside." Her gaze met his.

He didn't want her to face her father's ire if the sheriff was upset by their embrace. Neither did Dan wish to cause further disruption without cause.

"You are sure?" He furrowed his brows.

She nodded. "Thank you. For all you have done today." Rising on her toes, she pressed her lips to the side of his face.

Then she worked the latch and slipped inside with a long glance back in his direction.

His heart beat faster at the brief contact. And he watched her, eyes unmoving from her features, until she disappeared.

Impossible. How could he allow such to affect him on such a day as today? A day of mourning? How would he atone for his sin? Certainly not by doubling it!

What was happening here?

A crash and shatter brought Lily to full awareness. She shuddered. Pushing through a sleep-fogged brain, she searched for an answer. What could that have been? The last of the china? Another lantern? What did it matter?

Lily pressed herself farther into the thin mattress as if it would make her invisible.

Ma's shouts rang through the house. She had started early this morning. Was anyone there to receive her ire? Pa perhaps? Or did she rant against an unseen foe?

How long could Lily remain as she was? Hidden beneath the worn quilt? Dare she try her odds against Ma's non-existent patience?

If only she could disappear. But there was nothing to offer any protection beyond the threadbare covering she gripped now.

Ma's furious voice bounced through the small structure, filling the space. But her words were no more comprehensible than usual. Would it make a difference if they were? If Lily could give her what she sought?

No. Lily had tried that. Once. Or twice.

And paid dearly.

It was never enough. *She* was never enough.

Maybe Joseph had been right—the only answer was escape. Not that Lily hadn't considered it, longed for it, attempted it. However, the options available to Joseph and to her were not the same. And she had quite exhausted hers.

How many men had she put hope in...only to be set aside as she had been with Cutie. What was it? What was wrong with her?

Another loud clash. Ma's rampage continued. It was only a matter of time before she came in search of Lily. Could she sneak out somehow?

She rejected the thought as soon as it entered her mind. That wasn't possible. Ma loomed in the great room from the sound of things, placing her directly in the only path to the outside world. Lily didn't even have access to a window from her partitioned space.

What chance had she of escape then? Of leaving this God-forsaken house and taking her chances in the world? What opportunity was there for a young, unmarried woman if she tried?

She deflated. With no further education than she had—it was her parent's house to a husband's home, or...the unthinkable.

The blanket that made up one wall of her bedroom space shook.

Lily swallowed. Her time was up.

It was jerked to the side and Ma appeared, stumbling as she pushed it aside. "There you are, you ungrateful child." Ma's words were mumbled and slurred.

There wasn't a bottle in her hand, but there didn't have to be. Lily wasn't naïve. So, Joseph's death could not change her mother's obsession with the stuff. Not even for one day.

Lily's hands trembled as she pulled the quilt down past her chin. "Ma'am?" Why did her voice have to shake so?

"Get up and get to your chores."

Turning to slip from the palette, Lily's eyes stung. Could she not be permitted a few days to let the loss sink in? To grieve?

"I-I need to get dressed." She lowered her head but snuck a glance in her mother's direction.

That was a mistake.

Ma fumed, her features, already reddened, deepened in color as her eyes narrowed. "Dress? You spent your dressin' time lazing in the bed."

Stumbling forward, Ma grabbed for Lily's arm.

As much as she wanted to move away, Lily knew better. Even so, she winced as Ma's overgrown nails dug into her upper arm.

"I don't think anyone cares," her mother fairly spit out. "Is there any decency left in ya' anyway?" Ma cackled as she jerked Lily from the bed space.

"Ma, please!" Lily's heart ached at the accusation. Even after all this time, it was difficult to discern what words were her mother's and what was the drink. It stung.

Her mother half-dragged Lily toward the kitchen as she continued to struggle with her footing. She bumped into Pa's chair as they passed through the great room. Ma shoved Lily to the floor. Hard. The momentum allowed Ma to retain her balance.

Lily cried out as her hip knocked into the unforgiving wooden boards and her hand hit something sharp.

Shards lay scattered over the floor. Dark amber glass shards. A bottle? What would cause Ma to do that?

"Quiet," Ma hissed, as she pressed a hand to her temple. "You want to give my poor head a reason to ache?"

"N-no, ma'am." Lily scrambled to rise, nearly toppling again when she put weight on her right leg. She shifted to balance on her left.

"Now, get to them dishes. Your Pa will be home for his lunch later. And I don't want to be bothered."

Lily rushed for the sink, daring to look over her shoulder only after she started piling the dishes.

Ma turned, hand over her eyes, and picked her way through the mess to the dark recesses of her room. She didn't bother to close the door.

Moments later, Lily heard a bottle drop to the floor and her mother groan. With any luck, she would be in a sleeping stupor or passed out.

With any luck.

Dan entered the barn. It didn't matter how many chores he took on, or how he threw himself into his work, he couldn't push out his considerations of Lily. He'd been troubled most of the night.

Though sleep had eluded him the previous nights. It was because guilt dominated his thoughts. How different this was. And he felt quite a bit more guilty because of it.

He picked up a cloth and some oil. Then moved toward his saddle. Working to clean the piece might occupy his hands, but it left his mind open to his various musings.

His thoughts had not solely been on the man whose death he had been responsible for. The young man whose life had been cut short because of Dan's poor choices. No, his wandering focus kept returning to Lily—her sadness, her loss. And he let the weight of that lie on his shoulders.

But these were not his only contemplations of Lily. If only they were. His mind had dwelt on her fine, gentle features. He envisioned the way her tendrils of hair, stubborn, slipped from the pins that bound them. And how her eyes sparked when she drew near. Had he imagined it?

Yes, of course he had.

She had lost her brother, her closest friend. Anyone who had spent any time in Wharton City knew of their bond.

And it had been taken away, ripped from her far too soon. Joseph was so young. Too young.

Yes, it should have been Dan.

"You plan on rubbing the leather raw?" A voice intruded.

Dan turned.

Slim stood in the barn's wide opening. If not for Slim's thicker figure, Dan mightn't have known, as he was silhouetted against the sunlight.

Dan glanced at the saddle. For certain, he had continued to rub long after the oil had dissipated. He pulled back and cursed his thoughtlessness.

The crunch of dirt under boot told that Slim moved closer. "You all right?"

Dan sighed and nodded. He shifted away to put the cloth and oil back on the shelf.

"You don't expect me to believe that, do you?" Slim picked up the saddle from its post.

Why must Slim be so interested in Dan's well-being? What happened to the days when they teased each other and poked at one another's weak spots?

A good ribbing. That's what he needed. Wanted. Anything but this.

"Oh, I see. You've gone mute." Slim turned back to Dan, having stowed the saddle.

Dan shook his head.

"You can't run from this, you know." The humor had eeked out of Slim's voice. He was all seriousness.

Why'd he have to do that?

Dan met his gaze. Heat infused his core. He stood taller, straightened his shoulders. "I'm not running from anything."

Slim crossed his arms and held his ground.

Why should Dan care what Slim thought? Dan grunted and moved toward the barn door.

"Just keep on then...not running and all," Slim called.

Dan paused. But just for a moment. His hands curled into fists. Why did Slim have to be so presumptuous? Forget it. He picked up his step and continued on.

It had to be near lunch. Dan directed his steps toward the homestead. An anchor in his chest became heavier with each step.

Being in the house had become...difficult. The boss either didn't notice or didn't care. Dan didn't want to test which.

Drawing in a deep breath, he steeled himself for what he might find within. He climbed the steps to the porch and moved into the home's great room.

There was naught but the bustle of Cook and Amanda Miller preparing the noon meal.

Though he made every attempt to not disturb them, Amanda's voice cut through soon after.

"You're a bit early. Everything all right?" Her brows furrowed.

Was everyone so interested in his state of being? Couldn't they all just get back to the no nonsense way they'd always had with him?

"I'm fine," he said, forcing a neutral expression onto his face.

She shot him a smile, weak as it was. "Won't you sit?"

Crash!

The loud sound came from the back of the house.

Amanda turned her head in that direction briefly, before meeting Dan's gaze. "Dan, I don't think—"

He held up a hand to silence her as he reached for his pistol. It wasn't there. A silent curse for Brandon flew from his mouth. Why did his boss insist on taking it?

Shooting a look at Amanda, he saw that she noticed him reaching for his weapon.

But why shouldn't he? It wasn't a crime.

And they needed protection.

Shaking off the strange feeling of wrongdoing, he stepped toward the hall.

"Dan—" she called again.

He glared at her.

She quieted. Her breaths came rapidly. There was no way to hide it...she feared, too.

He quickened his pace and moved toward the far bedroom. The one that belonged first to her, then to Mariena, and now...to another.

The scuffling within quieted.

His own breathing came in gasps. He must get control of himself.

The palms of his hands became sweaty. He rubbed them on his trouser legs. His steps placed him outside the door.

All sound had ceased from within the room. What would he find?

Gathering all the nerve he had, he pushed the door open and burst into the room.

Brandon leaned against the far wall, hunched over, a hand to his forehead. Was he injured?

Dan saw no sign of blood or mar upon his person. And, as he swung around toward the other inhabitant of the room, he found the Apache brave upon the bed, staring at him.

CHAPTER 4

The Bargain

Lily moved through the café. Would anyone notice her limp? She had noted Mrs. Jackson's features of late had borne more than curiosity. Did the woman suspect something was amiss?

Perhaps Lily was a fool to think Mrs. Jackson wouldn't. After these past couple of years, coming in almost every day...most of the time with injuries of some sort.

Considering that, Mrs. Jackson was daft if she hadn't considered it strange.

Lily's face burned. A thick shame overcame her at this thought—that someone knew about her situation at home. Even someone as kind and caring as Mrs. Jackson.

Tugging at her collar, she tried as ever to pull the neckline impossibly higher. Was the mark covered? The hideous mar she had the misfortune to be born with?

She shuddered at the idea of it being bared for all to see. Now *that* would truly shame her. Terribly so.

But it would only be a matter of time before many things would change in that regard. For decisions had to be made. She had been thinking...and thinking in dangerous directions.

What could be worse—the continued abuse of her mother or the life of a saloon girl?

If only there were another way...

But there weren't many options open to her. And this was an occupation...a life she could run to. A life that could provide her an out. She did not welcome such, yet it would be *her* choice and it would be an escape. Not so different than what Joseph had done.

Joseph...

Lily blinked back tears as she stepped into the kitchen.

Mrs. Jackson stood at the stove, stirring pots of vegetables. "Quite the crowd today, hmmm?"

"I...um...yes." Lily turned away as she filled a plate with meatloaf, potatoes, and beans.

Mrs. Jackson watched her.

Aware of the woman's eyes on her, Lily did her best to straighten her shoulders.

"I have a hunch it's a bit more than Joseph got you down." The older woman's voice was soft. Kind. Excruciatingly so.

Lily sighed. Must she have this conversation?

Perhaps it should be sooner than later. Which would she prefer? Despite her best attempts, she sniffled.

Fabric swished. Had Mrs. Jackson turned? Stepped toward Lily?

"I...need to get this food to—" Lily started, moving to exit.

Mrs. Jackson relieved her of her small burden. "No such thing. I'll take that."

Lily opened her mouth to protest.

"You sit yourself down. It's high time we had some honest words, you and I."

Watching Mrs. Jackson retreat into the dining room, Lily chewed on her lower lip. So, it must be now? Dare she tell all? Or could she find a way to keep some pieces to herself?

Settling on the stool in the corner, she took several breaths. What might she say if not the whole truth? Didn't she owe the café owner the courtesy of that much? The woman had been so generous...more so than Lily deserved.

Mrs. Jackson returned before Lily was ready.

"There, now. We have a few moments to ourselves." The woman checked her stewing pots and came near to Lily. Her eyes set on Lily's face and she said, "Why don't you tell me what has you so troubled?"

Now or never, truth or fiction.

"I…" Lily hesitated, swallowing hard. Her lip trembled. Truth it was. "I can't stay in my parents' home."

Sobs overtook her, and she bent forward.

Mrs. Jackson's hand fell on her shoulder. The simple contact brought some measure of comfort. She sat and allowed Lily to let it out. A luxury. And a respite.

When Lily regained some control over herself, the woman asked, "What will you do?"

Lily lifted burning eyes to her employer, blotting them with a handkerchief that had appeared from somewhere. "I-I don't know."

Mrs. Jackson took her hand. "I know that's not true. You're a smart girl. I'll wager you've made a plan."

Lily bit into her lower lip until it hurt. Dare she speak it to this tender, God-fearing soul? What would Mrs. Jackson think of her? Still, the woman deserved more than a lie. Breathing in, Lily chose her words and spoke them slowly. "I have."

"And?" Sadness shrouded Mrs. Jackson's gaze. As if she suspected the worst already.

"I…don't have many options." Lily looked off toward the dining room. Maybe someone needed something. She had become remiss in her work. Rising, she said, "I should—"

Mrs. Jackson laid a hand on her knee. "They'll be fine for a few moments more."

Lily settled back on the stool, twisting the small lace cloth, suddenly interested in its texture.

"You were saying…" Mrs. Jackson prompted.

The desire to catch the woman's eyes, even briefly, was too great. Lily met her gaze and then shifted her regard to the ceiling. "There just aren't many options for a single woman. Not that would provide for my room and board."

Mrs. Jackson's hands became lax. Were they trembling?

Lily closed her eyes. She did not try to stop the coming wave of tears. "The saloon." The word was not much more than a breath. Barely audible.

Could she look at Mrs. Jackson now? As much as she attempted to work up her courage, she couldn't. So, when she opened her eyes, she set them on her wringing hands.

"You know you are not without friends." Mrs. Jackson's voice was low.

Lily closed her eyes once more. What did Mrs. Jackson think? That people were lining up to help her? Laughable. "Truthfully, Mrs. Jackson, I am."

The woman pressed a hand to her chest as she inhaled sharply.

Lily wanted to reach out to the kind soul, but her gesture felt useless. So, she pulled her hand back. "I know you would help anyway you can."

Mrs. Jackson's eyes, still widened, remained fixed on Lily. She nodded.

"But I can't—won't—put you out. Won't risk setting you in the crosshairs of my father."

Something passed over Mrs. Jackson's features. Awareness? Realization? Had this not occurred to her? Did she think she would take Lily in and all would be well?

Such a sweet thought, but impossible. Lily needed to be more than an arm's reach away from her parents. From her father.

The saloon, though deplorable in every way, would cut her off completely. Who would want a daughter back that had...

A voice raised from the dining room. The customers were in need of service.

Their little chat had pressed the boundaries of the patrons' patience. Lily did not wish to make them wait any longer.

"Excuse me, Mrs. Jackson. I am sorry to disappoint you. I truly am. But I have to do what I have to do.

Lily rose and exited the small room in one smooth movement. Then she was out to face her customers.

And her future.

Dan tied off his horse's reins. His pulse betrayed his determination to remain easy going about his visit this morning. Had it been a week since they buried Joseph? Every time Dan closed his eyes, the younger man's face was before his.

Only to be replaced by Lily's. Which sent his heart into a curious dance.

It shouldn't be tolerated. He was a louse.

He deserved to be punished for what had happened to Joseph. After all, he'd stood by and watched it all happen.

And then, he allowed his mind to dwell on the man's sister.

Intolerable.

But why did he find himself outside the café—his intentions set on seeing her? Oh, he might tell himself he only wished to ensure she was well, check in on her.

That would be a lie. He *wanted* to see her. If only for a few moments. Perhaps part of it was, in truth, to assure himself she was indeed well. Still, there was no denying that his being here had less to do with her health and more to do with his heart's pull.

He grimaced and fought the urge to untie his horse and move on. It wasn't right. How could he indulge such notions?

Glancing at the café's door, he was stymied. Should he? Dare he? But he had come this far...and he might should check on her. That, at least, was not self-serving.

Yes, he should. If only to fulfill his unspoken promise to look after her. That's what this was about—his desire to look after her. For Joseph.

He pulled off his hat and moved toward the door. A sick feeling in the pit of his stomach warned him not to use Joseph to veil his own motives.

Should he not proceed then?

But he had already stepped into the dining area. No use turning back now.

The café was busy. Especially for such an hour. Shouldn't the breakfast rush be over?

A din of grumbles filled the place. And no one moved about to serve them.

No one to serve them? Where was Lily? Was she unwell?

Dan strode to the kitchen, uncaring that it was off-limits to customers. He simply barged in.

Mrs. Jackson scurried about the small space, cooking as if her life depended on it. Sweat made her garments cling to her fuller figure, and her face had reddened.

What happened here?

"Mrs. Jackson?" Dan reached for her.

She bounded out of range as she grabbed for another pan. Did she even notice him?

"Mrs. Jackson," he said louder.

She swept hair out of her face and stirred scrambled eggs with one spoon while using her other hand to flip sausage.

"Mrs. Jackson," Dan yelled.

Her hands jerked, dropping the utensils. And she pulled back from the stovetop.

When she turned toward him, her eyes flicked in recognition and relief. "Oh, Dan. You gave me a fright!"

She went back to her cooking as if he hadn't spoken. Was he not more intrusive?

"Mrs. Jackson," he started, volume raised.

She held up a hand. "I hear ya'. I'm rather busy right now." Her features pinched as she looked at him. "Just be patient. I'll get to ya'."

"I'm not here for food."

Her brows rose. "I don't suffer too kindly to anyone in my kitchen, sir."

Had she not heard him?

He stepped closer to her. "Where is Lily?"

She gave him a long look before nudging him to the side and shaking the pan of bacon. "Gone."

Something had passed in her eyes before she turned away. Something Dan had a difficult time putting words to. Sadness? Regret? Disappointment?

"Gone? Gone where?"

Mrs. Jackson shrugged. But she paused for a moment and stared at the wall. She knew more.

He took a step closer. "What is it? What aren't you telling me?"

She shot him a look. "It's none of my business and certainly none of yours."

Dan looked at the floor and pushed out a breath. Why in the world did this woman have to be such a stick in the mud? He wanted to help. Couldn't she see that? What could he do to convince her?

Mrs. Jackson went back to her dance around the kitchen. He had been forgotten.

No. He would not be dismissed.

Moving closer, he set a hand over hers on the pan. "Tell me where she is."

Mrs. Jackson stopped and stared ahead for a moment. Then she looked at Dan. Moisture welled in her eyes. "She's gone and taken a job at the saloon."

No. It couldn't be. Why would she do such a thing? A weight hit the bottom of his stomach. This was his fault. Without Joseph, she had no hope. Was she acting out of grief?

He had to stop her. Somehow.

Lily slowed her steps. It was time.

She'd spent enough of the morning wandering, delaying. It only made this more difficult—this point at which she would cross from her world into *that* one.

And now she stood, just outside the saloon's swinging doors. Waiting. For what?

Did she wish for someone to stop her? Or for something to drive her onward?

She didn't know.

As the time passed, she became more certain this was all that remained for her. She rubbed her arm. The bruises from yesterday's encounter with Ma were still fresh; they still hurt. But the pain on the surface only alluded to the depth of the wounds within. Nothing could touch those. And nothing could heal them.

Was that why no one wanted her? She had been damaged—within

and without. Did that mark her as unloveable? And more—unable to love?

Yes, this decision, this future, was all that was left to her.

She glanced to the right and left. Did anyone watch her? Shaking her head, she discarded the consideration—it wasn't as if it mattered. After today, she would be leprous to the good people of this town. Never again acceptable. Not that she ever had been.

Commanding all the courage she could muster, she raised her arms and pressed into the saloon.

Inside, all was quiet. Did no one stir within this place in the daytime hours? She glanced about the space that she had never before laid eyes on.

Tables and chairs were spread throughout the room—not altogether unlike the café. Some of the chairs had been scattered from their places, a few upended. Broken glass littered the floor.

The raised bar had a myriad of small glasses strewn about. And there was an odd smell. Had no one bothered to clean? Perhaps it was a task completed in preparation for the day, not done after the evening. For certain, she would learn well enough.

"H-hello?" she ventured into the silence.

She stepped further in.

Something cracked underfoot.

Jerking to the side, she looked down. More of the amber colored glass.

Just like home, she mused.

What a thought. The saloon would be, in some ways, no different from home. But there were things that would be quite different—her job. And the number of bruises she would bear each day.

"What can I do for you, my lady?" a smooth voice laced through the scantly lit room.

Lily jerked her head up from her study of the broken glass to study the man who had appeared in a doorway beyond the bar.

The man, of moderate height and good build, leaned on the doorframe, clad only in trousers and an undershirt. Had she disrupted his sleep? It was nearly mid-morning.

She averted her eyes.

But his smile had been warm and welcoming. Charming almost.

"I-I don't know." Her face heated. What had brought her here again? Oh, yes—a job. Could she do this?

Footfalls on the wooden floorboards warned that he drew near.

"Well, you found yourself in the right place." The man's voice was rich and thick, like honey. It poured forth, soothing her worn nerves.

She peered up at him, tentatively.

He now stood directly in front of her.

Could she meet his eyes? She didn't have the nerve.

"Are you in trouble, darlin'?" His voice was soft, gentle.

She nodded but kept her eyes to his chin. Why would she admit such to this man? Something about him allowed her to put her guard down. Her hands settled on her upper arms, crossing over her chest, she felt strangely safe and uneasy at the same time.

He touched her chin, lifting her gaze to his.

His eyes were almost gray. Not as warm as his voice, but they seemed sincere. "Let me help you."

The touch of his fingers on her skin was tender. Her throat became thick. Was this someone to care for her? To take care of her? She never thought she would find it again. Least of all here...

His hand moved to the side of her face.

She swallowed. Hadn't she longed for someone to want her? To want to be tender with her like this? Yet...something in her resisted. But it was small—she could overcome that trepidation. In time. There wasn't anything untoward in his manner.

"You've been through it, haven't you?" He whispered, his eyes fixed on hers.

She nodded, letting her lids slide closed.

Would he embrace her? Let her lean on him? Or would he wait for her to come the rest of the way? Could she do so? Take that last step toward her future here and leave her past behind? It might not be so hard; it could be easy if...

The swinging doors of the saloon slammed open.

She jerked her head around.

The man ground out a curse.

Who would burst in on them? Something about her thoughts seemed hazy.

The figure that approached was tall and broad. Dan? What could he want? It was rather early to want a drink.

"Lily," Dan pressed out. Her name sounded like a warning more than an address.

"Leave her be, ranch hand." The tenderness in the barkeeper's tone had gone, replaced with a more forceful, grating voice. "Can't you see she's been through enough?" The man shouldered his way in front of her, blocking Dan.

Dan's eyes narrowed. "And I suppose you're the one who's going to help with that?"

The man opened his mouth, but Dan's ire seemed to leave the barkeep hunting for words. Did Dan intimidate him so?

What *did* Dan want? Was he here to rescue her? What for? Why would he care?

The two men now stood face to face, glaring at each other.

"Come here, Lily," Dan said, his voice only slightly eased. "I'll make sure this ruffian leaves you alone."

"Leave her alone? You got it all wrong. *She* came to me. And I intend to help the lady any way I can."

Dan grunted. "I bet you will, Silas. The same way you help all the ladies in your employ."

Silas squared his shoulders. "You talk as if my girls aren't well cared for. They've got everything they need. I look out for them."

Dan smirked. "I won't dignify that with a response."

Lily watched the muscles in Dan's jaw work. Why did he harbor such terrible feelings toward this man...Silas? He had been only pleasant to her.

Dan held out a hand. "Let's go."

She hesitated. What good would going with Dan do? Wouldn't she be in the same mess? How would he help with her mother? Her father?

"See that, Dan-ill?" the man sneered. "She doesn't *want* to go."

Dan's features tightened, but Lily saw something pass in his eyes. And she regretted her decision. He had helped her after the funeral, had let her release her grief on him at the news of Joseph's death...

Joseph.

What would her brother think of what she was doing?

Maybe she should let Dan help her. If only for today. There would be other days, other chances to talk with Silas.

Stepping to the side, she reached for Dan's hand.

His hard-set features broke for a moment—and in that moment she saw his genuine concern and relief.

He did care. If only just a little.

Silas appeared stricken. "Are you sure, little lady? You want to go with this brute?"

Dan wasted no time in pulling her to his side.

"I...it is best." She couldn't make eye contact with Silas.

Dan urged Lily toward the door.

"I understand." Silas's voice had taken on that buttery quality once again. "But if you ever need anything, I'm here."

Dan halted and turned. "You stay away from her," he ground out.

Silas shrugged, yawned, and stepped through the doorway to wherever it led.

Soon enough, Dan had led her out of the saloon and into the harsh sunlight where her intentions were bound to be exposed.

And questioned.

Dan gripped Lily's hand and pulled her along—across the planked walkway, around the General Store, and into the alley. Everything seemed tinted in red. Was he so angry? At her? At Silas? At himself?

As he ducked between the buildings, he released her hand. He took a moment to breathe against the worst of the tightness in his chest before turning toward her.

"What were you thinking?" he pressed out.

She stared at him, brows lowered, a picture of hurt.

He wanted to kick himself. Why did he say that? It must seem as if he blamed her. She needed an easy hand...unless he wanted her running right back to that weasel. Scuffling at the dirt, he looked down for a moment.

When he met her eyes again, she had wrapped her arms around herself, and she visibly trembled.

"I'm sorry." He lowered his voice. "I just...I don't understand."

She rubbed her hands over her upper arms. "I don't expect you to." Her lower lip quivered. Tears were sure to come. He prayed not.

"I...know I don't deserve to know. But I'd like to have some idea why." He held her gaze. "Why did that seem like your best option?"

Her eyes widened. "My *best* option? It is my *only* option." After the words shot out, she bit her lip and looked to the side. Did she regret them?

"Only option?" he said softly. "How can that be?"

She wiped at a tear. "You wouldn't understand."

How could this be her only option? Because Joseph was gone? Were her parents pushing her out? Forcing her to find a life of her own? Was that why Joseph had sought out a ranch hand's life?

Dan didn't want to ask any of these questions. Nor would she be apt to answer—such would be to her shame. She had reached an age at which many women would be married. Why hadn't she?

What had, after all, happened between her and Cutie? He shook his head. It wasn't any of his business.

Still, the fact remained that she needed a place to belong and she had no prospects. Would that Joseph were still here. He would know what to do.

Joseph.

Again, a reminder that this whole thing was Dan's fault. Perhaps, then, he must provide the remedy.

He swallowed and exhaled. "You're right."

She peered at him, a curious expression about her features.

"I can't understand what you've been through. Or what you're going through."

She looked at the ground and nodded.

Should he touch her in some way? Her arm? Her hand? She appeared so helpless. But as he lifted his hand, he decided against it. Perhaps it would be unwelcome. She didn't need that, she needed real help.

"But I can offer something."

Her eyes met his, a brow raised.

"It seems that because of...well, because of what's happened, things have become...unstable for you. And I want to help you, to be something...that is, someone you can rely on."

"Be what, exactly?" Her question was more...accusing than he'd expected.

He licked his lips. This wasn't something he had experience with. Or had prepared to do. He'd certainly never imagined getting hitched. Yet here he was...and he wanted to do it right.

How should go about it? On one knee? Or would a simple agreement suffice?

He shook his head. And let out a breath. Best to just do it.

Taking her hands in his, he pulled her closer. "Lily, I would like to provide a place for you—a home. With me."

"What are you saying?" Her eyes widened and her brows arched.

"I think we should marry."

There. He'd said it. Maybe a bit too plainly. But it was out there. Now, it was for her to accept or reject him.

His heart beat harder, thundering, crowding out all sounds around him. Why? This was but a simple arrangement. It wasn't as if he had anything at stake.

She searched his features. Did she seek out a sign that he played her for a fool? Would she play him for one?

After a few moments, she sighed. "You don't want to hitch yourself to me."

His brows furrowed. And he watched her, expecting defiance. Instead her eyes pled. For what? Some gesture, some assurance of his sincerity?

He would give it. But how? What? His eyes trailed to her lips. Dare he? Should he chance to touch his to them? Would that convince her of his earnestness?

Leaning forward, he pressed his mouth to hers. He intended it to be a gentle affirmation, but a heat sparked within and overcame him. Lifting his hands to cup her face, he claimed a deeper hold on her.

She released a whimper and grasped for his arms. To steady herself?

Her hands on him drove his desire for more. She seemed ready to supply. But it wasn't right. This wasn't right. It took some moments for his will to regain control, and he released her.

His hands slid to her shoulders. "I assure you, I do."

Her eyes were clouded as they met his.

"Will you marry me, Lily?" he rasped.

She nodded. Then fell into his arms.

He held her to himself.

And as he inhaled the sweet smell of her, he couldn't help but wonder if this arrangement was for her benefit alone.

CHAPTER 5

The Fallout

"Lily," Dan murmured after several moments. He was loath to disengage from her, but they were pushing the bounds of propriety. The last thing he wanted was to give the gossips more to wag their tongues about.

She stirred against his chest but didn't pull away. Did she enjoy the feel of his arms as much as he liked her being in them?

If only...

He wanted to press a kiss into her hair, to the delicate skin of her face...maybe even to taste her lips once more. With that thought, he loosened his hold. Such thoughts were dangerous. He must not let his mind wander so. Yes, she had agreed to marry him, but that didn't mean he could take undue liberties.

She looked up at him, a question in her eyes.

Why? Because he had loosened his hold?

"I, ah, think it best we speak with your father," he said, considering her features.

"My father?" Her gaze captivated him—the green orbs were flecked with gold. Mesmerizing. It would be best if he tore free from that connection now. He'd better not lose himself.

"I should have a conversation with him. Set some things between us."

"Must you?" Her brows lifted...as if this concerned her. The grip she retained on his shirt tightened all the more. Was that thought troublesome to her?

He stepped back. "I'd prefer to do so soon."

Her fingers let loose his shirt. They stood separated by an arm's length of space—both a relief and a challenge. She appeared so weak, so vulnerable.

"I do not ask that you go with me." He ached to reach for her again. Instead he set his hands to his belt. That was safer.

She clasped her hands in front of her waist and held them there. He couldn't read if his words offered relief or upset her more. Did *she* even know?

Dan glanced toward the opening of the alley. If anyone looked in and spotted them here, it would not be good for her reputation. It would be best if they returned to the walkway.

"Here..." He put a hand to her elbow and shifted to escort her in that direction.

She did not move.

"We shouldn't continue lurking in the shadows. People will talk."

Her eyes found his. She seemed defeated, deflated. Did she not care? What had her in such a state?

"What is it?" Would she tell him?

Turning toward the darker end of the alley, she played with the fourth finger of her right hand. Indecision seemed to plague her.

When she faced him again, her features were set. "I will go with you."

Curious—one moment she had been undecided, the next so certain. He'd give anything for a peek inside that mind of hers.

He nodded. When he tugged on her elbow again, she allowed him to lead her. They exited the alley and moved down the short walk of the main stretch until they arrived at the jail.

All the while, Dan worked in his mind what he might say to Sheriff McAllen. He wished he knew the man better. Or even knew Lily better.

What had brought her to this point? That she would be in the saloon? What occurred between her and her parents he couldn't venture to guess. Was he preparing to walk into a minefield?

He glanced at Lily as he knocked on the jailhouse door, wishing he had the nerve to pray for guidance.

Footfalls and movement filled the space within.

Lily looped her arm through Dan's elbow and drew measurably closer.

He looked at her. What was that about?

The door opened and one of the deputies stared at them. What was his name? Travers?

"Good day, Lily," the man said, tipping his hat with a sly grin and a wink.

She shivered almost imperceptibly. If she hadn't been so close to Dan, he would have missed it.

Heat stirred within him. What was this man insinuating? Or was this his idea of flirting? Either way, it wasn't appropriate and certainly not welcomed.

"Good day, Deputy," Dan forced out as he tugged Lily even closer. He wondered after his need to stake a claim on her in such a way. Then pushed it to the side. "We're here to see Sheriff McAllen."

"Who is it, Travers?" a voice called from further within. Sheriff McAllen's gruff baritone for sure. And he didn't sound ready to suffer foolishness. "I'm fearful busy."

Dan winced. He hated his luck.

The deputy looked toward the interior. "It's Lily and one of the Miller ranch hands."

"Oh? I don't have time for nonsense," Sheriff McAllen called.

Deputy Travers half-turned toward the couple and raised a brow.

Dan tired of the incapable gatekeeper. He shouldered past Travers, keeping his body between the oaf of a man and Lily as he pressed inside.

The sheriff sat at his desk, bent over several papers. His lunch sat to the side.

"What the—?" McAllen glanced up as they approached.

"Sheriff, forgive the intrusion. But I must speak with you." Dan's words rushed out. If he didn't say all of it quickly, he wouldn't say it at all.

McAllen eyed the two of them and pushed back from his desk. "This best be worth my time."

Lily's hand came up, resting on Dan's upper arm. Did she want to communicate something to her father? Or to Dan? If so, it was lost to him.

"Sir, I'm not good with words. And I don't see the point in dawdling. So, I'll get right to it." He took a moment to breathe.

"Well?" McAllen said, his voice sharp. "Spit it out."

Dan grimaced but pushed on. "I've come to ask for Lily's hand in marriage."

McAllen's eyes locked on Dan's and hardened. "Oh, you have, have you?"

"Yes, sir. I mean all due respect and I know we didn't have the proper courting period, but sometimes things are best this way." Dan fought for straight words and a confidence he didn't feel.

The sheriff stood, stepped around his desk, and walked to them. He looked Dan up and down before moving to stand in front of his daughter.

McAllen stared Lily down. She shrank even farther into herself. What was this?

"Tell me, Lily," McAllen said, his voice quiet, like the stillness of dark clouds before a storm. "Have you gotten yourself in a family way?"

"Pa!" she shrieked.

"Sheriff!" Dan said at the same time, inserting himself between the man and his daughter. "How could you say such a thing?"

Even as he glared at the man, something nagged at the back of Dan's mind. The saloon. Cutie. The deputy. Was Lily that kind of woman?

Did it matter? He had determined he would take care of her in Joseph's place. Wasn't it his responsibility? Besides, she had made no pretenses. No assurances. Nor had he asked for any.

McAllen turned toward his desk and waved a hand in the air. "Take her. With my blessing."

Dan looked at Lily.

Tears streamed down her face. Why had he suggested she endure this? He should have come alone. He wrapped an arm around her and ushered her to the door.

"But," McAllen called.

Dan paused.

"She's *your* responsibility. Not mine. Ever. Again."

Lily's trembling intensified.

Dan looked back over his shoulder, hardening his gaze. "That best be a promise."

He then shifted his focus to Lily's shaking form as he escorted her out of the jailhouse and into the open street.

What was he going to do?

Lily tried to calm herself. How could her father have said such a thing? Did he truly think it? That she had...?

She squeezed her eyes shut, but her tears made their way through.

Would she ever be whole? Or believe she was worth anything? How could she when her own father...

Glancing at Dan, she tried to decipher his features. They were set and seemed, on the surface, somewhat despondent. How could he not be? After what he had heard? What he must think of her? Yet, he had stood with her in front of her father...quite a bit more than she would have thought...or could have hoped for.

But now, his gaze traced the horizon, eyes narrowed, shoulders hunched slightly. Was he disappointed? Dismayed at the mess he'd gotten himself into? Why shouldn't he be? He'd hitched himself to a real mess by all appearances—a woman of ruin, as far as he knew.

Who would want her now?

"Dan," she said, willing herself to look at him, but finding she lacked the courage. "I don't want you to think that you..." A sob rose in her throat, cutting off the rest of her sentence.

He turned to her. "Don't want me to what?" His words were softer than she'd expected, more tender than he should be.

Did he watch her? The feeling of his gaze on her created a thick tension.

She swallowed. "I can...that is...I would...understand...if you..." Her words faded and her sentence trailed.

His gaze on her intensified. Had she offended? That was not her intention.

Wrapping an arm around her midsection, she dropped her head into her other, now lifted palm. What was the right thing to say? The right way to communicate what was in her? She longed to untangle him from this gnarled mess.

When she peered at him, his eyes were still on her. She wanted to look away but thought otherwise of it. His eyes held such depth. And such concern.

"What?" The word was so quiet, she wondered if he had spoken it. "If I what, Lily?"

Why did he have to say her name like that? As if he truly had a care? That might break her, crack through her well-built exterior. No, that couldn't happen.

She sucked in a breath. "If you decided not to follow through with..."

His eyes widened, and he pulled back.

"After..." She gathered her courage. "After what my father said."

"Let's not speak of what your..." He stopped and looked at the ground. It seemed as if he struggled to contain something hard within himself. "What Sheriff McAllen said. We won't speak of it again."

Lily tilted her head. Would he so soon dismiss Pa's words? Would he give her such grace? In words only? Or did his mercy go deeper?

That wasn't possible.

Hugging her arms to herself, she nodded and gazed off to the side. To what, she wasn't certain.

Silence hung between them. Would he fill it? Or should she?

She pressed upward at the front of her dress, at the cloth beneath the neckline. Was it still covered? Yes...the mark was well beneath the high collar's protective line. Her breaths came easier.

When the stillness between them became awkward, she looked up.

He stared at her. For how long?

With slow movements, he shifted. "Shall we?"

Where were they to go? Would he take her back to the Miller ranch? Treat her as if they were already wed? Was that why he was not concerned with her father's accusation? The Millers did not seem the kind of people to suffer such.

What then? Would they take her in? House her until such time as she and Dan would wed? That didn't seem likely either.

If they did…oh, the embarrassment, the shame she would endure. Must Dan tell them everything? Could she bear that? Did she have a choice? She met Dan's gaze again. His brows were furrowed.

"Please don't dwell on it, Lily." His voice was quiet but firm.

Did he think she struggled over Pa's words? If only there were space in her mind to worry over that. Oh, it would come. And it would be hard. But there were more immediate things…

"You must be tired," he said on a breath.

Was he weary? It wasn't yet noon. And still, because of her, he'd perhaps lived a week's worth of tension in a couple of hours.

All she could do was nod.

"I'll take you somewhere you can rest." He held out an arm, indicating she should walk toward the main road. But he did not offer his elbow. Was that telling?

She best not think too much on that. Here he was, taking her from the pit she'd lived in and offering her a means of escape. Why? Why would he be so kind? Because he cared? Or did he have some ulterior motive?

With tentative steps, she moved forward as directed, keeping her eyes down. Her future, her life, was once again in someone else's hands.

Dan lifted Lily onto his horse before pulling himself into the saddle behind her. With his chest pressed against her back, a rush of sensation, warmth, spread through his being. Pleasant and soothing, intoxicating even, he fought the urge to lean in further, breathe in deeper. Perhaps this draw, so enticing, could prove dangerous dare he give in.

Did she feel it, too?

"We'll," he said, clearing his throat as he attempted to clear his head. "…have to go after your things another time." Though he regretted the need to be blunt, he preferred to not have any misunderstanding about their destination. He would not take her to her parents' home.

She turned, her features now in profile. The wind whipped her red-brown hair. Soft tendrils grazed his features.

The temptation to reach up and set them back in place overwhelmed him. More so the desire to unsettle the remainder of her hair.

"There is nothing I want or need that I do not have on my person."

Had she stowed belongings elsewhere in town? At the café perhaps? He doubted it. What could her meaning be? Were there not things at her parents' home she wanted? Why, then, would she say such?

Her father.

She did not wish to upset or risk seeing her father. He couldn't blame her. Nor would he argue further. If there wasn't anything she wanted, he would let it be.

"As you wish," he murmured close to her ear.

Was it his imaginings or did she lean into him a bit more?

He would not begrudge it.

Jerking the reins, he set the animal in motion, and they were off.

When they had stepped out of the jailhouse, his first thought had been to take her to the ranch. Brandon and Amanda would take her in for certain. But was he, then, asking too much of their generous nature? Rooms at the homestead were filling fast. And one room was occupied by...the Apache youngster!

There wasn't any way Dan could justify endangering Lily by setting her in the same house with that brave. He wouldn't do it.

Then where? Where would she be safe? And cared for?

An answer seemed to rise to the surface of his thoughts. Perhaps it was too obvious. So much so, he hoped no one intending harm would discover her.

Decision made, he turned the horse and pressed heels to flank, urging the animal to put the town behind them. And, hopefully, the memories of the encounter with the Sheriff.

Several minutes later, Dan slowed the mare as the small cabin appeared in the distance. It stood only a third the size of the Miller homestead. But there was no need for this home to be of such enormity.

"Why are we here?" Lily asked, her voice tinged with apprehension. "Do you not live at the ranch?"

What had her so uneasy? He became concerned as her body tensed and she sat forward a bit, creating distance between them.

And he realized...

Did she think this was Dan's cabin? That he intended to take her into his home before they were wed? She thought so little of him?

Heat sparked within, shooting through him like a bullet. Though... she hadn't much occasion to really know him. He attempted to push that familiar fire down. Best to give her the fair shake she refused him.

That didn't mean he had to like it. "This isn't my home."

He dropped down the side of the horse and, without bothering to assist her, walked toward the small cabin.

Would she follow? She could manage, couldn't she?

The shifting of fabric behind made him curious. Had she come off the horse? Or was it the mare's restless steps disrupting the dirt?

Though he itched to satisfy his curiosity, he refused. He kept his eyes trained on the door. After taking the few remaining steps to the door, he knocked.

A muffled voice within assured Dan that someone was within.

And, moments later, the door opened, and Uncle Owen's face met his. "Dan! Good to see ya!"

The older man reached for Dan's hand. Dan gave it a firm shake. Uncle Owen winked. "What can I do for you? Nothing troubling, I hope."

"That..." Dan looked back at Lily on his steed. "Remains to be seen."

Uncle Owen's gaze followed Dan's. "Oh. I see."

Dan's eyes returned to Uncle Owen's. If he weren't in such a fix, he'd have laughed at Uncle Owen's comical expression—wide-eyed with a sort of grimace on his face. But Dan couldn't. He related all too well.

"We'd best have a sit down, then." Uncle Owen opened the door wider. Then paused. "Is she coming in?"

Dan closed his eyes. He'd best go back for her. "I suppose," he muttered.

"How was that?"

"Yes, sir." Dan turned and walked toward Lily and his mare.

He thought he heard Uncle Owen chuckle behind him, though it may have been his imagination. Did he only think so because that's what he expected?

As he neared Lily, he looked up at her. Her features were difficult to read—stoic, flat. Was she angry? Hurt?

Putting off engaging her for a handful of seconds longer, Dan gripped the horse's bit and urged the mare closer to the cabin. Once at the post, he reached for the reins to tie the mare off. But the leather straps wouldn't come.

He looked up.

Lily had them in a firm grip.

Staring at her, he tugged again.

She let them loose.

He lost his balance and nearly fell, catching himself at the last moment.

Of all the...

Glancing toward Uncle Owen, he noticed that the man had disappeared, leaving the door open. Probably the older rancher's hip. It bothered him from time to time. At least he hadn't witnessed Dan's embarrassing near-trip.

Dan looked back to Lily. She was halfway off the horse. Only...

She wasn't making any more progress. Her body had slid off to the side of the horse, and one foot sought the ground, but it seemed as if her other foot, or perhaps something about her boot, had gotten caught in the stirrup. She clung to the pommel and she was grunting.

Serves her right.

What a terrible thing to think toward a lady in distress. Dan wished he felt worse. Should he rush to her aid? Or wait for her to ask?

Everything in him wanted to assist, but he held back. Maybe his efforts wouldn't be well-received.

So, he waited. And watched.

She pulled herself up slightly. Then movement about the stirrup under her skirt commenced. And intensified. At last, she sagged against the animal as she cried out.

"Need some help?" Dan kept his voice steady, hoping his smile didn't sneak into his tone and betray him.

"Yes." The word came out on an exasperated breath. No two ways about it. She was at the end of her rope.

Coming alongside the mare, he stopped behind Lily and wrapped his right arm around her waist. Then, using his left hand to find her boot under the skirt, he searched for whatever had caught it.

A metal hook on the boot had become bent, and it latched onto the strap of the stirrup. If the horse had been feistier or gotten spooked, she would have been dragged.

His earlier thought to wait now seemed careless. And he was sorry. With greater tenderness, he eased her foot out and lowered her to the ground.

Once she had firm footing, he wanted to maintain his hold and apologize...somehow. If he could get past his guilt.

But just as she stood on her own feet, she pulled away. Did she know what a mistake he had made?

He deserved the brush off...every bit of it.

"Well?" She stumbled as she turned.

He reached out to steady her, but a sharp glare from her cut him off.

So, he addressed her question with openness. "Well what?"

She shut her eyes. "What am I to do? Stand out here and wait for you?"

He furrowed his brows. "No, of course not. Uncle Ow— Mr. Owen has asked us to come inside."

She crossed her arms and tapped her fingers against her opposite arm.

Was she so suspicious? Dan tired of it. "Mr. Owen is my boss's uncle. He is a close friend. A trusted friend. He and his *wife* are trusted friends."

Lily's stance softened. "Is his wife home?"

"No." Dan exhaled.

Lily's guard went up again.

He took a step toward her.

She moved back, but the post Dan had tied the horse to was just behind her. Her gaze set on him when her retreat was blocked.

He softened his tone. "I know you may not want to, but I'm asking you to trust me."

She watched him as she swallowed. Her eyes glazed over. Had she no fight left in her? Was that a good thing?

He set a hand on her arm, his touch light.

She jerked at the contact but did not move away.

That pierced him deeper than any dagger would. Emotion swelled within him. And through the thickness in his throat, he said, "I won't let anything or anyone harm you."

Nodding, perhaps a bit too quickly, she then shifted to face the door.

Though he had been awarded her trust, it felt like anything but a victory.

Lily stepped into the small cabin. Would it be dark and horrid like home? For certain it was no bigger. But as she moved into the space just beyond the door, she was ushered into a rather warm, inviting great room. Everything seemed bright and open. Strange, as the walls were just as closed in, but it didn't feel that way. She didn't struggle to breathe here.

Across the room, in a comfortable-looking chair by the hearth, sat Mr. Owen. Though the fireplace wasn't active with flame, it anchored the room.

There was life and love here. She could feel it—in the air, reverberating off the walls...despite the small size. It felt like home, though she was yet a stranger here. It was something she couldn't explain...but it didn't make her leery. Shouldn't it?

"Come in," the older man said, waving her forward.

Was she still standing just inside the doorway?

Dan maneuvered around her, pressing against her shoulder. He reached behind her and closed the door. "Thanks, Uncle Owen."

Dan continued into the room and settled in a seat near the man he seemed to know well.

Why did she stare at them? Was it the sense of home she had never experienced yet knew it to be this place? Or did she have some apprehension toward the older man?

She dismissed that thought. The man was as welcoming as his home. He put her at ease. Perhaps that's what disquieted her.

Forcing herself to step forward, she moved to the waiting chair.

Mr. Owen and Dan watched her every move.

The older man with a smile, as if he knew what was in her thoughts. Dan appeared concerned.

She must manage her expression. As she sat, she pressed a smile onto her features.

Mr. Owen shifted his focus to Dan. "Not that I don't appreciate the visit, son. But I hope there's something I can do for you two."

Son? Was this Dan's father? That didn't seem right. He had said this was his boss's uncle. She searched her memory...back to school days. Shamed, she found that she barely remembered Dan...but he was there, he had to be. Still, this man did not fit with the image she conjured of his father.

Distracted, seeking answers that had not been forthcoming, she realized the two men had continued talking.

"...so, I need to find a safe place for Lily," Dan said.

What had he said? Did he share about her father? What Pa had said?

Mr. Owen scratched his beard. "I wish Dorothy was here. She'd have a better mind about where we could..."

Dan's brows furrowed.

Mr. Owen laughed. "Surely you know her name ain't 'Cook.'"

Dan's cheeks colored.

It was strange to see him embarrassed.

Mr. Owen laughed harder. "You didn't!"

"I...guess I never thought about it."

"Least your honest." Mr. Owen shook his head. Then he turned to Lily. "Got yourself a good one here, missy. He'll never steer you wrong."

Truly?

Mr. Owen coughed. "As I said, Dorothy would know better where we could put her. But I'll go ahead and speak for us: she is welcome here."

Dan's shoulders relaxed, and he released a breath. Had he been so worried after her well-being?

"I'm to stay here?" Did she understand correctly? That Dan had pawned her off on this elderly couple?

"Yes, ma'am." Mr. Owen smiled at her. "My wife will be tickled pink."

"Oh…" Lily glanced at Dan and then looked away. How could he put her in such a position? "I don't mean to be a bother—"

"Not on your life, young lady. You ain't a bother."

She looked from one man to the other. "But I—"

Dan looked at Mr. Owen. "Let us have a moment, will you?"

The older man nodded. "I'll make some fresh coffee."

Mr. Owen rose with some difficulty and made his way, hobbling, to the kitchen.

Dan slid into the chair just vacated. Now next to Lily, he took her hand in his. "I need you to trust me. This is best."

She lowered her voice. "I don't wish to be an inconvenience." Though Dan sought her eyes, she couldn't look at him. Why did she feel so helpless? So…vulnerable?

Gentle fingers grazed her chin, urging her to face him. She met his gaze.

There was something deeper in his eyes, something she couldn't quite discern. But she wanted to.

She leaned forward and whispered, "Why can't I come to the ranch with you?"

He watched her. Was he lost for words? But then he did speak. "You'd be an inconvenience."

Lily widened her eyes and jerked her hand back, his words cutting through her already tender heart.

"That's not what I meant." He pushed out a breath and ran a hand through his hair. "You're not an inconvenience here or there."

She clenched her teeth, fighting tears, refusing to give over to them. But as she chanced a glance at him, she pushed out, "Then why can't I just stay there?"

He continued to eye her. Did he know of the war within her even now?

She prayed he would not pull back. Why would she do so? Why did she wish him to be near? Why did that seem important?

As if answering her prayer, he leaned closer. "That's just not possible."

She clenched her hands. "Why not?" The words did not have much force behind them.

"Just...trust me." His words were clipped.

The manner of his tone sliced through her, stinging as it cut. Her fight against her tears became futile. And one escape.

Why would he be so insistent? Was there something he didn't trust *her* with?

Dan covered her hands with his larger ones. "Lily, I..."

What did he care to say? Would he speak things that would endear him to her? She should not listen, yet she waited.

"I only want to do the best I can by you. *For* you."

This time it was she who sought his regard while he looked downward.

He continued, "I can't do that if you won't trust me."

In the silence of the moments that followed, she considered his words. And she knew he had been right—there must be some give and take. And he wasn't asking for much. Only hurt had kept her from seeing it.

She didn't have ground to stand on anyway. The truth was she had nothing. No one. And nowhere to go. He had been and was being generous. And this offer was a gift.

Nodding, she slid a thumb over one of his fingers.

He peered up at her, meeting her gaze at last.

The velvety brown she found there was so soft and deep that the world melted away. Her heartbeat slowed.

Perhaps her trust wasn't for nothing.

CHAPTER 6

The Discovery

No, Ma, no! Lily raised her hands, covering her face. How had she ended up right back where she started—at the mercy of her mother's intoxicated rages?

Ma swung the ragged edge of a broken bottle.

Lily jerked back, hoping against hope that the sharpened pieces wouldn't catch her skin.

Time slowed...

And just as Ma's weapon connected with Lily's arm...she startled awake.

Lily was not cowering in the corner at her parents' small cabin. Rather, she lay on a soft, clean pallet in the corner of another cabin. One that was warm and safe. *She* was warm and safe.

Somehow.

Movement on the other side of the large space gave her pause. She held her breath.

Water trickled and a pot clanged. Did someone work the stove? Definitely not her parents' home. No, this cabin belonged to Mr. Miller's uncle. Perhaps it was his wife stirring nearby.

She had returned later last evening. Much to Lily's surprise, the woman was not ill to find an interloper in her home, but pleasant and every bit as welcoming as her husband. As if she found extras about every day. But that could not be so—they hadn't the room for guests.

Mr. Owen and Dan had worked to make this space for Lily—her pallet and partitions. She settled back against the pillow. Images from her heavy, dark dream clouded her mind. Why should she fear such? Was there a chance Dan would not keep his word?

Because she had hoped before...only to be disappointed. Why should Dan be any different?

Something whispered in the recesses of her mind...insisting he was. Had he not taken her out of harm's way already? And he stood beside her, set on keeping his promise to marry her in spite of what Pa said.

Maybe...

"You up already?" It was the older woman's voice. Was it directed toward Lily? Her words seemed a bit far off.

"I wanted to help." Mr. Owen's deeper, raspy words joined his wife's.

"Oh, you didn't have to do that. You need your rest."

"Are you mothering me again?" His words were light-hearted. Lily could almost hear his smile.

"No such thing!" Cook protested. "Just doing *my* wifely duty, taking care of you, you old coot!"

"Now, you know I have no objection to you doing your wifely jobs." Was that a hint of playfulness in his tone?

Lily's features warmed. But also, her heart...to think of these two still in love and chasing each other after so many years. Where were their children? Did they have any?

Cook giggled. "Oh, you old charmer." Her words became muffled.

Were they kissing? Lily pressed a hand over her heart. How endearing! Would such sweetness ever be for her? Her mouth fell. Such wasn't likely. It may be that she and Dan could live amicably, even come to an understanding...but love? Wasn't that too much for someone like her to hope for?

Cook and Mr. Owen continued their exchange, but their voices had become muffled. Should she rise and risk interrupting them? Or let them linger in their moment?

She snuggled under the quilt and left them to their moments alone.

What would this day bring? Would Lily stay here with Mr. Owen and worry the day away? Or...might she convince Cook to take her to the Miller ranch?

Had Dan voiced his concerns to Cook over Lily's presence at the Miller ranch? Would the woman refuse to let Lily go? There was only one way to find out.

Lily slid from the pallet and stood. The makeshift bed had been rather comfortable. More so than she'd expected. Mr. Owen and Dan had done well.

With no other garments, Lily made short work of freshening up. Her dress, though wrinkled in places, had fared well enough. She reached for a split between the partitioning blankets and peered through.

Mr. Owen and Cook sat at the dining table across the small cabin, coffee cups in hand. Their heads were close together as if they shared some great secret.

Perhaps she best not disturb them. She moved back, ducking toward the pallet once more.

"Morning," the older woman called.

Lily stepped back through the opening, meeting Cook's eyes across the space. "Good morning."

The older woman had a broad smile on her face, as if Lily hadn't disrupted their morning routine.

"Sleep well?" Mr. Owen, too, seemed unfazed by her sudden appearance.

"Yes, sir. Thank you." Lily played with a wrinkle in her skirt.

"Come over and have a sit down. I'll pour you some coffee." Cook rose and moved toward the stove.

"Let me," Lily said, stepping forward. Why must her presence be such a bother?

"Nonsense," Cook scolded. "You sit right down, and we'll chat before I head out."

Lily settled into one of the two remaining chairs. How would she go about this? "Head out? To the Miller ranch?"

"Oh, yes. Gotta get them boys and young'ins fed. They got lots of work today." Cook poured the hot dark brew into a cup.

"Do they? Sounds like y'all might need an extra hand." Lily held up her hand. "Or two." She smiled as she lifted up her other as well.

Cook set the steaming cup in front of Lily. "Now, don't you go getting any wild hair ideas. You need to rest. It's probably best if you just stay put today."

Lily let her hands drop into her lap. Perhaps Dan *had* spoken to Cook.

"I've got Amanda...ah...Mrs. Miller to help. She does as she can. Though she is awful tired with the baby and all."

"The baby?" Lily worked to swallow the coffee she had sipped lest she spit it out. There was a baby at the ranch? What else did she not know?

"Yes, Mrs. Miller will be ready to have that baby come this time next month...no more." Cook beamed.

Lily drank another sip of coffee while thinking before she spoke again. How best to proceed without appearing too eager?

The two had almost finished their breakfast stuffs. Lily's stomach started to protest. She didn't have time for that.

Setting her cup down, Lily set her gaze on Cook once more. "I'm sure you are certain Mrs. Miller isn't *too* helpful. Seeing as she has to get ready for the little one. And rest."

"That is true." Cook lowered her own cup. "I can't seem to make her rest."

"Maybe there's just too much work and not enough...hands." A lilt to her voice pressed what she hoped was the right emphasis on the last word.

Mr. Owen chuckled.

Cook's brows lowered. "Which is where you come in."

Lily put on her most innocent expression, hand to her chest. "Why, I hadn't thought of that."

"Oh, posh!" Cook waved a hand.

Mr. Owen laughed out loud. When he quieted, he spoke, "Come on, Dorothy, give her a chance. You know she's right. Amanda needs good cause to stop and rest. Or she won't."

"Maybe she don't," Cook countered. "And even if she does, maybe I don't need the help. I was feeding them boys long before Amanda showed up."

Mr. Owen gave her a hard look, brow raised. "It ain't just the boys anymore. You got Amanda and them kids."

"And you're saying I can't handle it?" She stared at her husband.

Perhaps Lily shouldn't have pushed.

Either way, when Cook loaded her wagon to head toward the ranch, Lily *and* Mr. Owen were with her.

Dan looped a rope mindlessly. He had to find a way to get some sleep. And soon. It was becoming increasingly difficult to tend to his chores in his tired state.

Last night, he had been haunted once more by Joseph's death. Not even thoughts of Lily could overcome the darkness that pulled at him.

He looked down to find the rope slapped together in a jumble. Not what he would consider suitable. Nor would Brandon find it acceptable. Not that he was a hard man, but a fair man...he liked things to be done correctly.

Letting loose the excess, Dan went about winding the thick strand again, lending his focus to the task a bit more this time. And in a matter of moments, the rope had been looped properly and stowed.

After setting it in place, Dan pressed the heel of his hand to his forehead. Could he clear this cloud from his mind? Shaking his head, he attempted to sift his thoughts. It was no use.

The gentle rhythm of wagon wheels crunching on the earth neared. Cook approached.

Should he ask about Lily? Had she had a good night? Or did the strangeness of the new environment make it difficult for her to find sleep? Would Cook know?

He made his way out of the barn as the cart passed. And he was less than pleased at the sight—the cart held not one, but three riders.

Heat stirred in the pit of Dan's stomach. Why would Cook bring Lily? How could she not think better of it? And why would Lily go along with such? Did he not make himself clear—that she should trust him and remain far from this place?

The heat grew into a fire. He marched after the cart, following it as it slowed to a stop between the barn and the homestead.

As he neared, Uncle Owen worked to climb down. That bum hip gave him so much trouble. Dare Dan assist and make him appear even weaker? Or let him struggle? What would Dan want in his position?

The struggle.

Dan came around and helped Cook out of the wagon. Then he lifted his arms for Lily.

She set hands on his shoulders and leaned toward him as he eased her down. Her eyes found his—the green seemed to light up. Why? Was she so happy to see him? No matter how it laced a pleasant sensation through his core, he refused to let it squelch his anger. For she had wronged him. But that wasn't the worst of it.

After he set Lily on firm ground, Dan turned to ensure Uncle Owen was on firm footing.

Lily retained her hold on his shoulders.

He looked back at her.

She fluttered her eyelashes.

Did she wish to staunch his ire? Or did she play a game? Was that why she looked at him so? A flirt?

Frowning, he removed her hands from his person. And moved to Uncle Owen, not caring to note if she had been hurt by his dismissal. How could she? If she only wished to toy with him.

Uncle Owen and Cook stood to the other side of the cart and shifted toward the porch. Should he broach the subject with them now? Or later? After all, he had trusted them to keep Lily away. If he'd not cared, he would have just brought her here himself.

Their backs were to him, however, and they began their slow walk to the steps.

Perhaps later would be best.

Had he cooled enough to speak with Lily? Or maybe that was a conversation best had later as well? But as he turned, he found her standing directly behind him.

"Lily," he ground out, nearly swearing.

She seemed stricken.

"Don't sneak up on someone like that."

Her features fell. The flirt was gone. Her hurt was all that remained.

He gripped his belt. Because he felt stand-offish or to keep from touching her?

"Why...why are you angry?" She peered up from beneath her eyelashes.

"Why am I angry?" He spit out. Why would she ask that? As if she didn't know? "We...I...Did I not make myself clear?"

She blinked, her long lashes fluttering again.

He tried not to think of how innocent and attractive it made her appear.

"We talked about this." He pressed through clenched teeth. "I thought you agreed to trust me." His voice rose as his anger returned.

"I do trust you." She set a hand on his arm.

More flirting? Was that all he was to her? Another man to manipulate?

He removed her hand and let it drop. "Then why did you come here? When we agreed you would stay at Cook and Uncle Owen's cabin?"

Her shoulders deflated and she crossed her arms. For a second, she seemed thoughtful, perhaps a little lost. Then she dropped her arms to her sides once more and lifted her shoulders, turning her regard to him. "I just wanted to be near you. Is that so bad?"

Again, she batted her eyes.

Confounded woman! When would she understand this wasn't going to work with him? He didn't want to—wouldn't—play her game. "Yes, it is so bad. I can't take care of you if you won't trust me."

Her façade dropped. For a moment. Why?

This was Lily—raw and real, and vulnerable. And he relished it. Though he ached to reach for her, he held back. He lowered his voice. "And I can't care for you if you won't let me in."

Shrugging, her hands slid up to rub her upper arms. She was the picture of loneliness...of someone lost, perhaps even to themselves. And he wanted to help her. So much. But how?

"I...understand," she said, not looking directly at him, but somewhere over his shoulder. "I'll be more mindful."

He nodded, looking at the ground between them. "Thanks."

"I, um, need to help Cook in the kitchen." Without dropping her arms, she moved past him and to the porch.

He watched her as she went into the house. And then he realized—that must have been how she convinced Cook to bring her—the promise of help.

Maybe he wouldn't be so hard on Cook.

Maybe.

Lily wiped down the table. The day had progressed without much incident. What had Dan been so afraid of? Why would he want her kept away? Did he not want her here for his own reasons?

She shook her head. Maybe he didn't intend to marry her after all. Biting back the sting of tears, she worked at a sticky spot on the fine wood of the dining surface. Would he, too, abandon her at the last moment? And then she would have nothing left but to slink back to her parents' home. To the nightmare. Or perhaps to the saloon...

Drawing in a breath, she pushed down the rising fear. She was safe for now in the elder Millers' home. They seemed nice enough. Maybe they would let her stay.

If she could dream...

"You're going to rub that spot raw," a voice said from the direction of the kitchen.

Lily looked up.

Amanda Miller stood in the doorway, a smile on her face.

Lily stopped her vigorous movement. "I'm sorry."

Amanda shook her head. "It's nothing to worry yourself over. I only meant to tease."

Lily stood as the woman stepped toward the table, two glasses of tea in hand.

Amanda sat and indicated the seat beside herself. "Please, join me. Take a load off."

Watching her, Lily wasn't sure what to do. She shot a look toward the kitchen. The sounds within had fallen silent.

"Cook is making her rounds to the bunkhouse."

"Oh." The bunkhouse? Did she clean up after those men? "Perhaps I should help—"

"Nonsense." Amanda patted the table in front of the vacant chair. "I want to chat for a minute."

Why would Amanda wish to speak with her? Uneasiness danced in her stomach. Could she deny the mistress of the ranch?

"Okay." She stretched out the word as she sat, reaching for the tea. Gulping more than was ladylike, she wished for a napkin to blot her mouth as she pulled the glass away.

Then she met Amanda's gaze. The woman's eyes were kind, welcoming—just as Mr. Owen and Cook's home had been. Just as everyone had been. Was this typical? It had not been Lily's experience of the world to be sure.

"I understand that you and Dan are to be married."

"Yes," Lily pushed out somehow. So, the woman would start with the heavier things. Would Amanda be protective of Dan? Not approve of a marriage made for convenience? Did she even know it was made under such circumstances?

"He is a fine man. Hardworking. A good man."

Was he? He at least *seemed* to have a big heart. Lily rubbed the side of the glass, turning it as she watched the light from the lantern hit in angles against it. "Yes."

"And you two must know each other well...having been school-mates." Amanda took a sip of her tea.

Lily met her gaze. How much *had* Dan told her? Did he tell her the whole truth? Best to tread cautiously. "Somewhat."

"Oh?" Amanda's brows rose. Maybe Dan hadn't been so forthcoming.

Was this woman hunting for information? Or did she truly care to know Lily? It was difficult to discern. Her questions were prying... weren't they? Or could they be an attempt to draw Lily out? Did she want to come out?

"How well do you know someone at that age, after all?" Lily attempted to laugh it off.

Amanda smiled. "True."

Lily took another swig of her tea.

"We all have ways of disguising who we are." Amanda met her gaze. "Of protecting ourselves."

Lily fought to keep from spitting out her tea. What *did* this woman know?

"I certainly did." Amanda let out a long sigh. "I'll have to tell you about it sometime. But, as always, this baby has me excusing myself."

Excusing herself? The woman stood and moved toward the front door. Where would she go? The only things outside were the barn and... the outhouse. Oh, yes—the outhouse. Lily had been told that when the last months of childbearing came, one was frequently in the outhouse.

The door shut and Lily was left alone in the house—this large, quiet house. A rather massive home compared to her parents' or to Uncle Owen and Cook's. But so many lived here. Today, she had met Samuel, and Lucy, and Nisto—a desert Indian boy, whose sister had married Cutie.

Her heart stung as if the wound were fresh. Indeed, it might as well be. The pain she endured had been dealt daily. As if God intended to heap more injury on, Cutie had been the ranch hand Joseph was to replace.

Joseph.

How was he gone? It didn't yet seem real. Her heart still ached. A big part of her remained empty.

Would it always?

Banging sounds farther away startled her.

She jumped in her seat. Had she been so caught up? When her breathing eased, she swallowed and worked to calm her racing heart.

The banging continued. What caused it? Had someone left a window open?

She turned to her tea. Should she leave Amanda's here? Or clean it up?

The banging was rhythmic—too much for it to be the wind beating a shutter. But dare she investigate in someone else's home?

She waited. The moments crawled by. Yet, it seemed as if hours passed. Still, the banging continued. And as it did so, she became more convinced she had to know what it was.

Glancing at the front door, she hoped for movement, for an arrival that did not come. Would Amanda return? Or had she been caught up by someone? It didn't matter. She couldn't wait any longer.

Decision made, Lily padded toward the sound. It led her deeper into the house, past the great room and to the back hallway. The sound was definitely louder back here.

As she tiptoed down the hallway, the pounding intensified. Something in one of these rooms was amiss.

She had flattened her body against the wall. Why? Was she so nervous? Her hand in front of her trembled. Perhaps she should turn back, get Dan or one of the others and return. That would be best.

But...maybe it was nothing. Only the wind from an open window—blowing a shutter, a lid, something...

Wouldn't she seem the perfect fool?

Closing her eyes, she swallowed. And steeled herself. This wasn't going to spook her. She was stronger than this. Pushing onward, she soon stopped at the door second on the right—the sound was loudest here.

The latch had been turned opposite such that the door could be locked from the outside. And it was. Why? Had something...or some*one*...been locked inside? For what reason?

Once again, she hesitated, her body filled with a tingling sensation—something akin to the need to run. But she didn't want to run...in that moment, she wanted to know.

Widening her eyes and ignoring the layer of perspiration, she reached for the latch, her fingers shaking as the rush of a prickling sensation coursed through her.

There was a rush of movement. A hand landed on hers. She was pulled back from the door. Arms surrounded her.

She pushed. She fought. But she was held too firmly.

A voice spoke into her ear...demanding. The words made no sense as she fought. But she stilled. She knew the voice—Dan.

"It's me. You're safe now."

Relief washed over her and she clung to him. "Dan!"

He held her tight, holding her against himself.

Couldn't she just relinquish all her worries in this space—here in his arms? In his care? But she held back.

"What...what is in there? *Who* is in there?"

He pulled back far enough to look at her. "You should never seek that room again."

She furrowed her brows. What secret did he hide? "Is someone being kept against their will?"

He looked away.

She gripped his shirt, jerking at the fabric. "Tell me, Dan. I have to know."

His gaze met hers. "Trust me, the less you know, the better."

She struggled out of his arms. "No. I really need to know."

Dan blew out a breath. Would he tell her? Was he attempting to decide? After a few moments, he spoke, "It is a wounded Indian."

"Indian?"

He grimaced. Did he not approve of the Indian being here? Or of her continuing the conversation? "Yes. Like Nisto."

Did he think her devoid of thought? There was no way he believed what he just said. Even his features screamed the untruth of his words.

"Like Nisto?" she challenged. Her eyes settled on him and dared him to continue the lie.

He watched her, his gaze seeming to take in every nuance of her face. Then he pushed out a breath. "It is an Indian Brandon feels would be mistreated and misunderstood if brought forth."

Mistreated? By who? Lily narrowed her eyes as she considered what he might mean. Then she looked at him again and swallowed. "You mean mistreated by my father."

Dan met her eyes again. "Yes."

Her anger seemed to dissipate as her father's face came into her mind. She realized how tired she was. But she needed to understand. Holding Dan's gaze, she asked, "What do you think?"

Dan's eyes cleared, then darkened. "I think your father would not understand."

Lily bit at her lip. What a mess. And she had walked right into it.

A long silence passed between them in which she considered the fix they were in. When she glanced up at Dan, she noticed that his features had twisted into somewhat of a pained expression. Or one of guilt?

Was this what he had been afraid of? That she would find this? Did he think she might betray them to her father?

She moved toward him and placed a hand on his crossed arms. "I give you my word, I will not speak of it. To anyone."

His dark eyes lightened once more.

And a little more trust was built between them.

Dan watched the wagon pull out and disappear into the horizon. What was happening to him? He couldn't deny that a part of him didn't want to see Lily go. Even for the evening.

But it would be longer. He had spoken with Cook. Lily would not be back the following day. Or the days coming after that.

Though it bothered him that he would not see her as much, he was convinced it was for the best. What if she had opened that door? What if the Apache brave had gotten to her? What if—?

He didn't want to—couldn't—think further. The very images that started to form were too much. So, he pushed them to the side. And he was just thankful he had been there in time.

Still he wondered...was this just about the brave and Lily's safety? Or was he protecting himself, too?

It seemed that whenever he was with Lily, more of him succumbed to her wiles. It was true—he cared about her. Maybe even cared *for* her. Maybe always had. But this was more. His regard had deepened.

Was he risking his heart? There were times, such as when they had arrived earlier today, when it seemed she thought nothing more of him than just the most recent in a long string of men—something to conquer, a heart to hold. Was she trapping him with her flirtatiousness and nothing more? Indeed, how much truth had been behind her father's insinuation?

Despite these difficult thoughts, nothing would stop Dan from keeping his word. From protecting her in Joseph's stead. From marrying her.

Though perhaps it should warn him to guard his heart better. She maybe wasn't one to be trusted. Not if he was one more conquest, just one more man to be toyed with.

It wouldn't be the first time he had put his heart out only to have it trampled...time and time again. No. His relationship with his father had been little more than a string of broken promises and lies.

"What a day," a voice said behind him.

He shifted to see who approached, pushing down any sign of being startled. Must everyone sneak up on him today?

Brandon came to stand next to him.

"I'll say." Dan turned his gaze back to the horizon.

"She's something," his boss said. The words were kind; they seemed a compliment. Brandon was not one to tease.

"Yeah." Dare he share his thoughts? His boss was as solid as they came...always gave good advice. Then he remembered that Lily had come upon the Apache brave. Was he prepared to share that? Maybe not yet.

Brandon remained silent. He was never one to pry. Dan was thankful.

"Have you wired the judge yet?" Dan asked, perhaps a turn of subject could ease the torn feelings within him. About Lily. About his father.

Brandon looked at the ground. "Yeah. Haven't heard anything."

"You look as though you don't expect to."

"With Geronimo at large...all these massacres and killings, I don't know that a judge will care about our situation so much."

Dan considered his words. Geronimo and his raiding band had made life...beyond difficult...terrorizing Southeastern Arizona and Northern Mexico. The chance that Brandon's appeal for the Apache brave's fair trial would fall on deaf ears was good.

Not that Dan cared. The murdering Apache locked in the homestead would get whatever he deserved. Dan couldn't close his eyes at night without seeing the young brave strike down Joseph.

Dan shook his head. Not now. He'd have those images to contend with later. No need to entertain them now as well. "What will you do?"

Brandon looked at Dan. But Dan refused to glance his way.

It didn't take a mind-reader to know that Brandon had at least guessed how Dan felt. For certain that's why he'd taken Dan's weapon—for fear Dan would finish the job himself. Perhaps he would have.

"I don't know," Brandon said.

Dan heard movement. What was Brandon doing? Shifting his balance to another foot? Looking around?

Pressing his mouth shut, Dan swallowed any suggestion he might offer. The brave wouldn't survive two seconds under Sheriff McAllen's care. Not even if the sheriff couldn't put two and two together. There was no love lost between the white man and the Apache these days. Thanks to Geronimo.

"I think you should invite Lily to the Harvest Day festivities." Brandon's voice took on a lighter tone.

Dan rolled his eyes. Guess he deserved that. He'd thrown Brandon a conversation shift, after all. "I don't know."

"Why not?" From the sound of Brandon's voice, he was looking in Dan's direction now. "If you plan to marry her, you might as well be at social events together."

Dan glanced down and watched the dirt move as he shuffled his feet. Brandon couldn't understand. While people may not have liked Amanda's first husband, they hadn't had any reason to disrespect her.

But it would come, whether now or later. People talked. And they had their minds set about Lily's virtue. He could not escape being at least singed by it. Would he rather take that bull by the horns now?

CHAPTER 7

The Invitation

Dan watched as Slim and Brandon ushered the new ranch hand toward the homestead. Samuel had long since rung the dinner bell. But Dan didn't follow the men. He regarded the backs of the men as they neared the porch.

Had he been too standoffish with the young man? Perhaps he'd injured the boy's pride, insisting he was too young to take on such hard work. Was that truly Dan's challenge with him? Or was it something deeper?

Dan sighed. He couldn't help that whenever he looked at the youngster, far from a man, he saw Joseph.

It was difficult.

Too difficult.

Pushing a hand through his hair, he wished away the hour to come. Could he sit across the table from the youth and hold his own?

Dare he try? A tightness filled his chest. He rounded his shoulders to ease it. And found little relief.

"Boss," he called.

Brandon paused, looking back at Dan.

Slim held back as well, but Brandon motioned for him to take Eli on into the house. Placing a hand on the youth's shoulder, Slim picked up their conversation and led him onward.

A breeze blew past. It relieved the remainder of the heat on his body, stirred up from the day's work. The air had cooled just enough that it was discernable—time for the season to change. If the world went through its process, moving on, moving forward, why couldn't he?

Dan's gaze fell on Brandon. His boss watched him from where he had stopped. Did the man attempt to read Dan's thoughts? Maybe he could. It would be a big help—Dan was frequently lost even to himself.

Forcing his feet forward, Dan stepped toward his boss. "I...think I'll head to Uncle Owen's."

"Oh?" Brandon quirked a brow, coughing, as if to cover something. Surprise? Or perhaps a laugh?

Dan dismissed it, gazing off in the direction he would have to ride. "Yeah. I need to have a conversation with Lily."

"Sure." This time, Brandon didn't even seem to attempt to disguise his smile.

Dan looked down, but he couldn't stop his own smile. Though it was short-lived. Thinking of his conversation with Lily brought a trickle of nervousness through his midsection and a pleasant tingle over his skin.

How Brandon read Dan's growing regard for Lily escaped him. But the man seemed rather pleased. Would he feel that way if he knew...?

But he didn't know...*couldn't* know...would never know...what Dan did.

"At least eat first." Brandon said into the silence.

Dan glanced toward the house. The thought of staring at Eli throughout the meal, making any sort of conversation, knowing it should be Joseph in his place...

Stepping back, Dan shook his head. "I'd like to be there and back before it gets too late."

Brandon's face fell. Had he noticed Dan's attention drift? Could he discern Dan's thoughts? "Sure. I bet Uncle Owen's got something stirred up for dinner anyway."

"Yeah."

"See you in the morning." Brandon backed away, starting to turn.

"In the morning." Dan spun and walked into the barn.

It took little effort to prepare and saddle his horse for the short journey to Uncle Owen and Cook's cabin. Why, then, was his heart racing? Pushing that thought to the side, he mounted the dark brown mare. Then pressed his heels into her flank, bidding her forward and onward.

Soon enough, the small cabin appeared in the distance and he slowed the animal. He hopped down at the porch and tied off the reins. Dusk had fallen and the few lights from within burned bright.

Dan paused. He watched the movement of shapes inside. The figure in the kitchen was slender and moved gracefully—not the hobbled steps of Uncle Owen. Did Lily prepare the small meal?

Where was Uncle Owen? As he glanced around, Dan spotted the man's outline, almost hidden by the shadows, near the table. He pulled out a chair and sat as Dan watched. All seemed well enough.

Why should he break the spell of such a pleasant evening? Should he just return to the Miller ranch and wait until he could sup alone?

He peered through the window again, watching Lily. The pull within him to be near her dashed every thought that vied against his plan.

Dan stepped to the door and knocked.

He resisted the urge to lean back and look in the window off to the side once more. Instead, he worked to gather his scattered nerves.

Footfalls sounded, nearing the door. And, sucking in a breath, he prepared to greet his old friend.

The door opened.

"Good evening, Uncle Ow—"

Lily's flushed face greeted him.

"Lily..." He swallowed. Hard.

A slight tint to her cheeks highlighted the red in her hair and made her skin, in contrast, appear that much fairer. It stole his breath.

"Good evening, Dan," she said, her color deepening. "It's good to see you. Won't you come in?" She backed away from the door, providing space for him to step in.

But he didn't move. First tongue-tied, it seemed he was also frozen to the spot. Which Lily would he get—the real Lily or the one who put forth nothing more than feminine wiles?

"Who is it, Lily?" Uncle Owen's voice called from off to the left. "Did I hear Dan's voice?"

"Yes," she called; her features became a mixture of confusion.

"Why won't he come in?" Uncle Owen's voice rang out. Why did the man insist on embarrassing him?

"I...don't know." A noticeable crease had formed between her eyebrows. She leaned forward. "You all right?"

He took hold of his wits. His own features heated. "I...yes, I'm fine. Just...surprised. That is, I expected Uncle Owen."

"But you knew I was here." The furrow of her brows deepened.

How could he answer that without appearing all the more...what? Stymied? Flustered? Taken aback?

Was there any saving face? Perhaps...

He stepped past her and into the cabin's main room. "What is that wonderful smell?"

She closed the door behind him, but he forced himself to keep his gaze on Uncle Owen, not to look at Lily. It didn't help that Uncle Owen, brow raised, appeared every bit as confused as Lily had...and somewhat amused.

"Beef stew," Lily said, stepping forward to stand beside him.

"What?" What was she talking about again?

"That smell." Her face displayed her bewilderment. "It's beef stew."

He looked to Uncle Owen again.

Lily passed in front of him but kept her eyes on his. And she flashed him one of her sweet smiles.

Not this again.

"You asked after the smell?" She lifted an eyebrow.

"Oh, yes." Where was his mind? How could he forget so quickly? There must be a way to keep his thoughts on the present. He watched her walk to the kitchen. "It smells wonderful."

"Yes." Her shoulders shook a little. Was that a giggle? "You said that."

His face heated even more. Wouldn't Uncle Owen save him? He shot a pleading glare at the man.

Uncle Owen grinned from ear to ear. That old codger.

"Did I ask if I might...um...bother you for a bowl?" He shifted his focus back to Lily.

She offered him a half smile and a wink. "Not yet."

Her attention fell to the bubbling mixture in the pot, which she stirred with a wooden spoon. This only caused the aroma to fill the air in the cabin all the more.

Would she make him beg? As much as he hated giving into her playfulness, he couldn't stop the emotions coursing through him.

She turned, putting her hands behind her back, and leaned forward at the waist. "You are most welcome to it, Mr. Hayworth."

He smiled and nodded as he tipped his hat forward and off. Then he made short work of discarding it and his gloves by the front door.

The table had been set and Uncle Owen still sat, watching from his seat. But there were only two settings placed.

"Where can I find the..." he fumbled for the right words.

Lily stepped to the table with a bowl and spoon. Would he not be able to do anything to help? Did she realize how close she had come to him? He was overwhelmed with the scent of lilacs. From her hair?

She placed the dish and utensil on the wooden surface and looked at him. Her nearness warmed him. And cleared his thoughts.

But she tarried for a moment. Did she wait for him to say something? Or was it because she felt as he did?

After a moment, her chin tipped down and her brows rose. She waited for something. What?

"Thanks," he managed.

With a swish of her skirt, Lily moved back to the large pot.

He wanted to deflate into the chair. But he dared not. It would be too telling. Glancing at Uncle Owen, he felt the urge rising in him to say something that would wipe that silly grin off the man's face.

"Bring your bowls, boys. It's ready."

Dan reached across the table and grabbed Lily's bowl just as Uncle Owen stretched toward it. He offered the older man a crooked smile. At least this once, he would not be outdone. So, he jerked the bowl free of Uncle Owen's grasp and turned away.

He marched to the stove and handed the first bowl to Lily. Their fingers touched in the exchange, and he remembered what it was like to hold her, touch her smooth skin, to set his lips on hers.

"Can I have the other?"

"What?" He jerked himself from his musings.

"The other bowl," she said more firmly. Though her eyes on his seemed rather amused.

He pushed forth his bowl and fought to maintain his stance as Uncle Owen poked him from behind.

"Hey, quit holding up the line," the man said low.

In a matter of moments, they were all seated, and Uncle Owen lifted up a short prayer of thanks.

Dan had only taken a couple of bites of the well-seasoned stew when Uncle Owen announced he had finished and needed to check on something in the barn.

"Can I help you with—?" Dan rose.

"No, it's, ah, a surprise," Uncle Owen insisted. "Stay, finish your meal." He waved Dan back into his seat.

He sat but was not fooled by the old manipulator. Still, he could not deny he appreciated the moments alone with Lily. Perhaps it would be easier to ask her to the Harvest Day Festival without an audience.

Turning toward her, he smiled.

She looked at her bowl as her lips spread across her face. Did she, too, wish to be alone with him?

An awkward silence fell between them.

"How's the stew?" she asked, her brows upturned.

Did she want his approval?

"It's good. Great, actually. Best I've had."

She peered at him, biting at her lower lip. "Better not let Cook hear you say that."

"Oh, no. Never." He offered his most charming grin. Though it wasn't anything special. Nothing compared to some of the other men she'd...

He glanced opposite. Why would he let his mind wander so?

There was that awkward silence again. Stirring the remainder of the broth in his bowl, he chided himself and worked to gather his wits about him.

"Lily," he said, clearing his throat and shifting toward her once more. Why was it harder, asking this simple question, than it had been to propose marriage?

"Yes?" Her eyes widened as she met his gaze. Was she fearful of what might come? Expecting something unpleasant? Why?

She appeared so stricken, so lost, that he reached out for her, covering her smaller hand with his. He wanted to reassure her. But how?

"It's nothing much." Dan did his best to put a dismissive tone in his voice.

"Oh." Her gaze fell. Relief? Disappointment?

"I just...that is...I wanted to ask you about the Harvest Day festivities."

One of her brows arched. And her chest rose and fell more rapidly. What business did he have noticing that?

He refocused on her eyes. "Would you do me the...honor...of accompanying me?" Why had he hesitated on that word? Had she noticed?

The pause, albeit brief, before she answered was telling. It concerned him.

She did speak, her voice sweet and gentle. "Yes. That would be nice."

Her eyes were glassy. Did she mean what she said? Did she want to go with him? Or did she only feel obligated?

He withdrew his hand and hunched over his bowl once more.

And they continued to eat in silence.

That same awkward silence.

Was this but a foretelling of the future?

Lily handed Cook a wooden spoon and swiped her forearm over her features. They had been busy in the small cabin's kitchen—stirring, mixing, and baking all morning.

"How are those pumpkin spice biscuits coming along?" Cook glanced at the dough as Lily rolled it out.

"Just fine." Lily smiled. Why was she so determined to prove to Cook that she was more than capable? Something in her wanted the woman to see her ability and appreciate her for it. Maybe even admire her a little.

Mrs. Jackson had never given her a chance in the kitchen. And Ma had never cared.

Ma...

It had been too easy to forget...to put the woman out of mind while tucked away in this place...safe, comfortable. Had it only been a week since she'd last seen her mother? Since Ma had thrown her to the floor?

The scrapes on her hands had healed well enough. They always did.

But Ma's words...

Those cut deeper.

She shook her head. They wouldn't leave lasting marks either. Of that she was determined.

Lily traded the rolling pin for a biscuit cutter and made short work of twisting circles into the dough. Setting those to the side, she pulled the remaining thickness together, kneading and patting it out once more.

"You're awful quiet over there." Cook's voice broke the stillness.

"Just concentrating." Lily dismissed Cook's concern, excusing her wayward mind.

"Concentrating? Or *thinking*?"

Lily stopped. The rolling pin paused as it was. What *did* Cook know? Had Dan shared more than he should?

She turned her head toward the older woman.

Cook stirred her pie filling—adding a sprinkle of this and that. Did she ever measure anything?

Lily swallowed and looked at her own spices next to her biscuits, cut out with precision. How was she to answer Cook? How much dare she expose herself?

"I...have a lot on my mind. That's all." There. That should be enough. Lily turned back to her work.

"Want to talk about it?" Cook's comment sounded lazy and unassuming. Lily would wager it was anything but. She dropped the biscuit cutter. Grimacing, she bit her lip lest her frustration slip out. And as she knelt to collect the small metal piece, her hand met Cook's on the floor.

"My goodness, child. You're trembling." Cook's softened tone exuded concern.

Lily jerked her hand back. "It's nothing." She stood.

Cook rose beside her. "Why don't you sit for a minute?" Laying a hand on Lily's arm, Cook indicated the few seats around the dining table.

What was this? Didn't Cook need help getting the food ready for tomorrow's festivities? Why, then, would she be so worried about Lily? To the point she would put her to the side?

"You are not well," Cook said, her tone did not invite argument. And her gaze pierced Lily's hardening exterior.

Laying a hand to Lily's arm, she pressed Lily toward the great room. Lily jerked back, quite nearly facing off with the older woman. Her breaths coming in heaves.

Was Cook daft? Did she not understand the way things were? Lily needed to earn her keep. At the very least.

"Why?" Lily let out on a breath. "Why are you being so kind to me?"

Cook leaned back. "Why?" Her features could not have shown more surprise and hurt if Lily had slapped her. "Why ever would I not, child?"

Lily crossed her arms, uncrossed them, and then clasped her shaking hands together in an effort to still them. "I...don't understand what you want from me."

"Oh..." Cook looked at the floor for a moment. "I'm sorry I pried."

Pried? Did she think Lily offended by her questions? Lily opened her mouth to assure her that was not the case, but Cook cut her off.

"I'm sorry. I'm just an old fuddy dud, I guess. And I talk too much. I didn't mean to be a bother."

Lily shook her head, but Cook kept her gaze on the floor.

"Please, forgive an old woman her long held faults."

"I..." Lily grasped for the right words. But what could she say? Would she have to expose something of herself if she contradicted Cook? The woman so sincerely wanted to be absolved. How could she not? "All is forgiven. I am not angry."

Cook's eyes met hers again. There was moisture in the older woman's eyes. Had Lily's outburst truly bothered the woman so?

"Thank you!" Cook took her hands and patted them. "Please, take a minute to rest. I'd best set that pie."

Cook moved away from her and into the kitchen.

What was Lily to do? She had never known such kindness, such grace. Everyone in her life had always wanted something from her. No one ever gave without expecting in return.

What were these seemingly gentle people after? And what would it cost her?

Dan stood outside Cook's door once more. He had knocked. And now the seconds ticked by too slowly. They could not have gone already. For certain *she* would not have gone. Not when he had spoken with her about accompanying him. She wouldn't, would she?

But then again, he always believed his Pa. The man wouldn't leave. Wouldn't forget him again. And yet every Saturday morning, when Dan rushed from his room, he found only Ma's downcast face and thin excuses.

His doubt grew. Had Lily now also left without him? The breaths coming in had become shallow. He closed his eyes and filled his lungs before pushing the air out. This was different. Lily was not his father.

Perhaps he had not been clear. Hadn't he? Did she not wish to be seen riding to the festivities with him? The doubt within deepened, and his heart weighed heavier.

Then the door opened.

Uncle Owen's tired features greeted him. Must the man always seem so worn? It worried Dan.

The older man's brow creased, and he frowned. "I didn't expect to see you here?"

"No?" Dan's own lips fell. Doubt. Had she not shared their plans with Uncle Owen? "Didn't Lily mention I would be her escort to the Harvest Day Festival?"

Uncle Owen rubbed his misshapen beard. "Don't 'spose she did."

Dan blinked and swallowed. Rejection. It must be true—she wasn't ready to be on his arm yet.

"Ah, what do I know." Uncle Owen waved a hand. "Those two don't tell me everything. Come on in." He moved to the side.

Was there hope after all? Dare Dan give it credence?

Dan stepped around the older man and into the larger area. His nerves had gotten him so worked up for this. And she hadn't even bothered mentioning it to Uncle Owen.

He had made too much of this outing. More than she did.

And that was dangerous.

Glancing down at his best shirt and fresh-washed trousers, he told himself that he would have dressed so whether she accompanied him or not. It was a special occasion. The whole town would be there...celebrating.

Cook rustled about the kitchen, here and there, shifting this and that. Not that he expected anything less.

But where was Lily?

He glanced around the small cabin...and noted movement. The quilts surrounding her partitioned off pallet rippled. Was Lily within? Perhaps dressing for the day?

His face warmed, and he forced his regard to the floorboards. It wasn't appropriate for him to think on such things.

Footfalls from that direction drew his attention upward. She had stepped out. Maybe she had only needed to apply finishing touches to her appearance.

Now she was but an arm's length away. And she made no effort to cover her surprise.

"Dan," her voice seemed almost alarmed.

He fingered the brim of his hat. "You sound almost as if you didn't expect me."

"I...no, of course I did..." She straightened her posture and ran a hand down her skirt.

They stood in silence.

He raised a brow. Did she speak true?

"That is...I had thought you meant for us to meet there...that I should ride with Cook and Mr. Owen."

Both brows shot up. "I asked you to come *with* me. It was not understood, then, that I would come to fetch you?"

She looked to the side as she made a slight back and forth motion with her head.

What was that about? What kind of men had she been courted by that she…? But he knew. She hadn't quite been involved with the most honorable men.

He looked back to the floorboards and tried not to think about what that revealed of her thoughts of him. Was he just another of these lowlifes in her mind? Someone who would treat her like…?

It bothered him. More than he wished it to.

"As it so happens," he said with more force than he'd intended. "I did mean to collect you. And I *am* here…"

She focused on him then, still biting her lip. Was this more playacting? Yet another attempt to endear herself to him? But there was something in her eyes beyond that…beyond the emotions she fought to contain. Was it…hope?

Still, he wasn't ready to give himself over to such—neither to hold hope nor be the bearer of someone else's.

"Shall we go?" He clipped. "Unless you have other preparations?" He watched her. Would she give him some indication one way or the other? Or remain paralyzed to the spot?

"I'm ready." She stepped forward. "Let me grab my basket of biscuits for the meal."

She continued, moving to go around him.

He put a hand to her arm. "Allow me."

Her gaze shot to his hand and then to his eyes. A handful of breaths passed. Did she gauge the reason for his touch? Or his words?

She stepped back, letting his hand fall. "I thank you." Lifting her hand toward the kitchen, she motioned to the stovetop. "The biscuits are just there."

He walked into the smaller space, all the while wondering what this was between them—this awkwardness. And what presumptions she might have in that pretty head of hers? What would he do about them? What *could* he do about them?

Collecting the basket she had indicated, he then returned to her side, led her out of the cabin, and to the wagon. He didn't bother to ensure she followed. Did he tire of her so easily?

At the side of the wagon, he turned. She was behind him, as she should be. So much so, that she had to stop short to keep from bumping into him.

He grimaced. Then, after setting the basket on the rim of the wagon, he reached for her.

She stared at his hand.

Why did she worry so? What did she expect? But he was not prepared to play games. Stepping to her, he gripped her waist and lifted her into the wagon seat.

Not in a mood to talk, much less apologize, he all but tossed the basket in her direction.

It did not escape his notice that she held it with a firm grasp, almost tenderly. Why? Were the biscuits dear to her? Why should they be?

He dismissed such nonsense and walked around, loosening the horse's tied reins and moving to his side of the bench. And, in short order, he sat beside her, prodding the horse forward.

As the horse bore them toward Wharton City with a speed so slow he thought he might be able to carry Lily faster, Dan considered his actions. Who wouldn't be put off by him today? But he'd dared not encourage her more than he had. Or was that ridiculous? They *were* set to marry. Though, the way he had treated her, and the things set in motion in these few days, could affect the entirety of their marriage. That was a heavy burden indeed.

Maybe he wasn't fit to be a husband after all. He glanced in her direction.

She continued to look downward, at the basket of biscuits. Whatever for? What was so important about them?

Shaking his head, he shifted his focus forward again and worked his thoughts to other matters. Or tried to.

Goodness, that man can be fickle!

Lily watched Dan's back as he strode away.

After securing the wagon and horse, he had mumbled something unintelligible, and off he went.

The feeling that welled within her, threatening to overwhelm her... was all too familiar...more so than she cared to admit...this feeling of being...extra.

Not needed.

Or wanted.

Was it the truth, though? Had Dan changed his mind? Did he intend to break off their arrangement?

Why, then, had he made a point to ferry her to the Harvest Day Festival? To punish her? Perhaps he had planned to tell her in their unchaperoned moments that the engagement was off.

How did she end up here...again? What had she done—or said—that put him off?

She didn't know. She *never* knew. With any of them.

Of all the times men had set her to the side, she never once knew why. It must be something about her. Something in her that was just... un-loveable. Unwanted.

The world around her blurred. Or was it that her eyes became hazy? Yes, it was only moisture, pooling there, affecting her sight. Tears were soon to come.

She wiped at them. This wasn't the place to fall apart. No, that would only bring further embarrassment upon Dan and the Miller family.

Off to the right, the townspeople gathered. Tables had been brought out into the field. Even then, women busied themselves, laying out the spread of food.

She glanced at her basket of biscuits—the fruit of her labors. What would anyone want with them? Such a meager offering. They were probably dry anyway.

Lily set the basket on a nearby bench. Maybe a dog or other such animal might happen upon them. Better a meal for such an undiscerning tongue than to upset the stomachs of these fine people.

From her place near the livery, she watched as the womenfolk chatted and laughed. As if it came so easily to them, these day-to-day interactions—friendships, merriment. If only they knew how hard it could be for someone like her to reach out. Or how dangerous.

No one could understand.

No one.

To the left of the nearby church building was the graveyard. Joseph was there.

Her heart ached. She'd done a fair job of forgetting, of numbing herself to the grief. But it became too difficult, and she too vulnerable.

Her stride carried her closer to the small, fenced-in area. In only a matter of moments, she stood over the gray stone with 'Joseph Richard McAllen' etched into the face.

She didn't know whether she knelt or her knees gave out. Either way, she drew closer to the marker. Her fingers traced the letters and those below it—'Beloved Son.'

Beloved son? Why not also 'Beloved Brother'? Joseph had been so good to her. He'd been her rock, protector, best friend, and champion. And, without a doubt, the only person she had ever loved.

Perhaps the only man she ever would.

Her lower lip quivered. Fighting the sobs that pressed against her throat became more difficult as the myriad of emotions roiled within her.

"Joseph," she whispered.

The pain leaked out then. Her shoulders heaved as she cried. How could he leave her? Why did he have to?

She pressed the back of her hand to her mouth to muffle her whimpers. Why would she blame him? There wasn't anything he could've done. Nothing anyone could have done to prevent the horrid accident. If only...

No.

Such thoughts were not to be permitted...much less entertained. But she couldn't stop herself. For it came from deep within, and she felt it with all she had—if only it had been her.

Sniffling, she cringed. She must be wicked to think such. And question the will of God. Hadn't she distressed God enough? If He even cared anymore. If He ever did...

She gazed at the letters that formed her brother's name. How could she not wish such a thing? Joseph had been stronger. For certain, his life had more promise. His future wouldn't have lain in ruins as hers did at this moment.

"Such a shame," a deep voice behind her said, the words sliding out as smooth as honey.

She knew that voice. But rather than soothe her, it sent a chill down her spine. Must she turn? Face him? In this vulnerable moment? Dare she?

Footfalls in the dirt warned that he came near.

She wiped at her tears. Could she hide that she'd fallen apart?

"Life has dealt you a difficult hand, darlin'." The man was now standing over her. Did he not care to maintain a proper distance?

She refused to turn. But as she opened her mouth to bid him leave her be, nothing came forth.

"And where is that…troll? The one who fancies himself your keeper? Why is he not here in your time of need?"

She bit her lip. Hot tears pressed against her eyelids, threatening to spill once more. Dan had abandoned her. He didn't care. Not truly.

Twisting, she met Silas's eyes. "Leave him out of this."

Silas put a hand to his chest. "Forgive me, Lily. I did not mean to upset you." As he spoke, he stepped around her kneeling figure until he stood beside her. Then lowered himself until they were eye-to-eye. "I am only worried about you."

Was he? Or did he seek only what she could do for him? Such was the story with everyone in her life.

At least, in Silas's case, she wouldn't be beholden to anyone. She would earn her keep, and she wouldn't have to worry about being sent back to her mother. The terms would be clear.

Maybe…just maybe…it could be the answer…

CHAPTER 8
The Outing

Why had he let himself get so riled up? Dan leaned against a post and looked out at the gathering crowd. It just wasn't like him. He was always one to keep his head level. Or at least he tried to be. No matter what. Then why?

He let out a breath. Since Joseph's untimely demise...and then Lily's sudden entrance into his life, he hadn't been able to keep his own mind. Or maintain any manner of steadiness about himself. Nope. His emotions were all a jumble, as were his thoughts. What was that about?

Even things long buried had begun to resurface. It wasn't right.

He shuffled a boot against the edge of the planked sidewalk. As if he didn't know.

She challenged him—his way of life and the way he liked things. Impeded his easy manner, stirring something in him. It just wasn't good.

Still, he might need to apologize for his behavior. She didn't deserve to be treated with such disregard...or to be the brunt of his cantankerous manner.

He sighed. When would he learn? And when would he harness his heart?

Rumbling, though somewhat subtle, came in on the wind. Wasn't every soul in town at the festivities? What could it be?

He scanned the crowd. Only a few heads inclined to catch the noise. Most folks continued their merry making as if nothing were amiss.

The sound grew louder, and a desperate call cut through the din of voices. But the words were not yet discernible. Dan sought Brandon amongst the many faces. His boss had already started moving toward the edge of the group. He, too, must know something was wrong.

As the sound transitioned into hoofbeats, several others worked to quiet those gathered. Dan wished it were possible to stop them. Creating a panic would serve no one.

"Sheriff!" the man approaching on horseback called. It was the first discernable word.

Now that the people were no longer distracted, they had heard it, too. Whispers and gasps provided an undertone of fear.

There wasn't time to address that. Dan lengthened his stride and moved in the direction of the main street into town—as good as anyone's guess as to where the man would appear. It seemed to be the source of the sound.

Brandon was soon behind him, lagging by just a few paces. How many others were also following?

A man, face reddened and clothes disheveled, rounded the corner at the end of the dirt road. He continued to call out with all he could muster for the sheriff.

Dan stopped. A handful of men collected around him.

McAllen shoved his way through the small group, shouldering past Dan. Had he even noticed the ranch hand?

"What is this?" McAllen bellowed.

The stranger, heaving, jerked on his reins. But the horse had been run out. It would be a miracle if the animal survived.

"Sheriff..." the man rasped. His voice had become weak. Was the ride the only thing that ailed him?

Dan narrowed his eyes, attempting to take in all the information he could from his position.

"What's the meaning of this?" McAllen demanded, his gaze hard on the young man. The man did not receive outsiders graciously...especially those who caused such a stirring among his townsfolk.

"The..." He gasped for breath, sucking in air. Did he search for words? Or fight to form them? "...Apache...are...coming."

Apache? Dan looked left and right as if the Indians would appear—come out of the stores or over the tops of the buildings. Ridiculous.

Still, this man...he was a harbinger of great danger. What could the Apache want? Was it Geronimo's band? Did they come for the brave lying captive at Brandon's homestead? What could that mean for the Miller family?

The cluster of men around Dan shifted and grumbled amongst themselves. Some hurried away. To prepare? To run? What did they intend?

McAllen stepped closer to the stranger still astride who had risked much to bring them this warning. "You best speak true. I don't look kindly on those who disrupt the peace in my town."

The man appeared stricken; his features contorted. His eyes rolled back in his head and he fell forward, slipping from his horse and falling at their feet.

Some of the men jerked back a step, but McAllen held his ground. In the middle of the man's back, just to the left of his backbone, an arrow protruded.

How much time did they have before the vengeful Apache swooped upon their small town? Time to get the women and children to safety? To ready and arm the men? Dan looked at his boss.

Brandon shook his head. Because he pitied the stranger? Didn't think he would make it? Or didn't think *they* would?

McAllen's deputies stepped forward and lifted the wounded, perhaps dying, man.

"Take him to the doctor," McAllen ground out. "I want answers if he ain't dead."

Brandon elbowed Dan and stepped back. As he moved away from the small crowd of men, a ruckus started about what to do.

Dan followed his boss, and they slipped into an alley. Soon they were back in the field near the church where the women and children remained, unsettled.

As a collective, their eyes fell on Dan and Brandon as they appeared from around the back of the café. Dan's heart raced. The responsibility for so many weighed heavy on his shoulders.

"We have to get these people to safety," Brandon said, his voice firm, steady.

Dan's gaze followed the lines of the structures—both manmade and natural—around the area. Where might they find shelter? It must be somewhere from whence they could protect *and* fight?

And where was Lily?

The thought came unbidden. His concern should be for the group as a whole, but he couldn't shake the nagging feeling that she wasn't safe. He hadn't seen her since their arrival earlier. Where had she gotten off to?

He glanced toward the livery. Was that...? She left her basket there. But why? If she had dropped the biscuits at the livery, perhaps she had not bothered to join the gathering at all.

It seemed he couldn't breathe. His heartbeat became erratic. And panic rushed through him. Where could she be? This was no time for her games. He needed her. He wanted her to—

A piercing cry split the air. A war cry.

Dan's time for considering had gone.

The Apache had come.

Lily tore her attention from Silas. What had happened at the town's center? The group, huddled moments ago around the picnic tables, rushed this way and that.

A strangled voice released an odd cry.

She turned to Silas.

His eyes widened, and he rushed at her.

"Wh-what's going on?" She held up her arms. Would he attack her?

He sidestepped, attempting to move around her.

She blocked his path. Why? Shouldn't she let him go?

His eyes darkened. For a moment she feared he might plow over her. Perhaps she deserved no better. Instead, he clamped a firm hold on her wrist and dragged her behind him. Did he give such care for her safety? Or did he simply not wish to risk the delay of her resistance?

"Hurry, if you want to live. And for Pete's sake, be quiet!"

She grabbed at her skirt even as she tripped on the hem. It became difficult to keep up, but she dared not pause, for Silas's mood had grown foul.

He jerked her up the couple of steps leading into the small church. Would they be safe within? Was it wise to be inside alone with him?

There wasn't time to follow those thoughts, much less protest, before Silas shoved her through the door and shut it behind himself. He spun, then crouched below the back window and peered out.

"Silas, I think we—"

"Quiet," he seethed. "Are you trying to get us killed?"

She drew back at his flash of anger, pulling into herself. Something rubbed against her leg and she whirled around, prepared to fight off an onslaught. Her hands connected with solid wood—a harmless pew having been the victim of her backward movements.

Laying a hand over her heart, she pushed out a breath and forced the ones that followed to be even. There was no need to get carried away. Perhaps there wasn't anything to this disturbance in town. At least, nothing she need be concerned with. Had Silas taken advantage of the moment?

She peered at him, only a few feet away. He appeared to be truly worried—watching from his position, ducking and preparing for any sign of danger. Would he, after all, protect her?

All stilled for a moment. It was in the air. And she knew—there *was* something to his concern.

Shots fired.

She knelt low. Oh, that she had the gumption to slink to the altar and plead with the Lord Almighty for her life. But she remained as she was, paralyzed.

Further sounds, each more alarming than the last, came from the direction of the main street—gunfire, men and horses screaming—and then nothing.

Had whatever altercation ceased? Or was it because she now clamped her hands over her ears?

After some moments of nothingness, she opened her eyes...when had she shut them? Hesitating but decided, she lowered her hands.

Still nothing.

Perhaps then the skirmish had ended. And Silas...?

Was gone.

Gone? He no longer squatted by the window.

Her gaze swept the church. Nothing. She was alone.

The door, however, was wide open. Banging, in fact, against the stair landing's rail. Dare she?

Her thoughts were clouded. Maybe too much for the best decisions. But she couldn't remain here. That was certain.

Rising, she moved to the open door. The field beyond the church was empty. In fact, there wasn't a soul as far as she could see. Where were the dozens who had gathered moments earlier in celebration?

She stepped onto the stairs, laying a trembling hand on the rail. Was she so shaken?

Why shouldn't she be? Moments later, she set her feet on the ground.

Voices in the distance reassured her that she wasn't truly alone, that others were there but farther away. Should she walk toward them? Or seek shelter in the church once more? Maybe give into her curiosity and search for the townsfolk?

Before she'd fully considered any option, her legs carried her away from the small church building. Into the wide-open field. Into vulnerability.

The voices became louder and then quieted in a rhythm she couldn't discern. Everything seemed surreal. Even the world started to spin. Only now she had nothing to hold onto.

"Lily?"

She looked around herself. The voice calling to her was near. How was that possible? Was there hope?

"Lily!" The strong, masculine voice filled her senses. So loud. From where?

She turned. *Dan.*

Moisture filled her eyes. She was safe.

He moved faster than she thought possible. As if he knew she would soon falter.

And, just as he approached, she did, falling into his arms. He held her firmly.

"Lily, thank God." He spoke into her hair.

So, he *did* care.

He leaned back and looked into her face. His features spelled relief, but they soon shifted. Something akin to pain contorted them. "Where have you been? Where did you run off to?"

Why would he scold her so? Couldn't he see that she held to her dignity with rather thin threads?

"I...I..."

"This isn't a game." His voice was gruff. "You could've been killed."

That pained expression touched his features once more. He may sound angry, but his eyes betrayed him.

Only...

Her tight control on her emotions slipped. Why would she think she could master such an overwhelming force? She hadn't the strength. Not any more. "Where were *you*?"

He jerked back. "Me?"

"Yes! Where were you when I needed you?"

His mouth became a thin line. Could that be guilt holding his tongue?

"If it hadn't been for Silas, I..." She shook her head. Her vision blurred as tears fell. "I don't know what would have happened to me."

"Silas?" His features darkened.

That, she saw quiet well enough.

"You were with Silas?"

Had she revealed too much? Did she care? She pressed her lips together and let it wash over her. He could judge her all he wanted. Didn't he already? And he might push her away. Or set their agreement aside. But he would *not* paint her the wrongdoer when she had been innocent.

She straightened, throwing back her shoulders and pulling free from his grasp. "*He* rescued me."

Dan blinked. Would he be as stunned if she had slapped him?

"He pulled me to safety." Why mention that Silas may have only done so to save his own skin?

Dan set a hand to his belt and blew out a breath through his teeth. "I thought you weren't going to associate with that man anymore."

She folded her arms across her chest. "I can't choose who comes to my aid, now can I? Especially if *you* are not to be found."

He looked off to the side, into the distance.

Though she stood in place with everything she had left, she was thankful he had no way to see into the inner workings of her mind. Or that under her skirt her knees shook.

When he turned to her again, his features had loosened somewhat. "I'm sorry I wasn't there, I—"

"Please..." she said, letting her gaze fall to the ground, her voice not much more than a whisper. She could handle his brashness so much better than the tenderness. "Take me back to Cook and Mr. Owen's."

She sensed his eyes on her for several moments after. Would he continue this interchange? Insist she hear him out?

"All right." His tone had softened, but there was something else in his voice. It almost sounded like hurt.

That pulled at her. Only just though.

She was too much of a tangled mess. So much so she wondered if anything or anyone could find a way to undo the knots. And set her free.

Dan wished he had the way with words so many other men seemed to. Men like Silas. Fine words dripped from his lips like honey. Always had. Even as a boy.

Young Silas had been the source of more than one schoolyard tussle for Dan. Rarely was Silas on the receiving end, but he was more often than not the instigator—with that mouth of his. Spilling sonnets in some cases, poisoning with accusations and dripping with venomous taunts in others. Dan still remembered some of his choice jabs. Well placed, he had to admit. They found their mark and got the reaction Silas wanted—a bloodied and bruised 'Dan-ill.'

Dan pushed those memories to the side, but he was certain the lines on his features had deepened. There wasn't time to dwell on the past. Not when his future lay in shambles. Not when Lily sat beside him... hurting.

And this time *he* had been the source. An ache tore through him and the cavernous pit within him opened once more.

Would there ever be an end to these feelings? Could he stamp them out? Did he want to?

He looked at Lily. What could he say? Were there words that would matter?

Her head was down. She stared at the basket in her lap, her hands grasping the handle so firmly her knuckles paled.

"I'm...sorry I didn't get to try one of those biscuits."

She peered at him, curiosity filling the green irises, which had dulled. Did she doubt his words?

He turned his attention to the horse. "You must've put some effort in to..." To what? What did he intend to finish that thought with?

She shifted the basket to her knees.

"I..." Did he imagine her words? She cleared her throat and spoke, "I wouldn't mind if you had one now."

He looked at her. Was this some kind of truce? Her features were set —neither giving way nor holding firm. She betrayed nothing of what she may or may not feel.

He dipped his head, a short movement. One he wasn't all that certain of.

She inclined the basket toward him, lifting the cloth.

Should he reach for one? Or would that be too bold?

"Here." Picking out one of the golden-topped morsels from within, she held it out to him.

He accepted it, all too aware of the places where their skin touched.

She must have been, too. For she pulled back at the contact before resettling the basket.

But he couldn't tear his eyes away as he took the first bite. He hadn't quite expected how much he would enjoy the well spiced, somewhat sweetened fluffy biscuit. It had been tended to with perfection and baked with precision.

He put the back of his hand to his mouth as he savored it. His eyes slid closed as he took in the different flavors. Far from even a passable cook himself, he enjoyed the skills of a good one.

"You like it?"

Opening his eyes, he found Lily gazing at him, hesitating, sneaking a look here and there, but keeping her focus on arranging and rearranging the cloth.

"Like it? Lily, I've never tasted anything quite like it. I'm amazed."

Her cheeks colored. Could his compliment bring out such a reaction? Did she care so much for his opinion?

His mouth spread into a smile. "You have a gift."

She looked away as her fingers skimmed across the handle. When she met his eyes again, she turned away again. "I don't know about that."

"Don't discount yourself so easy." He held up the biscuit and took another, larger bite. Just as delicious as the first.

When he set eyes on her once more, she had caught hers on him as well, and the corners of her perfect lips had tipped upward.

It mesmerized him. And he remembered the taste of those lips. Only so well. They had been soft and sweet. And so tantalizing. He wished for another moment...another chance to be near her, to lean in and...

Her brows furrowed.

Had he said something untoward? Did his features betray his thoughts?

"Is something wrong?" Lily's smile fell.

"Wrong?" The moment became heavier.

"You stopped eating."

The muscles in his shoulders released. Nothing to worry about. He looked at the remainder of his biscuit. "Oh. I was just...my mind wandered."

One of her eyebrows lifted. Did she not believe him?

He pushed the rest of the morsel into his mouth and grinned. The horse slowed, drawing Dan's attention forward. Uncle Owen and Cook's cabin lay just ahead. He minded the horse until they stopped.

Instead of dropping out of the cart, he turned to Lily. Was he being too bold?

Her eyes widened. Did she fear what he might do? Was she not ready for the things he wished for? How could he put her at ease? He would never push for anything she didn't want.

Putting on the sturdiest smile he could manage, he searched for the right words. "I only wanted to say…"

She leaned in an inch.

His voice trailed. Was she so eager for his words? The silence stretched until he could gather himself enough to finish. "I…ah…I don't think I can let you take those biscuits."

She covered her mouth with her hand and her shoulders shook. "The biscuits? You need the biscuits?"

He nodded; laughter vibrated in his chest as well. "If you don't mind, that is."

Her eyes sparkled in the setting sunlight. "I'm pleased to let you have them."

"Thank you." He slid over to the edge of the bench, preparing to drop down.

"On one condition," she said, laying a hand to his shoulder.

He jerked around, searching her features. What could she want? "Yes?"

She bit at her lip. A gesture that made her appear innocent, thoughtful, and much too endearing.

Was she uncertain about her request? It made him more curious. His stomach seemed lighter in that moment. And it was all he could do to restrain himself from touching the silken hair that somehow remained pulled up despite the goings-on of the day.

"Would you…come to dinner? Tuesday night? I'll check with Mr. Owen and Cook, of course, but I'd like it if…that is, I'd appreciate if—"

He smiled. The way she stumbled over herself only increased her allure. Giving in to the impulse, he reached forth and grazed the hair just above her right ear, his fingers skimming her cheek as he did so. "Of course, I will."

Her eyes met his. And everything stilled. The moment thickened. Became more intense.

Dare he press his lips to her rosy ones? They parted as if she could read his mind. Did she wish him to?

He wanted to. So much.

How could any man hold back at such an invitation?

But he didn't want to be just any man to her. He slid his hands under hers and around the handle. Placing the basket on the floorboard, he then captured both of her smaller hands and brought them to his mouth, pressing a kiss to the backs of her fingers.

She sucked in a breath.

He, too, was aware of the increasing intimacy of the moment. But he refused to push further.

After releasing her hands, he dropped from his seat, walked to her side of the cart, and helped her down.

The feel of her body so close to his threatened his resolve once more. But he pulled back, placing her hand in the crook of his elbow. If it took every ounce of determination in him, he would show her how a gentleman should treat a lady. How she should be treated. How his *wife* should be treated.

Lily submerged a linen dress into soapy water, rubbed it against her washboard, lifted it, and then pressed it down again. She had assured Cook she would have the clothes hung out to dry before midday. Even if she hadn't promised, she needed to be finished in time to start on dinner.

Dan would be coming tonight.

Her skin tingled. From the cooling of the water or from thoughts of Dan?

She had not seen him since the Harvest Day festivities two days past. But she had kept herself busy—planning the menu, finishing her new dress, and cleaning around the cabin.

Uncle Owen tired of her frenzy and had gone to the Miller Ranch with Cook that morning. It was nice—having the place to herself. Oh, she missed his kind smile and genial companionship, but she had to admit she'd accomplished more without the distraction.

Pulling the last garment from the basin, she rung it.

A horse whinnied from somewhere behind.

A horse?

Was someone there? Who? Had Uncle Owen come back?

She turned but could not spot anyone from her vantage point at the rear of the cabin. Perhaps whomever had arrived waited at the front side of the house. Or maybe near the barn. Should she try to assist them? Was that wise?

Her stomach turned. And her skin prickled. It may be an intruder. Come with a mind to thieve the place. Or worse.

Nonsense. It's only Uncle Owen.

Setting the now-clean dress in the basket, she lifted the small burden. Now on to the line, time to hang these out to dry.

The horse let out another protest. It did not seem pleased. That wasn't like an animal in Uncle Owen's care. Or Cook's.

Lily froze—the thought none too comforting. Her breaths came harder. Something heavy fell on her chest.

Who would come to the cabin for any other purpose than a visit? It was a small, rather humble home. Surely, no one could expect to gain much from such a simple house—no riches, for certain.

Still, the bumps on her flesh would not calm. Something was amiss. Should she run? Hide?

Pushing down such overwrought thoughts, she set the basket down and moved to the side wall of the house. Her hands trembled, and she caught hold of them.

What was she doing? She was no brave frontierswoman! This wasn't like her. How would she react should she come against an intruder intent on harm to this property or her person?

Still, she crept around the house. Would it not be wise to seek safety in the field beyond? Her mind screamed for her to do so. There was little chance she could, in fact, face down a thief. She hadn't the courage.

No matter her trepidation, she moved on, feet carrying her around the side of the cabin. She stilled for a second, her chest rising and falling —too much and too fast. Closing her eyes, she gathered what courage she could muster. And, holding her breath, she peered around the corner.

A dark chocolate horse stirred several feet away, tied to a post. Its rider was nowhere to be found. Lily scanned the area, but to no avail.

The thickness in her midsection rose into her throat. What if the encroacher had slipped into the cabin? Or the barn?

With no idea where he could be—or what the intruder wanted—she had not the fire left within to continue her ill-advised venture. No, indeed, this was a bad idea.

Whirling, she decided to do what she should have from the start—run.

Turning and moving, she halted, suddenly face to face with...

"Ma!" Lily fell back.

She struggled to remain on her feet. A futile effort. In the next moment, she landed on her backside. But not for long. Her legs were under her in the next moment.

"Thought you would run from me, did ya?" The woman spat out. Her words were punctuated more than Lily thought possible. Had she sobered up?

"Ma, please...I just...I wanted to—"

"I don't care what you wanted. What about your family? How could you abandon us?"

"But Pa said—"

"Don't you slander yer Pa." The words were spewed out as the older woman stepped closer. How could it be that Ma towered over Lily? Was she so tall?

It became difficult for Lily to maintain her footing. She leaned heavily on the wall as she skirted away. "Please, I didn't mean to—"

"Ungrateful girl." Ma ground out the words through clenched teeth. A claw-like hand struck forth and captured Lily's wrist. "Don't you know you owe me *everything*?"

Lily bit into the inside of her mouth as her mother's unkempt fingernails dug in. Crying out in pain would not serve her. She had learned such the hard way.

Ma twisted Lily's hand, jerking the young woman's body with it.

"And you run off with the first pair of fine eyes that looks your way."

"Ma, please—" Lily reached for the hand that held her, attempting to remove the vise-like grip.

The older woman dragged her closer. Where did her unearthly

strength come from? "He doesn't love you. Never will. None of them did. You know why?"

Tears poured down Lily's face. She hoped Ma would think them evidence of the pain. Not the truth. That there were intense emotions coursing through Lily.

She couldn't let Ma know how such affected her. For how could she block the words? Or deny their truth?

"You're worthless," Ma rasped into her ear. "Worthless."

Lily shook. If only she could protest. Or argue. But no fight remained within her. History spoke for itself—no one wanted her. Not for more than what she could do for them. Why would Dan be any different?

Ma shoved her to the ground, releasing her.

Lily cried, holding the injured limb to her chest.

"Don't come skulking to my door when he discards you." Ma's voice had calmed. It was eerie. "I won't have you either, you wretched child."

Curling into herself, Lily let the emotions wash over her. She didn't hear her mother depart. But she was all too aware when she was alone once more.

CHAPTER 9

The Connection

Yet again, Dan found himself in this place...unable to keep his mind on what he did. His thoughts strayed and strayed often...to *her*. To her features...hadn't he memorized their angles well enough? Her hair...the simple touch had proved it to be silken and softer than anything he'd ever felt. And to her lips...that brief contact of days past haunted him, creating a need, a hunger. For more.

So much more.

Glancing at the stall floor, he realized he had raked all the hay into a large mound in the middle. Not exactly what he had aimed for.

He sighed. Was he so useless in this state? Picking up the tool, he poked at the small hill and began spreading the bedding.

An hour later, and with much continued redirection of his thoughts, he finished the two remaining stalls. And so, a job that should have taken half the time, was finally done.

"You still in here?" Brandon's voice rang through the barn.

Couldn't Dan duck behind one of the walls and hide? Maybe that was asking too much. No, he'd best face his boss and take his due.

"Yeah. Still here."

Brandon paused by the stalls, crossing his arms. "Now, that doesn't sound like you one bit." The man's brows furrowed. "Something worrying you?"

Dan shook his head as he set the rake and shovel in their place, still avoiding his boss's eyes.

"You feel okay?" Brandon's tone became more serious. Did he now worry after Dan? Think perhaps that Dan was ill?

Guilt slammed into him. Why must Brandon be so concerned? The man, a few years older than his ranch hands, played the elder brother to them. That made it worse. How many times had Dan prayed in his youth for even one day of his brother's time?

Dan shifted the tools' handles. Making extra sure they were well settled in their places. He just couldn't make himself look at Brandon. Why had his boss come to the barn again?

"I'm fine." He shrugged. "I just...can't get my head in the right place."

Brandon's silence stretched. Uncomfortably.

Dan closed his eyes. Would he be forced to say more?

"Ah, you're *distracted*." There was an unmistakable smile in Brandon's voice. Perhaps even a little laugh as he grabbed his saddle.

Dan's face warmed as he coughed. He fought the urge to deny his boss's insinuation. But he couldn't. Could he avoid it altogether? Change the subject?

Brandon adjusted his saddle on the sawhorse and reached for a brush.

Dan drew in a breath as he grabbed for a rope. "Any word from town?"

The boss maintained his firm stance, but his features scrunched. "Town?"

"Yeah..." Dan worked the rope between his hands, letting it out. It needed recoiling. Yes, it was a mess. "About the Apache raid."

This time, the silence filled with tension.

Why had he broached this subject? He could kick himself for his lack of forethought. Unable to stop himself, he lifted his eyes. A quick glimpse of his boss's grimace spoke volumes. "What do you think they wanted?"

This was no veiled speak between them. Brandon knew what Dan asked. Did the Apache seek out the brave kept in the Miller home?

Brandon's jaw tightened. But he didn't answer. Just worked his brush over the leather of the seat.

Dan looked away. He had gone a step too far. He examined the fibers of the rope.

The stillness stretched between them once again, and Dan knew he needed to break it. "Boss, I didn't mean to—"

Brandon's gaze jerked up from his work. "I intend to do what I must to protect my family. *All* members of my family." His tone invited no further conversation on the matter.

Dan had known Brandon thought of him as family. Even if he hadn't said it. Still, the way this man took up for him...

Only Dan's Pa had ever done that. Even his own brother had only ever seen Dan as a nuisance.

Brandon looked toward the barn's entrance and let out a long breath. "I intend to see the brave gets fair treatment." His gaze leveled on Dan once more before he went back to cleaning the saddle. "Under the law."

Dan swallowed and looked at his hands working loops in the rope. This—the law—is where the rub came, as far as that brave was concerned.

"So, we'll wait 'til the judge comes through in the next couple of weeks." Brandon spoke as if that were the end of it. He leaned this way and that as he moved around the saddle.

Dan nodded without looking up. Why did he press Brandon? This had been discussed. The lines had been drawn. Still, he pushed. Why?

Looking at the rope, now wound, he wanted to vanish.

"If it's all the same to you," Brandon said, tipping his hat's brim upward. "Tell me what your trouble is with Lily."

Dan jerked upward. How—?

He shouldn't be surprised, though. The man knew him well. As well as anyone.

His dry hands fumbled with the rope. Sucking in a deep breath, he then let it out slowly. "That...is a big question."

"Is it? Or does it only seem like it to you?"

Dan shook his head, he pressed on a smile he didn't feel as he glanced up. "What?"

"Often times, things aren't as complicated as we make them." Brandon rubbed the leather with a cloth.

Was Brandon right? Was he muddling things? "And just why would I do that?"

Brandon shrugged. "Not wanting to show your hand, I suppose."

Dan slackened, almost dropping the rope.

"So, you put on your poker face."

Dan balked. *Ugh.* Were they going to talk about feelings now? "Boss, I'd really rather not—"

Brandon waved a hand. "I get it. But I'll tell you this..."

Dan wanted to slip through the slats in the walls and disappear.

Still Brandon continued, "There aren't many things you can't overcome if you care about her."

Dan searched for a response but came up empty. He turned and hung the rope on a peg.

Brandon set his brush to the side. "And if you care about her, you should get to know her...hear her story. From her."

Dan looked at his boss, narrowing his eyes. What *did* he know about Lily?

Brandon lifted the saddle and hauled it back to its place among the others. "Things turned around for me and Amanda when we had time for just us. No excuses, no reason not to be honest."

Dan watched Brandon's back, trying to recall every interaction between Lily and Brandon. Did his boss know something?

"It's about time for supper. I'd best head in." Brandon slapped Dan's shoulder and moved past him.

But Dan remained where he was.

Brandon glanced back. "Think about what I said."

Dan watched his boss as he continued on and out of the barn.

Was there something Dan didn't know about Lily that he should? Could he let go of his suspicions and allow Lily to explain her past?

More, could he truly open himself to what was right in front of him? Let these things in the past remain there and allow for hope of a better life ahead take hold?

Either way, it was time to clean the day off himself and head to Cook and Uncle Owen's. Just thinking about Lily, of being with her, being near her, thrilled and agitated him at the same time.

Lily stirred the warming pot of beans, watching the softened, slender green strips move with her spoon. They swirled at her bidding. The light caught on tiny waves in the liquid as the broth rippled.

Even as she pulled the wooden utensil free, the gentle sway continued. It mesmerized her. Or was it that she needed such a distraction. She widened her eyes.

How would she make it through this dinner? This evening? She had nothing left in her. Nothing to give.

Not to Dan. Not to anyone.

Might she release him somehow? Turn him from this ludicrous idea of marriage? It wasn't as if he truly wanted her anyway. No, it must be his misguided thought to rescue her.

She bit at her lip as it trembled. How could she let him sacrifice his life, his future for her? Wasn't she just as her mother had said? Worthless.

"There's his cart," a cheery voice called.

The voice behind Lily and the accompanying movement jerked her back to reality. Praying Cook wouldn't discern anything amiss, she straightened and wiped at her eyes. "Oh?"

The older woman paused as she reached for the oven but soon abandoned her mission.

Lily shifted, sensing Cook's gaze on her.

"You all right, child?" It wasn't so much a question.

Shrugging, Lily set the spoon down and turned to the water basin. "I'm just tired."

Cook's silence stretched. For Cook, the long silence was more than awkward. It was also quite unlike her.

Lily's eyes slid closed, and she shook her head. Why must Cook pry so? Breathing in, she opened her eyes and turned, facing the older woman. Perhaps that would prove something.

Cook's brow creases deepened.

"I'm just tired," Lily insisted, her tone sharper than she'd intended. Wishing back the words, she then decided to leave them. She wasn't Cook's concern after all.

The stairs beyond the front door creaked.

Whipping her head toward the sound, Lily's heart jumped into her throat.

Three knocks thudded on the solid wood.

Dan. Had to be.

She forced out the breath, releasing it slowly. There could be no more delay.

She peered at Cook. The woman's expression had not changed—so skeptical, so worried.

Lily ached. How long before Cook saw the truth, saw Lily for what she was—an unwelcome burden?

"Just tired, huh?"

Anger slid through Lily's weakness. She didn't have time for this.

Shoving off from the basin's stand, she moved to receive her guest. She crossed the room and swung the door open.

Her breath caught.

Dan had cleaned up.

Real nice.

Real, real nice.

He was quite handsome. And tall. His hair, no longer covered by a hat, had been combed back and out of his eyes. Now unhindered by stray hair, those eyes searched hers—striking and warm at the same time.

What did he see?

Her hands flew to her own hair. She hadn't made any effort with her own appearance. Several strands had fallen out of her coif. And as she smoothed down her skirt, she became all the more mortified at the number of disheveled places.

His brows arched and his lips spread into a charming smile, showing teeth that were whiter than she'd expected. "Shall I...come in?"

"Oh...of course!" She stepped backed to allow him entrance to the great room. Were her heavy breaths as noticeable to him? Her chest seemed to rise measurably with each inhale.

She pressed a hand to her neckline, ensuring all remained as it should. The mark was covered. A flush rushed over her features and she averted her gaze, praying he wouldn't notice.

He ducked as he entered the cabin. How had she not noticed that before? But his nearness now made her all too aware of the broadness of his frame.

"Welcome, welcome," Cook said. She appeared just behind Lily as Dan strode past.

Lily looked off to the side. Cook would see for certain.... more than Lily wanted her to.

"Thank you for having me." Dan 's voice seemed to resonate in the space.

Lily turned, but his words were directed at Cook.

"Why don't I see you 'round here more often?" Cook poked his arm.

Dan's gaze moved to Lily. "Not sure I've had a good reason. But I think you'll see more of me from now on."

Lily dropped her regard to the floor as her face heated. She pushed the door to its frame but was blocked.

"Hold on there a minute." It was Mr. Owen's voice. Did he push at the door?

Indeed, as she ceased her efforts, he widened the gap.

Had she hurt him? She jumped back, only to bump into Dan.

He steadied her. His larger hands on her were comforting, secure... safe.

Something deep within her longed to melt into them. Would that they could be there for her always...

Couldn't they?

No. She could not...*would not* cajole him into a marriage he didn't want.

Still, his hands remained on her upper arms. Must they? She'd regained her footing. Why then, did he keep his hold on her?

Shifting to look at him, she caught his eyes. The soft brown stirred something exciting in her yet soothed raw nerves at the same time. Would his touch always bring such a war within?

If only she could turn into him, put her hands on his, draw closer, and...

"Sorry, Lily." Mr. Owen's apology loomed nearby. "I didn't mean to startle you."

Drawing in ragged breaths, she eased away from Dan and faced Mr. Owen. "I-I assure you, sir, I didn't intend to shut the door on you."

Dan's hands fell from her.

She had to contain a shudder.

"Of course, not," Mr. Owen said, a smile on his face and in his voice. "Let's speak no more of it." He nodded to Dan. "Glad to have you. Smells good, doesn't it?"

"I was thinking the same thing." Dan grinned.

"Don't just stand there, Lily," Cook called over her shoulder as she rustled toward the kitchen. "Get them menfolk settled at the table."

Lily allowed herself a quick glance at Dan.

His eyes lit up.

Her lips turned upward. Just a bit. Before she reined in some control. "We have our orders, I suppose." She stepped toward the dining table.

Dan's longer stride brought him closer to her as they neared their chairs.

It unnerved her.

What, indeed, would this evening bring?

Dan watched Lily across the table. What rambled about in her head? She was quiet. Too quiet. Had been the whole meal.

It was more than just that Cook and Uncle Owen jabbered on, dominating the conversation. Even Dan didn't have much opportunity to speak up—save a comment here and there. Still...

There was more to it. As if Lily cared little to contribute. Even her posture belied a glum spirit—shoulders slumped, face angled downward.

Why? Had she not wished him to come? She *had* invited him.

Even as he watched, she fidgeted, shifting from side to side.

Could she sense his scrutiny? Did it bother her?

Standing, she grabbed her plate.

All eyes were on her, silence filling the room.

"I..." Her features reddened. "I only thought to clear the table."

Cook rose. "Let me help you." Her attempt to soften the abruptness of Lily's movements did nothing to ease the awkwardness.

Uncle Owen was on his feet in the next moment, relieving Lily of her burden. "I can help with this. Why don't you young folks enjoy the fresh air? It'll be dark soon."

Lily opened her mouth, but no words came forth. Did she seek to protest?

What should he do? Take the opportunity offered him? Would that make things worse? Or was it a chance to root out what bothered her? A small voice warned... This might only open the way for more rejection, yet another blow to his already bruised heart.

No, he had decided. He *would* move forward with this. And here was a chance to reach out.

It may be his *only* chance.

He stood, his gaze searching out Lily's. "Shall we?"

She met his eyes but didn't hold his gaze. Pulling her regard away, she played with the fingers of her opposite hand. "Truly, Mr. Owen, I don't mind, I—"

Dan stepped around the table and set a hand to Lily's elbow.

She jerked it away, shooting him a harsh glare.

He pulled back. Had he offended?

Her chest puffed. She appeared ready to take off, run if he dared move another inch.

Holding his hands out so she could see them, he assured her, "I didn't intend to overstep. I'm sorry."

Her breathing slowed and she nodded.

Dan glanced at Cook and Uncle Owen. They seemed just as surprised at Lily's reaction.

He focused once more on Lily. "Would you...mind taking a short stroll with me? The sunsets on this piece of land are quite a sight."

She watched him. Did she believe he would take advantage? After all she had known of him?

That stung.

Her eyes glistened.

He pressed down the offense that rose within. There was more to this. Much more. Something deeper moved behind the tears forming even now. Something making her afraid...of *him*?

"Go on," Cook urged. "Have a fine walk."

Lily looked at the opposite wall.

What was in her head? An ache filled his chest, and he wondered what, if anything, might have happened. Had he done something? *Said* something? It was all he could do not to reach out to her, pull her to himself...

Cook lifted the gathered plates and moved to the wash bin as if all were settled.

Uncle Owen watched the pair for a moment longer. He shot Dan a wink and jerked his head in the direction of the door before moving to help his wife. Encouragement?

Dan took a quick breath, prayed for courage, and shifted, inching closer to Lily.

Her hands were fisted together, her knuckles pale. Was she scared of him?

He wanted to soothe her in any way he could. But he wagered his touch would not be welcome.

Looking at the older couple in the kitchen, their voices lowered as they put their heads together, he was assured they had turned their attention from the dining area.

Dan cleared his throat.

Lily jerked. Her eyes met his.

He lifted his brows. "Shall we?" Were his words as gentle as he hoped?

She, too, glanced at the pair by the wash bin. And let her gaze linger. Would she refuse?

Perhaps he should bid her farewell. Better he put an end to the evening than suffer outright rejection. He opened his mouth.

She sighed as she turned back to him. Her wide eyes regarded him once more.

There was something else there...behind the veneer of disinterest she was putting forth. The green shimmered, and he saw it. Pain? Mistrust? He couldn't make it out.

She blinked and it was gone. Replaced by a coolness that had not existed before. Would she now dismiss him?

He settled back on his heels and waited.

She nodded.

She *what*?

Her brows furrowed. At his surprise?

Forcing a smile, he offered his arm.

Another pause. Did she consider the gesture? With some hesitation, and apparent determination, she unclenched her hands and placed one in the crook of his arm.

He then tugged her toward the door with gentle movements.

She followed. Though she kept her features set and downcast.

Soon enough, they were outside beyond the small porch and facing the setting sun. There they remained. All was still and quiet, save the myriad of natural sounds around them.

What was he to do? How would he reach her? He peered at her. And his breath stopped.

She was a vision in the fading rays of daylight. The hues of pinks and purples shimmered against the red of her hair, bringing out hints of strawberry. Her hair had been pulled up, but several strands had escaped.

He itched to touch them. But he dared not.

Her eyes were closed, and her chin lifted slightly, as if she relished the gentle breeze that fanned them. Did she? As she breathed in the cool air, his next inhale burned. Had he been so delayed in taking in a breath?

"Lily, I...," he started. But he soon lost his thoughts.

She opened her eyes, the green reflecting the light of the dipping sun as well as her hair had been. It stole his words.

As the silence lengthened, she turned toward him. Her hands rubbed her upper arms. Was she chilled? The evening was rather warm, save the welcomed breeze.

Her gaze on him did not linger, she shifted her focus to the ground soon after.

Why did his arms ache so incredibly? Why the urge to pull her to his chest and hold her? If she needed him, she would tell him, wouldn't she?

She pushed out a breath and dropped to the ground.

Did she slip? He fell to his knees beside her, hands on her.

Jerking away, she moved as far from him as she could. "Don't touch me!"

He pulled back. Why would she—?

Her face was a picture of fear. Pure fear.

What had he done to bring that about?

Holding his hands out where she could see them, he hunted for words. "Lily, I don't..."

She drew her knees to her chest and wrapped her arms around them.

Again, his heart hurt for her. She seemed so small, so fragile.

"I don't know what's going on here."

She ducked her head into the space between her knees and her chest. Now, even her features were no longer visible.

His hands moved toward her but hovered over her. Not touching, but he could not stay back. "Did I...?"

She whimpered.

"Lily, did I..." He could hardly force the word out. "...hurt you somehow?" A pang shot through his chest. Had he? How? He searched his memory for something, anything.

For some moments, she didn't move. She wasn't going to answer.

He sat back on his rear, wiping a hand down his face. What else could he do?

She shook her head. Then, with slow movements, her face lifted toward him. Her features were a mess—raw, reddened, contorted in pain.

Raising on his knees again, he leaned over her.

She sucked in a breath.

He halted, careful not to lay a hand on her. But his eyes would not be stopped. His gaze did a quick examination.

There...at the edge of the dress's neckline...a mark. Someone had injured her.

She lifted a hand to the place and pulled at the lining of the fabric.

His hand shot forth, holding her back from covering it. "Let me see."

Lily pressed against his hold. "No!"

More tears fell. Her cries became less timid, more fearful.

"Let me see," he insisted, anger welling in him. He could not contain the rage bubbling within. "Who did this?"

She slumped to the side, using her shoulder to escape his hands as she fell against the ground on her side. "You don't understand."

His fists held him up. A deep burning within him threatened to erupt. Indeed, he wished for someone, or something, to unleash it upon.

"What wouldn't I understand?" he seethed. "Why you would protect someone who would hurt you?"

She continued to cry.

"You're right, I don't understand."

He settled on his rear, setting elbows to his knees and dipping his head. As much as he wished to give into his anger, that wasn't what she needed. But what did she need from him if not that? *Lord, help me. Give me guidance.*

And something that seemed rather impossible became possible. The intense heat evaporated—slowly, but for certain. As he took in measured breaths and exhaled, he felt his muscles relax.

"I'm sorry, Lily," he said, looking at her form, still lying on the ground beside him. "That wasn't about you."

She, too, stilled.

He leaned toward her. "Hey, I want to understand. I do. And...if there's something...anything I can do to help, I'll do it."

She sniffled.

"Lily?" He fell back, reclining against his elbow, stretching out beside her.

She had quieted.

"Talk to me?"

Movement at last. She rubbed at her face. But with it, came a nod.

His heart beat strong again.

She pressed against the ground as if attempting to sit up once more.

As he shifted to rise to a seated posture as well, he offered a hand to assist her.

To his amazement, she slid her fingers into his grasp. He soon noted why. She worked to cover her injury as she rose.

Now sitting once more with skirt arranged, she snuck a peek in his direction.

He offered her a small smile, which he hoped would be encouraging.

"It's just that..." Lily started. Her voice sounded so small. Was she whispering? "...what you saw is, um, not actually a..." She shot a quick glance at him again.

He furrowed his brows. What was she trying to say? Would she ever say it?

She closed her eyes and pushed a breath out. "It's not an injury. It's a birthmark."

He cocked his head. Surely, she fibbed. What he saw had been...

Her eyes caught his and her shoulders dropped as she looked heavenward. Then she released the neckline of her dress. Not that it did anything. That only revealed the edge of the mar on her skin.

What game was this? Did she think this would dissuade him?

"Well?" Her gaze was on him again.

"Well what?"

"Don't you want to see it for yourself?" She eyed him. "So you know it's as I say?"

How could he respond to that? He dared not ask her to lower the bodice of her dress. Not one inch. That would be...

With no further encouragement, she tugged at the neckline the slightest bit to expose only a little more of the mark. Just enough for examination.

He leaned in as close as he dared. The mark was circular...at least what he could see of it made it appear so. It seemed as if something had burned her. But it was almost in a state between incident and healed... which could not be true, with her handling the fabric over it such as she did.

Meeting her eyes once more, he wished to ask...something. But what?

She looked away.

Why? It was as if she were embarrassed. Of a birthmark?

He reached out a hand, set it upon her shoulder, and rubbed his thumb over the portion of the mark that was visible.

Her breath caught and her gaze sought his again. There was a question in her eyes. She sought something from him. Something he was ready to give...assurance.

He closed the gap between them and pressed his lips to hers, his hand never leaving her shoulder, his thumb still on her birthmark.

Pulling back for a moment, he breathed, "Do you know how beautiful you are to me?"

She set a tentative hand to the side of his face and drew his lips to hers once more.

Indeed, the evening had not gone as Dan had thought.

Lily sighed as she brushed her hair. Dan's kiss still lingered on her lips. She closed her eyes and remembered how secure she had felt in his arms. How safe. How well she fit. Almost as if she belonged.

She allowed herself a moment to relish that feeling. Perhaps a drawn-out moment.

Hugging her arms around herself, she loved the warmth in the core of her being. Because of him. Because of his care for her. Yes, he truly seemed to have a care.

Her fingers found the locket that ever hung around her neck. Another sensation washed over her. This one all too familiar—fear, mixed with loneliness. An emotion that felt much more at home.

She worked the old latch on the locket and looked at the aged picture within—her grandmother. She and Joseph were the only people who ever loved her. Ever spoke kindnesses to her. Memories of the woman's soft hands were just that. There was no lingering remembrance of her actual touch. Just the knowledge that her touch was not harsh, did not dig into her skin.

Neither did Dan's. His fingers had grazed her skin, his every contact was gentle, only firm enough that she knew it to be sure.

Then why was she crying?

Wasn't his regard as sure as his embrace? There seemed no sign of his flight. Of his turning.

Yet...

She had thought such before.

A sinking in her chest brought with it a wave of nausea. Had she not learned by now? Her mother was right. None of them would stay. Not even Dan. Men had proven to her over and over again. They cared only for what affections she provided.

The kisses, which moments before were relished, now became regretful. What had she done?

She gazed at her grandmother's features. Though there wasn't a smile upon her face, her eyes belied the joy that was ever-present within her.

What would she say to Lily? Would she scold Lily's empty headedness as Ma did? Or would she encourage Lily to open herself? See what happened on the picnic the next day?

After all, she had agreed to join Dan on a picnic tomorrow. Should she just as well give him the benefit of the doubt? Perhaps...

Still, there was a part of her that wondered if any thought to persist in this hoax of a marriage was selfish. If she shouldn't release him. For his sake.

Did he deserve to be hitched to her? To her problems?

Did anyone?

She settled on her pallet, burying her face in her pillow. No, it wasn't right to keep Dan in this ill-thought-out agreement.

She must release him.

She must.

It was the only way.

Dan's every nerve tingled. From the moment he awoke to the time he opened the door for Lily, helping her into the wagon, and now, riding so close to her their shoulders brushed. He never felt so alive.

Did she feel it, too? How could she not?

If the moments they shared the night before were any indication, she did. For she had responded, indeed, giving every bit as much as he did. It had surprised him, pleasantly so. Did she care for him? Had he unleashed something within himself he had not realized was there under the surface?

He peered at her. She had not pulled her hair up today. Only secured the top portion back. Most of her gentle waves had been left flowing down her back.

How was he to keep his thoughts straight? His fingers ached to dive into the shining red river. Would it be as smooth as he imagined?

She met his gaze. A smile turned her lips upward.

Did she know what he thought?

The wagon rocked. Had the wheel hit a rut?

He jerked his attention forward as she hooked an arm through his.

How was he to concentrate like this? Thankfully, the wagon righted itself on its own as the horse continued forward.

He turned and offered her a smile.

Her cheeks colored, and she pulled back.

She didn't have to. He hated that she did so.

How would he make any headway like this? As he shifted his focus forward, he spotted his pre-selected spot for their picnic just ahead. He pulled on the reins to slow the horse.

Soon enough, they stopped some feet short of a small stream. This was the place. *His* place. Where he came to think. And, for whatever reason, he wanted to share it with her.

He looked at her, watching as her gaze wandered over the horizon. Her awe was palpable as she took in the scenery from this perspective.

There were several rockfaces visible from here—buttes set against the skyline. Cacti dotted the landscape as well as bushes and grasses. The browns and greens played off each other, with the occasional intruding yellow plant. All earthy, to be certain, but warm, inviting, and calming. Something he very much needed.

He let it soothe his worn nerves.

"It's...amazing!" she gasped.

Glancing at her, he released a long breath. "It's my favorite spot," he admitted. "I come here often."

Her gaze met his. "I can see why."

Those green orbs were wide with wonder. "There cannot be many such places in all of Arizona." She turned back to the view before them, drawing in as much air as she could manage before letting it out.

Did she, too, find solace here?

"What a place!" She spoke with resolution.

He altered his regard to the scenery as well. It was true. In his mind's eye, he pictured a homestead, just to the right. And he, fishing with a boy. Lily stepping from the cabin with a young girl tugging at her skirt and an even smaller one on her hip.

Did he want that? A life here? With Lily? Even after the mess that his family was? After his years of determination that he would never... *never*...venture down that road?

Yes. He did.

Very much.

He looked to the reins in his hands, overwhelmed with emotion. Too much to let her see. Dare he show her? Would she respond in kind?

Peering toward her, he found her eyes upon him. An invitation?

Moving to her, he captured her lips. She melted to him with a small sound. Her hands gripped at his shirt. Yes, she wanted him as much as he did her. It drove a hunger within that threatened to overtake him.

It was she, in the end, who pulled back.

He had nearly lost himself in her. Under some sort of spell for certain. His hands ran along her back.

She no longer held to his shirt, her head down.

Pressing a kiss to her forehead, he longed to maintain the connection.

"Did you...um...bring something to eat?" Her words didn't do much to penetrate the thick haze around him.

"Hmmm?"

"For our picnic?" She laughed. Somewhat of a nervous laughter.

He straightened. "Oh...of course." She must be hungry. How could he be so daft? Here he was pawing at her, and her stomach needed nourishment!

Tearing himself away, he shifted and dropped from the cart. Then, after helping her down, he grabbed for the blanket and basket.

"Where shall we set everything?" Lily inquired.

"I have a place in mind." Dan offered a smile. "Follow me." He reached out a hand and waited.

She looked at his hand as if she feared it might bite her.

He laughed. "I promise...it's not a coyote."

One side of her mouth turned upward. Why had she become so uncomfortable?

After a moment, she slid her fingers into his hand and let him lead her away from the wagon. They moved closer to the stream but turned to journey along its banks.

Once they reached a slightly elevated stretch overlooking the stream and the vista, Dan paused. "What do you think?"

"Yes," she breathed. "I do like it."

He smiled, well pleased with himself. Then he went about setting down the blanket and picnic basket.

This time, however, when he offered his hand to assist her, she ignored it. She stepped onto the spread-out fabric surface and settled herself to one side.

Curious.

But he shrugged it off, sitting himself near the basket and pulling out the foodstuffs. Mrs. Miller had helped him pack the basket. She had even been a part of choosing what he should bring.

As he watched Lily's face light up at some of the more delicate food items, he was relieved he had conceded to Mrs. Miller's finer taste.

"Did you make these?" Lily held up what appeared to be a small pie. What had Mrs. Miller called it? A tart?

Dan settled onto his rear. He shook his head with a little laugh. "I must confess...Mrs. Miller was a big help."

"Oh." Lily's face fell.

Was she disappointed? It seemed so.

"But I assisted," Dan was quick to add.

Lily's eyes met his. A slow smile crept onto her features. "It is very fine."

Dan nodded. "Thank you. I wanted everything to be right."

She looked away.

Was something amiss? Everything between them had started to seem a bit uneven.

He set the food to the side and scooted closer. "Have I done something wrong?"

She sat straighter. "What do you mean?" Her eyes fell to her hands in her lap.

He wanted to let it go and get back to their picnic. But something wasn't right. Remembering the images that played through his mind earlier, he knew he had to fight for that future. If he wanted it. No matter what.

Laying a hand on hers, he pushed on. "It just seems that...you are not well with me. Not truly."

Her gaze shot to his eyes. Something stirred there. Something that wasn't altogether pleasant.

But she held back. And the more the moments ticked by, the more it seemed the emotion welled within her.

He longed to reach forth and gather her to himself. Though he fought it. That would not serve either of them. She needed the space. And he needed answers.

Shifting her regard to the stream, she wiped at her face. Had a tear fallen? "It's not..."

He held his breath, waiting.

Nothing.

"It's not what, Lily? What won't you tell me?"

She bit at her lip. Her hands gripped into her skirt. Such that her knuckles turned white.

"Lily, I..." he started, reaching for her hands.

Jerking them out of range, she rose. "I can't..."

His gaze followed her. What was happening here? Can't? Can't what? He opened his mouth to voice his question, but she cut him off.

"I can't marry you, Dan. I'm sorry. I release you from your obligation." She spun and rushed off.

Lily hurried away as fast as she could. Where she would go, she did not know. All she knew was that she had to get away. She could not let him talk her out of it. This was right. He needed to be free of her. Of the burden that she would be to him.

Footfalls crunched the dirt behind her. Her heart sank. Of course, he would follow. How could he not? He was honorable and gallant and everything she hoped for in a man but didn't deserve.

"Lily, wait!" he called.

She pushed her legs to move faster. Tears blurred her vision.

"Where are you going?" His words were quieter than they should be. Had she pulled that much farther ahead of him? Or did the wind drown him out?

What did it matter? She had to go. Had to get away. Somehow. She couldn't face him.

"Lily!" a hand fell on her shoulder.

She halted. What was the use? Where could she go out here? Best to face him as well as she could. Would she be able to convince him? She must try.

"You can't mean that." Dan's kind voice was firmer than she wanted it to be. More determined than it should be. Didn't he want to let her go?

She should speak. Turn him away. But her tongue wouldn't work. The words wouldn't form.

"Look at me, Lily." He took hold of her upper arm and turned her.

As soon as he laid his grip to her arm, on the very place where Ma had dug her nails in, Lily could not stop the whimper that forced its way out, though her hand pressed to her mouth to quell it.

Now facing him, her eyes attempted to take in his reaction. It was not good.

His brows met, furrowing across his forehead. "Are you hurt?"

All she had to do was shake her head. One lie. One among many. But she couldn't. Hot tears poured from her.

"Lily, talk to me." His voice was desperate. He pulled at her sleeve, raising it as high as it would go.

Jerk away. Fight him. Don't let him see.

All thoughts fell moot. For she could do nothing but stand and watch his reaction as he found the bruises left by her encounter with her mother.

The concern in his warm brown eyes sharpened into intense burning anger. His features tightened; his mouth became a thin line. "Who did this?"

She dropped her face. How could she tell him? The shame...

He lifted her chin. "Who did this?" he insisted, his words tense.

Scrunching her features, she sobbed.

"Your father did this, didn't he?" Dan ground out.

She covered her face with her hands. Shouldn't she tell him? But maybe this was best—for him to think her father dealt the wound. The scars Pa left on her may not be physical, but they were just as real.

"Last night..." he started, his breaths coming deeply. "When I asked if you were injured..."

She dropped her hands. This would not be good.

He continued, eyes piercing her, "You said nothing about this... nothing but your birthmark."

Spent and weary, she nodded. "Yes."

His anger, still very real on his features, gave way to something else —hurt. Was he hurt at her omission?

Shouldn't he be? He trusted her. Believed her. Offered her the world, and she continued to hold back from him.

She nodded again. "Yes. I have not been truthful."

His shoulders remained tense, his muscles taut. What did he wait for? What of her? What did she need in order to come out of hiding?

"And you deserve better." She faced him full on. At last.

He didn't speak for a handful of moments. And then sighed and said, "As do you."

She considered his words. Was that true? Did she deserve better than her own deception?

His body relaxed, and he let his hands lower to her elbows, resting there. "And so, I, too, have something I must share with you."

Her heartbeat quickened. Would he, after all this, cut her loose? Speak words that would end their betrothal?

Could she bear it?

She closed her eyes. Did she have a choice? No.

"Come with me." Dan drew her closer and led her back to the picnic blanket. "I want you to sit."

Something rushed through her, wanting to naysay him, to insist he speak now. But she decided it best to heed him. And listen.

Her path, once again, was out of her control, and at the mercy of the man she hadn't meant to give so much of her heart to.

What was he to think? Dan was angered. Hurt. Among so many other things. To say that the picnic was *not* going as expected, would be an understatement.

Settling Lily and then forcing himself to sit with space between them was difficult. Still it was best.

But the deception...the secrets and withheld truths from the evening before tasted all too familiar to him. And it did not rest well. The bite of it ran far deeper and stirred up memories far more hurtful than she could know. Dare he speak of them? He wished for her truthfulness... not just for these bruises, but also of the years past. How, then, could he not offer her the same?

He took a breath and pressed his anger down. This was a time to be honest. To let her know the whole truth about things. And let everything work out how it would.

As he opened his mouth, she interjected.

"Please..."

"Yes?" Was something else going on? Were there other injuries? Could he maintain his calm exterior if so?

"I need to...*want* to...share with you." Lily seemed so vulnerable in that moment. Her eyes became wide and her skin had paled, if only slightly. "About my life. About my...parents."

Would she speak of the abuse doled out by her father? Could he stand to hear it?

He took in a breath. If she wanted to share it, felt it needed to be said, he would listen. Did she wish him to know as a way of being honest with him? That thought warmed his core.

Nodding, he kept his tone soft. "Go on."

She let out a breath and adjusted her sitting position. Her legs went out to her right side as she sat up on her left hip.

Pulling a gold chain from underneath her dress's neckline, she produced the locket dangling on it. "This," she said as she worked the latch, "is my grandmother's portrait."

She leaned forward a bit, and he moved toward her so he could see the woman's picture.

"She is a lovely woman," he commented.

Lily gazed at the photo. "Yes. She is. And was most kind. Especially to me."

Dan smiled. Not that Lily looked at him.

"The day my grandmother died was the last day I knew what it was to be treated with love and tenderness. Except by Joseph."

Guilt filled Dan for the role he had played in Joseph's demise. And his brows furrowed. She couldn't mean that no one else in her life showered her with love. Not even her mother? Did her mother also fear Sheriff McAllen? Would he raise his hand to his own wife?

Lily shut the locket and let it fall. "My childhood afterward was marked with..." She paused. Her words caught, and her lip trembled.

Dan wanted to reach out to her, to touch her and offer her comfort, assure her that it was in the past, that no one would hurt her again. But something held him back.

"Fear. And pain." Her eyes filled with moisture.

He looked down so she wouldn't see things in his eyes he didn't want her to. Could she handle his pain and anger right now?

She wiped at her eyes. "Never a moment of peace. Or safety."

He glanced at her. "What about your mother? Could she not stop him?"

"I never knew when...or where...but I knew it would come," she continued.

Had she heard him? It seemed as if she had not. Still, Dan tried again. "What about Joseph? Was it the same for him?"

She looked down. "Sometimes. Not always." Lily rubbed her face on her shoulder. "It was never good for him. But it wasn't constant torment."

"Did he try to help you?" Dan worked to keep the emotion out of his voice. He didn't want to judge. It wasn't his place. But he did.

There was no answer for several moments. "We each lived in our own hard place. And we were each other's only friend in that time. Only we could understand."

Their closeness made a lot more sense. Dan nodded. The sibling relationship and its necessity seemed clearer.

"Then he left. For the ranch. And then..." Her breaths tripped. Sobs followed.

Dan moved to her and put his arms around her. Without thought, without decision, he did so. Drawing her near his chest, he embraced her. "It's done. It's in the past. You are not that girl anymore."

She sobbed harder as she gripped his arms.

"And no one...not your father, not his goons...*no one*...is going to hurt you. Ever. Again."

Turning her face into his chest muffled her cries, but he felt every one of them. Still, he held her and let her release her pain. All the while, making an oath to himself, to God, to her, that this would be so.

Lily was spent. How long had she cried in Dan's arms? She did not know. But it had been for some time.

Should she be embarrassed? Only she wasn't. She felt comforted, safe—the same things she always felt in his embrace.

Did she know this...*this*...could be so good? Could be so wonderful? More...could she stand to let Dan go now that she had released nearly all of her heart to him? What, if any, would remain if he were to put her aside at this point?

She feared there wouldn't be much left for her to make a life with. So, she must do what she had feared—trust him.

Pulling back to look into his eyes, she found in his gaze the depth of concern there for her. It was raw. It was real. It was right.

Dan paused. Was he, too, caught in the moment? Or just indecisive?

She reached a shaking hand to the side of his face. And laid her fingers across the scruffiness there.

He did not smile. If anything, the depth of his regard became deeper. How was that possible?

Leaning away to sit with a small bit of distance between them, Dan looked to the horizon and seemed to consider it. It was a bit odd.

She swallowed. Should she speak?

The silence stretched. And she opened her mouth to say something, but he spoke first.

"My father was never around."

That seemed a rather strange thing to say. But she sensed there was more coming. So, she settled into her seated position and waited.

"He wasn't much for cards. But chuck-a-luck turned out to be his first love. And he was obsessed."

Lily lowered her head. She had heard how gambling could swallow a man's soul. Leaving an empty shell, if anything, behind.

"He always felt his big pay-off was in that next game."

Biting her lip to keep from speaking out against such hurtful ways, she worked to let Dan speak.

Dan sighed and looked at his hands, splaying his fingers and examining his callouses. "My Ma took on any sewing and laundering work she could just to keep us fed. He played away anything he could earn."

Lily fought the urge to nay-say such behavior. How terrible for his poor ma. What a childhood that must have been!

"Didn't keep me from wanting to spend time with him though. He was always making promises...'let's go fishin', boy, I'll teach ya how to catch the big ones,' or 'I'm headed in to town, let's go pick out something for your ma.'" Dan shook his head and looked down again. "Never happened. He always woke before dawn and headed off to Tombstone or Tucson where the best gambling houses were. Wouldn't see him 'til Sunday night."

Her heart ached for the disillusioned little boy, so much stolen from him.

"Then Ma got sick. Maybe...if only he'd been around...if we'd noticed sooner..."

She put a hand on his arm then. "You can't think like that. Your ma wouldn't want you beating yourself up, would she?"

Laying his hand over hers, he closed his eyes for a moment. But his brown orbs met her gaze once more soon after.

"Lily," he breathed. "There is something I have to tell you."

What could he say that would bring him so much concern? Should it worry her?

"I need you to understand," he choked out. "That I care for you. So much."

She nodded. Why did a warning sound in her head? In her heart?

He leaned forward and kissed her. His hands on her face and their lips the only points of contact between them.

Lily responded. It was a simple, sweet kiss that held promise for the future. And it soothed the uncertainty within her.

"There's more," he said, his eyes holding hers.

More? What further hardships had he endured? Could she hear more? She wanted to ease his pain as he had hers. Leaning closer, she whispered, "Dan, you don't have to—"

"Now," he said, drawing back. "It can't wait."

She watched emotions play across his face—determination, pain, sadness, guilt... What was this?

He pulled in a long inhale and met her gaze. "Lily, *I* am responsible for Joseph's death."

CHAPTER 11

The Breakdown

Lily pulled away. "What?"

Dan loosened his hold on her, letting her go as he looked on, guilt written on his features.

It couldn't be true. It just couldn't. "W-w-what do you mean?" She stammered.

He ran a hand through his hair.

"You can't be serious!" Her heart thundered, and her hands shook.

"I wish it weren't so, Lily. But I can't change it. Joseph's death was my fault."

Lily gripped the fabric of her skirt and took a few breaths. "I'm going to need you to explain to me what you mean."

Dan leaned away and looked toward the stream.

Would he now not meet her eyes? Could he not?

"We were going around the Miller property—the ranch, the surrounding area. I showed him everything about the place."

Lily began to feel light-headed. She forced her breathing to slow.

"He spotted a bedroll...well, what I thought was a bedroll. But it turned out to be a person." Dan glanced back at Lily.

She raised a brow.

"We should've gone for assistance then and there. I wish we would have."

Lily couldn't make her heart stop racing. This must be the Apache brave that...that... There was the faintness again.

"But we didn't. *I* didn't." Dan's gaze traced the horizon. After a few seconds, he continued. "We investigated it ourselves."

Another pause. Dan muttered something under his breath. A curse?

Then he continued. "When I realized it was an Apache, I tried to warn Joseph to stay back. But he was so worried because the brave was young."

Lily's heart ached. For Dan's pain. For her brother. For the whole situation. Could she bear anymore?

"But I knew better. I should have ended it. Or pulled Joseph back. Or something. *Anything* but what I did."

Lily wanted to say something, but her throat was tight, too tight for her to speak.

"Which was nothing...I did nothing but watch while that brave..." Dan seemed to come back to himself and realize that Lily sat beside him.

Dan let out a long breath. "I wouldn't blame you if you hated me. Or if you never want to see me again." His head dipped, and she could no longer see his face.

Her thoughts swirled—Joseph's face, the imagery of the actions Dan described to her, and Dan... Was he guilty of the crime he leveled upon himself? Or did he heap condemnation upon his conscience? *Was* he responsible for her brother's death?

Or was Joseph's death an unexpected incident? The sole act of the Apache brave? Could Dan have prevented it? Could anyone?

Dan rose and walked to the edge of the raised area, arms crossed, back to her. Did he await her verdict?

What was it? Had she accepted it in her heart?

Standing, she took the steps that would put her behind Dan's taller frame. And, placing her hands flat against his back, she spoke. "You did everything you could."

He set his head in his hand. "I should have known the danger was so great. I could have stopped it if—"

"How could you?" Her voice was firm. More so than she would have expected.

Dan continued, "But if I had only—"

"I forgive you." She cut him off, leaning her head against his back.

He turned to face her, setting his forehead against hers. In the silence, he stood with her. But did he believe her? Would he?

She lifted a hand to his neck, caressing the skin there. "Now forgive yourself."

So, the picnic didn't go as Dan planned. It ended even better than he could have hoped. The heaviest weight had been lifted from his shoulders. Lily knew all of it—his father, his pain, Joseph—*and* she forgave him! It was so freeing.

Now, they headed back to Uncle Owen and Cook's cabin. Lily clung to his arm, pressing as close as she dared to his side. They were happy.

Was this love? It seemed so.

But he had never known love before. Perhaps it was best to be cautious in declaring such an emotion.

The sun had begun to set as Dan reined the horse in upon nearing the small cabin. Turning to Lily, he pressed a kiss to her hair.

She closed her eyes and murmured something he couldn't distinguish. But it sounded lovely.

If only they could stay in this moment forever. The night would not stay away that long, though.

He hopped down and walked around the wagon to assist her. Not at all hating the feeling of her in his arms once more.

She smiled shyly. So innocent—unsure of herself, of how to respond to his displays of affection. As if...

As if she had never known what it was to be loved. Or known by a man.

How could he have ever thought her ruined? It was now all too obvious she had not been misused by other men. Those rumors he had bent his ear toward were just that—rumors.

He put out an arm for her and strolled toward the front door. All the while wishing their time was not ending so soon.

A gentle tug drew his attention to her face. Her smile seemed a bit more mischievous in that moment.

"Shall we...enjoy the sunset this evening?" she put forth.

"We shall." He was glad to concede as he turned them toward the hillside.

There they stood, side by side, arms linked, as the sky once more burst into a myriad of colors. It was beautiful.

Lily set her head on his shoulder. "What would it be like to be married at sunset?"

Dan had not considered that. He did not know how one went about planning wedding ceremonies and that type of thing. Did she?

He leaned toward her, speaking into her hair. "We'll need to start making a plan."

She shifted. Nervous? Or worried?

"When you're ready," he added.

Looking up at him, she met his gaze. "I think I'm only hesitant because..." Her features reddened.

"What?" he whispered.

She looked away.

He gave her arm a gentle squeeze. "Tell me."

Staring straight ahead, her face became bright red. "Because I don't know about..."

Dan furrowed his brows; he had no idea what had Lily so uncertain.

"You know..." She snuck a peek at him only to look away again.

He shook his head. "I know about what?"

She sputtered. "The...*after*." The last word was barely audible.

But he caught her meaning. And her innocence made him smile. He pulled her close and spoke in gentle tones. "You have nothing to fear from me."

A timid smile crossed her features as she dropped her face into his shoulder once more.

"But we can wait if you would prefer. Though I will admit, I'd prefer not to," he said softly.

She snuggled to him all the more. "Truly?"

"How can you doubt it, Lily? You must know I do not wish to say good-bye to you tonight. Much less any other night."

Raising her features to his, she lifted up on her toes and kissed him. Dare he have hoped to find such happiness? And here it was. In front of him.

When they parted, he looked into her eyes. "Say yes, Lily? Say you will become my wife in two Sundays."

She nodded, a light filling her eyes he did not remember seeing before.

His lips met hers again.

The deal had been made. The date had been agreed upon. And now, their attachment had been sealed.

Lily couldn't imagine all that Cook and Amanda had said about the wedding clothes. All she had to do was hint that the ceremony would be occurring soon, and the two women were bursting at the seams, they were so full of plans.

Even now, Lily followed Amanda's expanded form around the main street of Wharton City. The woman talked excitedly about the things they might find at the General Store.

Lily worked to keep up with her. How was that possible? The woman must be slowed by her burden. When would the baby make its appearance? She had imagined it would be by now. Was the woman carrying twins?

"Here we are at last!" Amanda said, waving Lily forward as if Lily did not recognize the General Store.

Lily nodded and stepped to Amanda's side. "Yes, indeed."

"I just know we'll find the perfect fabric for your dress," Amanda chattered on as she maneuvered her way around people exiting the building.

Of course, the rancher's wife had to be more careful inside the store as she worked her way around the shelves and bins. But she was a woman on a mission, heading straight for the fabric section.

Lily stayed with her, lest she find herself left far behind and without a say.

Amanda picked through the selection as Lily neared. She held up varieties of cream, white, and ivory colored cloths.

Nonsense! What an impractical choice...

"Amanda..." Lily interjected, but her attempt trailed as Mrs. Miller held the fabric options up to Lily's skin, making as many different faces as there were choices.

"No...maybe...not with your skin tone...too bright...too dull...not quite right..." Amanda continued on.

"I..." Lily tried again. She grabbed for a couple of the samples, hoping to get Amanda's attention. "I didn't think I needed a new dress."

That stopped Amanda. Her eyebrows drooped. She appeared rather disappointed. "Didn't think you needed a new dress?"

"Yes." Lily's voice didn't have much strength. She so appreciated Amanda's care. But she didn't want all this fuss. Hadn't Cook and Amanda worked tirelessly enough to provide her with three new dresses after her relocation to Cook's home? She couldn't ask them to now make her an new, even more extravagant piece. "I planned to wear my best dress. Not have a new one made."

Amanda blinked. Was she so disbelieving? "But, dear," she said, putting a hand on Lily's shoulder, "your dresses won't accommodate a bustle."

"A bustle?" Lily's confusion must have been spelled out on her features.

"Of course. They are the height of fashion. And I insist you be in style for your wedding." Amanda held up another off-white fabric.

Lily pushed it down. "But Dan likes my blue dress. And it's my favorite."

"*White*," Amanda stressed. "White is the color of the day for wedding dresses."

Looking out the window, Lily sighed. Was there any way to get through to her kind heart and well-meaning ways? Lily didn't want it—the big bustled white dress that she'd never wear again. And who would pay for such an extravagance?

Amanda set the bolts of fabric to the side and put a hand on Lily's arm. "This is overwhelming, isn't it?"

Lily nodded. Maybe that was it.

"I'm sorry." Amanda's gaze softened and her voice was sincere. "I don't mean to push. We all love Dan and you, and we just want everything to be done right."

Was Lily's way not right? She frowned.

"Here." Amanda looped a hand through Lily's arm. "I have an idea about these colors."

Colors? They were all white. That wasn't color. Lily pushed her thoughts to the side.

"Let's go to the café and get something refreshing. Perhaps we can sit for spell and just talk?" Amanda caught Lily's gaze.

That did sound good. Really good. Lily offered Amanda a smile and helped her out of the General Store.

As they crossed the wide dirt path to the café, they heard a strong voice call out. "If it isn't the prettiest two women in all of Wharton City."

Lily didn't like it.

But Amanda smiled and turned. "And there's that handsome husband of mine."

As Lily turned, only somewhat satisfied that they were not being preyed upon, she spotted Mr. Miller and Dan. Then she let out a relieved sigh.

The two men approached from the general direction of the church. Had they completed their errand with the preacher already?

Lily, too, offered her sweetheart the broadest smile she could. Her cheeks were pained her mouth spread so wide.

Mr. Miller picked up his pace to catch his wife. He gave her a quick kiss and inquired after the baby.

Dan neared, and Lily couldn't hear anything further between the Millers. The look in his eyes stole the entirety of her attention.

"How was shopping?" He stopped in front of her, leaning in to sweep a kiss to the side of her face before pulling back.

She wanted him to put his arms around her, to greet her with a different kind of kiss. But it would not be appropriate until they were wed.

It would not be long…less than two weeks.

His brows rose. He sought an answer.

An answer?

Had he asked her something? Oh, yes. About the shopping.

She glanced at Amanda. The woman had become caught up with her husband.

"It was…good." Lily chose her words with care.

"Good?" Dan seemed concerned. Why? Did it matter to him how her shopping was?

"Yes."

"I had thought women rather enjoyed shopping." He smirked.

She dipped her head to hide any display of emotion. "Yes, well… perhaps I don't."

His arm came around her shoulder, and he directed her away from the center of the large path.

She lifted her face. Did a coach come down the road? Or a cluster of horses? Nothing appeared to be amiss. But as she watched, he drew her to one of the planked sidewalks, away from passers-by and away from the Millers.

"What's going on?" Dan's eyes searched hers. Here he was, concerned again. Sweet as it was, she could manage some things by herself.

"It's nothing." She waved him off.

"You sure?"

She smiled. "Nothing I can't handle."

He ran his fingertips along the side of her face, as if he were putting a stray hair in place. But it was only an excuse to touch her.

Not that she minded.

His gaze trailed movement further away. "Though I'd rather not, I suppose I should share you with the Millers."

She closed her eyes, smiling, letting his admiration wash over her.

"To the café." He raised an arm in the direction of the eatery.

She nodded and moved that way. It would be good to see Mrs.

Jackson again. Maybe speak with her about the wedding supper. The very thought made Lily tingle all over. Or was it Dan's nearness?

How good life was! After all that happened…things had turned around.

The Millers entered the café up ahead, and Lily smiled to herself. She counted herself fortunate to have made such friends. They were loyal and kind. Good people. Not like those that had only followed along with her for what could be gained.

So much in her thoughts, she only just missed bumping into the couple coming out as she approached. She stepped to the side in an effort to dodge the collision.

A hand grabbed for her. Dan? Did he mean to keep her balanced?

But the grip on her arm hurt. The vise-like hold more familiar than it should be. Her spine was struck with a wave of ice.

Though she needn't lift her eyes to determine the identity of her attacker, she did. To find the boring gaze of her mother.

Dan noticed Lily's parents a moment before Mrs. McAllen's hand struck out for Lily's arm.

He wanted to jump between the women, but his legs wouldn't move. Why was Lily soundless? She hadn't made a noise—not in surprise, not in pain. Though her twisting away from the contact to her person belied that it was, indeed, causing injury.

Sheriff McAllen reacted faster than Dan, placing hands on his wife's shoulders and urging her forward, out of the doorway and to the side.

Mrs. McAllen did not acknowledge him, but allowed him to move her as he willed. And she dragged a helpless Lily along.

Why did Lily not free herself? It seemed as if she had become paralyzed.

What of himself? Why did he do nothing?

Jerking Lily in toward herself, Mrs. McAllen's harsh voice let loose on her.

Sheriff McAllen stepped closer, as if trying to speak to his wife without drawing more attention. Why? Was he uncomfortable with a public display? Did he prefer all done behind closed doors?

And Lily's mother? Was she angry to be left alone with the sheriff to bear the abuse by herself? Pouring out her ire on Lily would not be tolerated.

Finding his voice and his nerve, Dan wedged himself between Mrs. McAllen and Lily, creating space somehow.

"Mrs. McAllen, take your hands off Lily," he demanded.

The woman glared at him. There was poison in her eyes.

Sheriff McAllen's gaze, too, landed on Dan, but his was one of confusion. That was curious.

"Dan..." Lily said under her breath, her words murmured and whimpered. Was she fearful for him? For herself?

In front of which parent? Because her father did not seem the bigger threat in the moment.

"What did you say?" Mrs. McAllen crowed. She jerked Lily's arm.

Lily worked to maintain her footing.

He swallowed. Then shook his head. There was no reason he should be afraid of this woman. None.

"I told you to release Lily." He said the words deeply, almost growling. They vibrated in his chest.

"So, *you're* the one?" The woman narrowed her eyes as she peered at him. "The unlucky one."

What was he to do? He did not wish to force her hand from Lily's arm. But he would do it if he had to.

"You have *no* idea," her voice all but cackled. "No idea..."

The woman was starting to sound unsteady...unstable. What *was* going on here?

"I will tell you one last time—let her go." Dan leveled his gaze on the hand that held fast to Lily's arm. He watched the muscles in the hand contract.

Lily seethed and her knees buckled as the pressure increased.

Dan swept his hand in. He made contact with Mrs. McAllen's hand.

She released Lily. And struck at him.

Lily fell to the ground.

Stinging. Burning. On the side of his face.

Sheriff McAllen pulled at his wife.

She roared.

McAllen moved off with her.

But Lily...

On the ground. Crying.

He knelt beside her, placing a hand on her back. Would he ever make sense of what had happened here?

She lifted her gaze to his. Her eyes were reddened. "Dan, I'm sorry... I'm so..."

"It's all right." As he spoke the words, he wasn't sure he meant it. Was it all right? He reached for her arms and, with gentle motions, helped her to her feet.

Once upright, she seemed more able to gather herself. And she looked to him again.

Her eyes widened. "Dan! Your face..." She pressed a hand to her mouth.

The side of his face still stung. He raised a hand to it.

Lily halted his progress. "No. It's bleeding." She pulled out a handkerchief and held it toward him.

"Wait," he held up a hand.

But she was not deterred. She dabbed at the site that now throbbed. As she pulled it back, he spotted the bright red upon the once white fabric.

He held her wrist. "Now you've ruined your handkerchief."

She fidgeted with the cloth, looking down at it. Did she avoid his gaze now? "It is nothing of importance."

Dan watched her. It tore at his heart to see her struggle so. But how could he deny that she had lied to him yet again.

Was it such a comfortable thing for her? If so, how many more lies had she told? What, if anything, was true?

His feelings for her were. But if they were based on fabrications, were they real?

Her eyes met his again. "Dan, I didn't tell you about my mother—"

"No, you didn't." He cut her off. Feelings that had been resurfacing for weeks rushed through him. He would not become a victim trapped in a web of lies again...he *couldn't*.

She closed her mouth. Tight.

Surprised by his response? Why? He had bared all to her. She knew...she *knew*...and yet...

Dropping her hands to hip level, she let her gaze fall as well.

He crossed his arms over his chest and did nothing as she moved a couple inches away.

"It's just that I...couldn't." Her gaze lifted for a moment. Eyes that filled with moisture begged him to listen, to believe.

His hurt refused. How much longer, how much more could he put his heart out? How much more could he afford risk and then discover it was all a sham? Best to cut his losses now. "So you say."

Her mouth fell agape. Shocked? So was he.

And he had few choices at this point. He needed to protect himself.

Swallowing, he looked at her.

She struggled to maintain eye contact. That couldn't mean good things.

He sighed. "Lily, there is that point where a man has to save what's left of himself. That point..."

She drew in a ragged breath.

"...was one lie ago." He spoke the words with more confidence than he felt. For inside, he crumbled. At this conversation, at what just happened, at watching her fall apart in front of him.

Her eyes slid closed, and she dropped her head. And her shoulders shook. Hard.

Yes, this relationship did mean something to her. That made it all the more painful for him. And it almost enticed him to stay.

All of this, coupled with the knowledge of what she'd been through at the hands of her parents...made his decision villainous. How could he turn a blind eye?

But the thought of being left, his heart vulnerable...only to be trampled, was too much. He couldn't. Maybe he was too broken himself.

Something within warned that she had nowhere to go...but Uncle Owen and Cook would not let that be the case. They would see to it she was looked after.

"Stay here. I'll make sure the Millers see you to Uncle Owen and Cook's."

And then he did the hardest thing he'd ever done. Even more difficult than the words he had just spoken.

He turned and walked away from her. Left her a shattered mess.

For this, he doubted he could ever forgive himself. No matter the reason.

CHAPTER 12

The Reality

Dan stared at the ceiling of the bunkhouse. Had he slept at all? With every breath he felt that same ache he had when he walked away from her.

And when he closed his eyes, her face was there. Her green eyes, glassy and sad. How could he have caused her such pain? It tore at him. He would not make it through this unscathed.

Then it *had* been the right choice. Yes. It must have been. If it was so difficult now, what if he'd stayed another week? Or let the wedding happen? When his heart...his life...was hopelessly intertwined with hers?

And any hope of separation lost. Yes, he had made the right decision.

Then why did he feel so awful? So...empty?

What was the use? He did not have hope of any sleep at this hour. It wouldn't be long before the others would wake. Perhaps he might clear his mind with a short walk.

Sliding from his bed, he pulled on his clothes and boots. He was as ready for the world as he could be.

The door creaked on his way out. Cutie had always been the one to oil these things. Maybe he should take up that task. Later.

He stepped outside and drew in the early morning air. As it filled his lungs, he did not find it as refreshing as hoped, however. It fairly stung. His inhale ended in a fit of coughing.

Guess he deserved that.

Even as he narrowed his gaze, the sun would not show itself. There was but a faint rim of light on the horizon.

Dan leaned against the fence and watched it grow—the brightness both widening and lengthening as the day approached. But he cringed as the light cast away the shadows. What would be revealed?

He pushed back from the fence, turning his back to the ever brightening sky, and walked toward an open field. Why was this so hard? Hadn't he only done what he'd thought best?

To have his heart left in shambles.

Dropping his head, he folded his arms across his chest. Brandon often talked about God and how they could pray to the Almighty. Dan wondered if He truly cared.

Sure, God cared about people in general. But about Dan's life? Dan's choices? Why would a being with so much power and infinite knowledge have any consideration for Dan?

It seemed utter nonsense.

Grass rustled behind him. He spun, immediately on alert.

Brandon came from the direction of the homestead. "Whoa," he said, holding up his hands. "Didn't mean to startle you."

Dan nodded, but soon turned back toward the field.

Brandon stopped beside him.

The Millers hadn't said anything to him at dinner last night. Brandon assured Dan that they had gotten Lily back to Cook's cabin safely, but they seemed to sense that Dan was in no mood to speak of what had transpired.

Would Brandon violate that now?

Brandon cleared his throat.

Dear Lord... Dan did pray. *Please don't put me in this position.*

"I received word that the judge we wired for arrived in Tucson on yesterday's stagecoach."

"Hmm," Dan mumbled. Judge? In Tucson? Seems they might have their trial after all.

"And I thought you could help me take that Apache brave into town today."

Dan's gaze shot to Brandon. Take the brave today? Into a mess of a hornet's nest for sure. "What about Sheriff McAllen...?"

The words trailed. Lily's face appeared at the mention of the man's name. Why must he come in contact with her father again so soon?

McAllen would be mad something fierce to discover Brandon had kept this from him—first the judge coming and then the brave. Did Brandon think landing both in his lap at once was such a good idea?

"In for a penny, in for a pound, I guess." Brandon shrugged with a smirk on his face.

"You're in for something, that's true." Dan's gaze remained serious. This was no joke.

Brandon smacked Dan's shoulder. "What say we get that brave ready to go before anyone else wakes?"

Dan remained as Brandon moved off a couple of steps.

Brandon looked back at his ranch hand. "What is it?"

Dan considered his boss and friend. And remembered this was his *boss* before all else. Was it his place to question?

No. It wasn't.

So, he nodded and followed Brandon to the homestead. They entered the larger house.

As the front door shut behind them, Dan heard a wagon coming down the long path into the ranch.

Cook. Had to be.

What kind of state would she have left Lily in? Was Lily as restless as he had been the previous night? Or perhaps had a fitful sleep, without dreams? Fit only for tossing and turning? Plagued with images of him and how she missed him...

Dan jerked his head forward. This would not serve him...thinking about her like this. It could only lead to obsession.

Brandon looked back from across the great room. "Something wrong?"

Shaking his head, Dan picked up his step and joined Brandon as he moved down the hallway.

Brandon halted just outside the room in which the brave was held. He reached for the latch.

Dan grabbed his boss's forearm.

The slightly older man's gaze was on Dan, a question in his eyes.

"Do you have a gun?" One of them should be armed. And Dan hadn't been allowed to have his revolver on the ranch since the brave had been held here.

Brandon shook his head, his brows furrowed.

Dan grimaced. "One of us should."

Brandon looked as if he would protest. Then he released the latch and held up a finger. Without a word, he darted further down the hall and into his and Amanda's room, stepped within, and reappeared in a handful of seconds holding a pistol.

Dan nodded as Brandon neared. This was best. And as his boss closed the distance, he reached the gun out toward Dan, but paused.

Quirking an eyebrow, Dan hoped to communicate his shock. Would Brandon still not trust him? Did he continue to think Dan would harm the Apache? That hurt.

Something passed across Brandon's face. Indecision? Concern? Whatever it was, he pulled the weapon back to himself. And indicated that Dan should work the lock and latch while he stood at the ready with the weapon.

Dan was deflated, but he nodded.

And, when Brandon appeared ready, Dan unlocked and unlatched the door before opening it.

They needn't have worried; the Apache brave was still secured and in bed. Though he sprung, awake and alert as they entered.

His eyes went wide and wild. But as Dan stepped back and took in the situation, the youngster spotted the gun and leaned away as well.

He almost seemed ready to comply with whatever Brandon needed him to do. How had his behavior been whilst they cared for him? Did he know where they were taking him?

"What does he know?" Dan asked.

"More than I think we realize." Brandon lowered his revolver.

Dan shot him a harsh glare. "What are you doing?"

"I'm getting him ready."

"Keep that handy," Dan said, nodding at the gun. "Remember what he—"

"I *do* remember." Brandon leveled his gaze on Dan. "But you should remember that we've been interacting with this *boy* for weeks with no incident."

Dan fumed. But he had no recourse. He could do nothing but watch, ready to strike as Brandon moved to the Apache brave, untied him from the bedpost and secured his bonds behind him. Brandon then pushed the youngster to stand.

Why was it that in that moment the brave did seem so young? He couldn't be more than ten or eleven. How could he even wield a knife? Or be in possession of one? But Dan had seen what he was capable of. He would *not* let his guard down.

Brandon prodded the brave closer to the door, to pass by Dan.

The brave paused and looked up at Dan.

Dan's heart beat harder, his every muscle tensed for action.

But as the brave sought Dan's eyes, he said, "I sorry. For friend. For death."

Lily stretched and pulled the mug of coffee closer to her chest. Cook had come out of the cabin and found her on the porch, awaiting the sunrise.

How long had she been here? Cook had wanted to know. But Lily hadn't an answer for her. The moments had passed into hours. She had lain down for some of the night, but not much. The attempt to sleep had been torture—nothing to distract her. Just she and her thoughts. And those were quite loud.

Convicting. Shaming.

Speaking of her deserved guilt. And never before had she agreed more that perhaps she had earned what she had gotten.

Yesterday, the moment all her fears were realized when Dan put her aside, her world crashed down. But as she sat with her thoughts, trying to see things from his perspective, she believed she could understand.

Would she trust herself with something so precious as his heart? No, he had done what was best. Hadn't she even longed for him to free himself from the ill-fated connection?

How much had changed in such a short time. When she began to think beyond herself...began to hope...began to dream...that something more could be in her life. That God might be so kind.

But if God existed, it was only to punish her. Surely.

The door creaked behind her.

She didn't have to turn. It had to be Mr. Owen...with Cook already off to the Miller ranch, there was no one else it could be.

"Dorothy warned me you'd be out here."

Lily nodded but didn't trust herself to speak.

"It is quite a sight."

She let her gaze drift to the horizon, long since full of color. It was beautiful. But she wasn't ready to acknowledge that anything held meaning for her anymore.

"Quite a sight all right. Quite a sight."

Lily took a swig of her coffee. How long would Mr. Owen stand there and fish after something? Couldn't he just move on with his chores? Leave her to her humiliation?

"Don't you think?"

She sensed him staring at her. He was a wonderful, fatherly figure. But she didn't need that right now. She needed to be left alone. Why didn't he see that?

As much as she wanted to be angry, she couldn't fight the tears that filled her eyes. One finding its release.

She wiped at it.

A handkerchief appeared to the right side of her head.

Looking up, beyond the kind offer, was the wrinkled, smiling face of the older man who only meant well.

Lifting trembling fingers, she took the cloth offered.

"Thank you." Her voice was weaker than she feared it would be. Now he'd never leave her be.

"I'm not much of a busybody." His voice, raspy with age offered. Though it seemed somewhat hesitant.

She nodded.

"But I do have two good ears."

Turning, she looked up at him.

"If...you need to talk." He shifted and set a hand on the door's latch. Would he, then, leave her now?

She regarded the hillside once more. Did she want for solitude? Or would sharing bring her peace?

Could she hope?

"Mr. Owen?" she called, looking over her shoulder as he pulled the door.

He paused and opened it a bit wider. His brows quirked.

"I...would like that very much."

Stepping through the door, he put out a hand toward her.

She slipped her fingers into his and let him assist her to her feet.

They moved inside where she began to unload a lifetime of hardship and shame in the hours that followed.

As she finished, fingering the locket around her neck, she let the silence linger. She wanted Mr. Owen to fill it. To say something. But he sat as he had for so long, gaze intent on her, features unreadable.

How did she sound to him? Would he agree she was the villain? That Dan had done the wise thing? Perhaps he would even wish her out of his home.

Her hand clamped around the small trinket, clinging to it as if it were the only thing grounding her. Was it?

When the chain tugged against the back of her neck, she let loose her grip. The necklace was not so sturdy that she could be firm without risking it's undoing.

She brought her fist enclosing the precious piece of jewelry to her lips. And let her eyes close. How could she face Mr. Owen anymore? For certain, he thought on how to dismiss her. Such a thing went against his kind nature, but he must. Should she relieve him of the burden?

As she opened her mouth to do so, his voice cut through the stillness.

"That is...quite a lot. More than any person should have to go through."

She let her head drop as she nodded. Yes, she had put Dan through it.

Drawing in a breath, ragged as it was with emotion, she searched for a strength she feared she didn't possess. Not anymore. Where would she go? Who would she be?

Mr. Owen leaned forward. "Do you have a plan?"

She tried to speak. But nothing would come. So, she shook her head as her eyes filled. Was her life as good as forfeit?

"You deserve a happy ending here."

Her head jerked upward, her gaze catching on Mr. Owen's. Happy ending? Did he not think to put her out then? Why ever not? Had she left something out of her story?

His eyes widened. So, he caught her surprise.

"I..." A shake overcame her. "I can't image how you could think I..." She pressed her hand to her mouth once more and sealed her eyelids against the flood.

The floorboards creaked, and she sensed that Mr. Owen moved closer. When he spoke again, his words were softer, but from a place beside her. "You and Dan, perhaps more than *anyone* deserve it."

Weathered, larger fingers fell on her other hand, still in her lap.

"If you will take it."

She opened her eyes, not caring that tears flowed. As much as everything in her fought his words, nothing in his gaze betrayed them to be anything but truth from his point of view.

"I know that man loves you. Else he wouldn't've got so riled." Mr. Owen's eyes seemed to shimmer all the same.

Lily lowered her hand, and her locket rested once more against her dress's bodice.

"Do you..." Dare she ask what was in her heart? If she spoke it, the dream would be real. And it would be in danger of being thwarted.

Mr. Owen waited. Something in his small smile encouraged.

"Do you think there is still a chance?" Her words must be too quiet for the older man to hear.

"I would bet my life on it, young lady." Mr. Owen's eyes sparkled.

And hope once again found a place in Lily's heart.

Dan slowed the wagon as they neared Wharton City. "Where am I headed, boss?"

"Go to the jail."

"Sure thing." Dan tugged on the right side of the reins and urged the horse to maneuver in that direction. *Right into the den of wolves.*

As they passed down the main street, Dan spotted Sheriff McAllen standing outside the Jail with another, somewhat more distinguished man. What? Had the judge arrived already? Were they late? Or did Brandon know this would be the case?

Dan pulled the wagon to a stop in the area beside the jail. Now he had a better view of McAllen's interaction with this stranger. It did seem as if he pandered to the man. Not that he'd ever seen the sheriff "make nice" before. Perhaps this was what it looked like. It seemed rather awkward.

Brandon grunted as he shifted across the wagon bed, his hand on the arm of the Apache brave, somewhat towing the boy along.

McAllen and the gentleman, who was certainly the judge from Tucson, looked their way, but Dan made short work of dropping from the bench and stepping to the back. He helped Brandon get the brave from the back of the wagon before he chanced a glance toward the waiting men.

The sheriff's expression was hard and pointed. His accusation clear. Though they didn't need it.

They knew he would not be happy about their deception on either count. And now they would pay the price.

Tugging the shuffling brave, who seemed rather hesitant in that moment, Dan and Brandon approached the sheriff and judge.

Brandon lengthened his stride to move ahead. He tipped his hat toward the more well-dressed man. "Brandon Miller. I'm hoping you're Judge Ethan Anders."

McAllen appeared as if he would grind his teeth to the gumline, but he kept his mouth shut. All the better to keep grinding perhaps.

The newcomer stuck out a hand in Brandon's direction. "Guilty, Mr. Miller. You must be the man I'm looking for."

"That would be me, your honor. I sent for a judge."

As Dan watched their interchange, he noticed that Brandon did not look once at McAllen. That did not keep the sheriff from staring nails at him.

"This is one of my ranch hands, Daniel Hayworth. He was also a witness."

Sheriff McAllen's widened gaze turned on Dan then. Dan didn't dare look, but he could feel it. For certain, he could feel it...like searing heat.

"Witness to *what*?" McAllen's words were tight. Did he even open his mouth?

Brandon glanced at him. His features remained neutral. Was he attempting to decide what, if anything to say? Or how much to say? He let out a sigh. "To the killing of Joseph McAllen."

Sheriff McAllen's face reddened. He made unintelligible noises and glared between Brandon, Dan, and the Apache brave. "You mean..." he said, his voice shaking. "This...this is the...savage...that..."

Brandon stepped between the sheriff and the brave, his shoulders rising as he stood taller, cutting off even McAllen's ability to see the boy clearly.

"You know you needed to hand him over to *me*," the sheriff said. His words were calmer than Dan would have expected. Was he numbed by the situation?

Dan didn't trust the emotionless tone. It seemed eerie.

Brandon's mouth stayed level, as did his gaze. "Beg your pardon, Sheriff, but there was little chance of this boy getting a fair shake."

McAllen's eyes narrowed.

"Without a judge," Brandon added. "I wanted us to do this right and proper. Just so."

McAllen's hands had curled into fists, and his arms shook as if he sought a target to unleash his fury on. The brave would be his choice.

Dan was certain he wasn't the only one to see that. One glance at Judge Anders, and he saw the man seemed to be taking a pretty good measure of the situation.

"Gentleman," Judge Anders's firm voice pressed into the space. "Now is not the time. I see why I was called for. And I agree, there should be a fair trial. But this is not it."

Brandon nodded but did not lower his guard.

Nor did McAllen let loose his anger.

"I have to make a decision about how to keep this..." The judge waved a hand in the direction of the Apache boy.

"Apache brave," Dan offered.

The judge nodded his thanks. "Yes, Apache. We need to keep him somewhere...in custody...but where he'll make it to trial *safe* and *intact*."

Sheriff McAllen shot Judge Anders a hard look. So, he wasn't quite thankful for Anders's assessment.

What would Judge Anders decide? How could he keep the brave in custody? But not guarded by McAllen's men?

"You have good men, Mr. Miller?" Anders asked, looking at him.

"I'd trust any of them with my life, your honor," Brandon said, standing a bit straighter.

"Judge, you can't be serious—" McAllen started, voice raised.

Anders held up a hand in McAllen's direction, cutting him off. Then he said in a gruff voice, "I will do as I see fit, Sheriff."

He watched McAllen for a moment longer as the sheriff shifted and squirmed a bit.

Was it so wrong that Dan enjoyed it as much as he did? Finally, someone put the man in his place. He only wished that Lily could see this. Just remembering how McAllen had spoken to her the day Dan asked for her hand...

Dan shook his head. No, he couldn't allow those thoughts to continue. They would lead where he could not follow. Could he not get away from her?

"This is what will happen." The judge spoke again. "We will put the boy in the jail."

Dan watched Brandon. His boss bit at his lip to keep from speaking out. He admired the man's control.

"But," Anders said, looking between Brandon and McAllen. "There are to be two men at guard and *only* two—one deputy and one ranch hand."

Now, McAllen and Brandon exchanged looks. Neither seemed entirely happy. Why would they be? They each had to give up part of their control and trust.

Not something Dan would be eager to do when it came to McAllen either.

The judge appeared rather pleased with himself. Smile and all. "You've got a ranch hand here, Mr. Miller. Is there a deputy on duty, Sheriff?"

McAllen nodded. "Yes, sir."

"Excellent," Anders's smile broadened. "First watch starts now."

Brandon and Dan shared a look. This wasn't quite what they'd planned for. But Dan would do what was needed.

Dan side-stepped toward the brave, but Brandon cut him off.

"I'll escort him into the jail." His boss's tone did not leave any opening for comment or question.

Dan backed up and followed.

They had to cross in front of McAllen as they moved toward the jailhouse.

Dan watched the sheriff as they neared. He wasn't the only one.

Judge Anders stared the man down as well. "Where is that deputy of yours?"

"Travers," McAllen called.

The deputy Dan had come to despise stepped out of the jailhouse. "Sheriff?"

Travers took in the situation. A sneer appeared on his face as he laid eyes on Dan. So, the feeling was mutual, was it?

"You and this...ranch hand...are going to be guarding this...Indian." Sheriff McAllen didn't bother looking at the Apache again.

"Sir?"

The sheriff rolled his eyes. "Deputy," McAllen said, voice rising again. "This Indian will be secured in a cell. You and the ranch hand will guard him until you are relieved."

"Me and the ranch hand?" Travers made no attempt to hide his confusion.

Meanwhile, Brandon, the brave, and Dan waited just outside the jailhouse, waiting for the deputy to permit them to enter.

"Yes, Deputy Travers. That is what I said. You and the ranch hand. Now, secure the criminal," McAllen said, a growl emitting from his throat. "Or must I do it?"

"No, sir," Travers said, perhaps louder than necessary. "I'll get the prisoner taken care of." Then the deputy caught Dan's gaze and scowled.

Dan didn't care. There was no consideration lost here between them. No surprises there.

After the brave was settled in the cell, Dan was given a chair and a place to sit at post. The deputy had his own station already. Brandon left his pistol with Dan for good measure.

Judge Anders then insisted that McAllen and Brandon accompany him to the café for some refreshment. There had never been a more uncomfortable, reluctant departure as far as Dan had ever known.

It was only surpassed by the awkwardness of the space remaining in the jailhouse.

The passage of time eeked by. Too slow. With the lack of sleep he'd had, Dan began to fear for his ability to remain alert.

Until the door burst open.

And Lily ran in.

Lily scanned the jailhouse. She'd been assured Dan was here.

Stepping within brought back memories—most she'd rather do without. And as her gaze landed on Deputy Travers, she grimaced. Any memories of him were certainly not good. He had been a source of unpleasantness for some time.

"Lily?" It was Dan's voice.

She turned toward the sound.

He rose from a chair in the corner, to one side of the jail cell farthest to the right. His frame stretched to its full height as he stood, reminding her how capable he was of protecting her, of sheltering her from so many things. The low-life Travers not-with-standing.

As she watched Dan, she worked to speak. But her voice wouldn't come. There was a thickness in her throat.

Dan's gaze stayed on her. His thoughts were difficult to discern. Brows furrowed and mouth downturned, he seemed concerned. Because he worried about her? Or because he didn't want to see her?

She looked to the floorboards. Could she gather some courage if she broke eye contact?

"What are you doing here?" His voice soothed and challenged at the same time. How was that possible? His footfalls on the hardwood confirmed he continued to draw near.

That only made her shiver. Was she nervous? Excited? Or just overcome?

She had to remember why she was here. There may not be another opportunity. To speak with him. To tell him. To bare her heart.

When she lifted her gaze, he had stopped only an arm's length away. How could she concentrate with him so close? She wanted to lean into him, melt into his strength. If only that were possible.

She opened her mouth but found herself unable to speak.

The creases in his features deepened. "Is something wrong with Uncle Owen? Cook? The ranch?"

"No," she pushed out. She was doing this all wrong. "All is well."

His shoulders relaxed. As did his facial muscles.

"Then why are you here?" His voice had a bit of a bite to it.

"It's just..." she said, all the more hesitant under his intense scrutiny.

But she had to do this. She had to have courage. For him. For their future.

Straightening her shoulders, she pressed out words that she prayed had more strength than she felt. "That is, I had to speak with you."

One of his eyebrows lifted. Would he grant her the chance to speak? Would she let him deny her?

She started to insert something more, but Dan shot a glance toward Travers.

"By all means," the deputy said. "Please, go on."

The muscles worked in Dan's jaw. "I'd rather you step outside."

"Not a chance, ranch hand." Travers crossed his arms. "I ain't goin' anywhere. Sheriff says I'm s'posed to guard this here Indian, and I intend to do just that."

Dan looked at the cell.

Only then did Lily notice the young boy in the jail cell. Who was he? Why were they guarding him?

"But you are welcome to step outside," Travers shot back. "Or you could let me and Lily alone. Maybe I have unfinished business with her myself."

Dan jerked toward the man as if ready to throw a punch.

Lily grabbed for his arm. "Dan!"

He halted but kept his narrowed gaze on Travers.

"Don't let him rile you up. He's not worth it." Now her voice had the firmness she'd wanted.

Dan glanced at Lily and nodded.

Travers snickered.

"You watch yourself," Dan said through clenched teeth.

The door to the jailhouse opened once again.

Brandon stepped in. And though he attempted to keep his face neutral, surprise passed over his features before he rid himself of any trace of it. "What's going on here?"

Lily ducked her head. What terrible timing. Perhaps this wasn't the best plan. Dan had a job to do, and she was distracting him.

"Nothing, boss," Dan said, his voice calmer than she'd expected. "Lily stopped by to check in."

Lily peered up as Brandon's gaze looked over the three of them.

He seemed to weigh whether or not to believe Dan's report. Either way, he must have deemed it acceptable, for he said, "Good timing. I came to relieve you. Can you go back to the ranch and let the others know we're taking shifts here? I'd like Slim out here just after lunch."

"Yes, sir." Dan nodded and took hold of Lily's arm, steering her toward the door. He paused by Brandon and handed off a pistol before urging her out the door.

"Don't forget what I said," Travers called.

"Don't *you* forget," Dan fairly growled. His hold on her arm tightened almost to the point of hurting as they moved into the yard beyond the jailhouse.

Once outside, Dan released her and continued walking to the waiting wagon and horse. She picked up her pace to keep up.

"I wanted to..." she called.

He turned.

She slowed and stopped. "I needed to talk."

Looking at the ground, he let out a long breath. Then met her gaze once more. "About what, Lily? I don't know that there's anything to talk about. I said my piece."

Blinking, she paused for a moment.

Long enough, it seemed, for him to return to readying the horse.

She stepped closer and touched his shoulder.

He jerked around so fast it made her take a step back.

Though nerves threatened to overtake her, she forced confidence into her voice she wasn't sure she felt. "You might have." Why did her words shake so much? "But I didn't."

Dan had one hand on the horse's bit. The other moved over his face. Would he give her the chance she so desperately wanted? Needed? Or dare she take it?

That was best.

"I am sorry," she started before he could stop her.

He looked at her. Then opened his mouth. Would he not let her continue? So, she pressed on.

"Yes, I lied to you. It wasn't that I meant to mislead you or betray your trust. You've got to understand how stuck I felt...how ashamed..."

He considered her. "I *have* to?"

"I think you should. I was in a hard place. Can you see that?"

As he paused, the silence rested between them for a moment. Should she speak on? Or let him respond?

"Can you not see that I offered you everything I had to give, and you couldn't trust me with all of you?" His words were given simply.

They stirred her heart. But she couldn't overlook that he would not step out of himself and see things from her perspective. She had done as much. Why couldn't he? From deep within her, a fire was lit. A spark, a flame that had long sought to defend her. And long had it been snuffed. No more.

"As if you are so perfect?" she muttered.

"What was that?" His brows furrowed.

"Why must you refuse to see?" she countered.

He just stared. Was he surprised she would fight for herself?

"I have apologized. But you...you won't take one moment to try and understand the life I lived. In the dark. In silence. In pain."

Dan's eyes narrowed. He said in a gruff voice, "Are you finished?"

"No. I take back what I said before. I can't expect you to understand. You never could, and you never will."

"Lily—" he started.

"No," she cut him off. "I have nothing further. And, as you've said your piece, I will bid you good day, sir." She turned and rushed off.

"Lily!" he called after her.

But she continued until she was some distance away.

He did not follow.

CHAPTER 13

The Taking

The horse beneath Lily pressed onward as she leaned forward. She had never been so angry, so hurt...

Never.

Why would he... ?

How could he...?

And then to just walk away. Or...to let her walk away. Did it mean that all was lost? That whatever they'd had was gone forever?

If he wasn't willing to fight for it, how could she? It wasn't as if she could save it on her own. What could *she* do? Drag him to the preacher one week from Sunday and insist he speak vows?

Tears blurred her vision. The broken promises and shattered dreams were in pieces. Nothing would make it right. No one could put them together again.

She slowed the horse.

It obeyed, as if it were ready to hold for a moment.

How long had she pushed the animal? Did she risk running the mare too hard?

Glancing this way and that, she did not see any familiar markings. Was she out of place?

She'd intended to return to Mr. Owen and Cook's cabin. It was as good a place as any to sit for a minute and determine her next course of action—if there were to be one.

But she couldn't even do that. She pulled back on the reins. The horse resisted stopping completely, sputtering and nickering.

"Shhhh," she soothed. She only needed a moment to gather her wits. They couldn't be too far off the path.

The mare urged forward, straining against the bit. And then moved onward.

"Calm down," Lily commanded. "Give me a minute."

The horse outright refused, continuing on as if Lily hadn't spoken.

This time, she allowed it. What was the use anyway? Perhaps the animal knew the way home.

As the mare plodded on, Lily couldn't help the emotion that settled into her chest, creating a tightened space there. Then it rose, filling her throat. It came out in sobs.

What use was she if she couldn't even make it from one place to another? Truly, she was useless. More so than this thoughtless animal.

The gentle movement of water caught her ears, and Lily's earlier hope vanished. So, the horse only wished for a drink. Infuriating beast! Not so smart after all.

She paused.

The mare was now at the side of the stream.

Lily slid off the horse. *Not so smart after all.* Maybe it was Lily who wasn't so smart. She had made quite the mess of her life. Even after she was offered the very chance of escape she had desperately wanted.

Couldn't hold on to that, could she? She had to ruin it.

Why, God? Why must you punish me? Aren't you done yet?

Dan looked upon the stone in front of him—his mother's. He didn't know why he felt so compelled to come here after delivering Brandon's message to Slim, but he did.

Didn't even bring flowers. Some such nonsense if ever he heard of it. Flowers.

What was he even doing here? Was he supposed to talk to the stone? To the mound of earth?

Ma wasn't here. Hadn't been here for a long time. Not since that night...

There was a stinging in the back of his nose and a tightness in his throat.

"I'm sorry, Ma. You deserved better."

He let the silence become fuller. And allowed the sadness to overcome him. It was his due.

How could he let himself fail someone so dear? Could he risk failing again? Hurting again? Grieving again?

"I thought I saw you out here."

Dan turned. His father waved from the front door. He found a small smile for the old man and lifted a hand. This was going to be... interesting.

His father nodded and slipped back inside.

Shifting his focus back to Ma's gravestone, he thought back to those blissful days when she was well. She did her best to provide some measure of laughter and lightness despite everything. At least those moments with her had been good. Right.

Only then it wasn't.

What else could he say? To her carved stone? To himself?

Nothing. Nothing would make it right again.

No. But he owed his father a visit.

Standing, he whispered his love to his mother, hoping that somewhere God saw fit to let her know. Then he turned and walked into the cabin that had been his early home.

"I started some coffee," Pa said from the stove.

"Thanks, Pa. Sounds nice."

The older man looked at his son. "It's been a while, boy. What's kept you?"

Dan shook his head. Why did his father pry? He didn't have the right to ask such.

"It's that girl, ain't it?" Pa smiled. "Don't think Owen hasn't mentioned her."

Dan sighed. "I'm glad he's over here checking in on you."

"We have to keep a watch over each other." Pa pulled the pot off the stove and poured the coffee. His hands trembled as he did so.

"Let me get that." Dan stepped to the stove.

"I can manage." Pa elbowed Dan away. He gripped the coffee mugs and moved ever so slowly toward the small table.

His shaking was bad, though. Worse than Dan remembered.

Still, as much as he spilled, Pa got the cups to the table with most of it still inside.

"Thanks." Dan sat and took a swig of the hot brew.

"You got anything to tell me about this girl?" Pa asked, easing into a chair as soon as Dan pulled the rim from his lips. "Am I gonna need to get my suit out?"

"No, Pa. I'm afraid not," Dan looked at the dark liquid. He couldn't even glance at his father. These moments made up most of their time together. So difficult. Still, Dan had promised Ma...

"No?" The way Pa's voice rose, he sounded confused.

"What has Uncle Owen told you?" Dan lifted an eyebrow.

"I dare not betray a confidence." The older man raised his cup.

Dan rolled his eyes. He was thankful for the friendship between the two older men. And even more grateful that Uncle Owen and Cook lived not two miles away—close enough to keep an eye on Pa. The man needed minding.

"Good Lord willing, you'll get it worked out."

"What makes you think I need to get anything worked out?" Dan sat straighter. What was his father saying?

"Don't take this the wrong way, son. But you sure do like to help people. That's a right good quality. You'll go out of your way to do what you can for someone in a mess. But when it comes to people, you keep them at arms' length. You know what I mean?"

Could that be so? Dan considered it until he became uncomfortable. Then he decided he wouldn't permit the man to make judgments about him. Pa hadn't earned the right.

"Ah, just think on it. Now, finish up your coffee and take me to the ranch to see them youngins."

Dan downed the rest of the beverage with a long swig. "I'm waiting on you."

"Let's go!" The man struggled to his feet.

And Dan struggled to let him do it himself. Pa could be stubborn. How much longer would it be, though, before he would need more help? Best not to think on such things.

Dan rose and opened the door. In a matter of moments, he and his father were well on their way to the Miller ranch. He did not wish to think on Pa's words, so instead he thought about Samuel, Lucy, and Nisto...and how excited they would be to see Papa Hayworth. It had become an increasingly rare event.

As they neared the Miller homestead, Dan noted that everyone, it seemed, milled about outside. And not in a festive way. They seemed excited, yes, but more frantic.

They looked at his cart with eagerness. As he approached, however, their expressions dulled.

Brandon was the first to his side of the cart. "Lily," he exclaimed somewhat breathless.

"What?" Dan asked, looking at his father as if he would understand.

"Do you know where Lily is?" Brandon asked more clearly.

"No." Dan's chest was struck with a sharp pain. Know where Lily was? He spotted Uncle Owen and Cook a bit farther away.

Cook's eyes were reddened. From crying? Was something wrong?

Brandon turned away.

"Boss," Dan called, perhaps a bit too forcefully. He dropped from the cart. His tone remained just as demanding when he asked, "What's going on?"

Brandon put a hand up. "We aren't sure of anything yet. She didn't go back to Uncle Owen and Cook's. And we just thought she might be with you."

All the feeling seemed to drain from Dan. Everything except an overwhelming fear.

Again, Brandon attempted to turn back toward the gathering.

And again, Dan caught him. "So, no one knows where Lily is?"

When Brandon faced him, he was stoic and maintained a neutral face.

That was never good.

Brandon shook his head. "No."

Dan blinked as if that could erase the haziness from his vision. In a handful of seconds, it did clear.

Oh, Lily, what have you done?

Lily ran a hand along the horse's side and let her gaze linger on the horizon. What would the rest of the day bring? After the mare had her fill, would they find their way home? Or find more trouble out here?

A stirring in the brush beyond drew her attention. Was something there? A wild animal? Someone who wished her harm?

Her heart pounded, and she moved closer to the horse. But did not take her eyes off the shrub.

Shifting again.

The wind? Not possible.

Someone was there.

She grabbed for the pommel of the saddle. But as she turned, several riders from the west came around a butte not so far away.

They came fast.

Pulling, she attempted to lift herself up.

A hand clamped on her shoulder, jerking her down and turning her. Now, her back was to the horse.

The animal protested and side stepped. If the rough hands were not holding her, she would have fallen.

She dared open her eyes—when had she closed them?—and looked into the face of her captor.

An Indian. With paint on his face.

She had heard many stories. Were these war markings?

He tilted her chin up and examined her as if she were an item for purchase.

Clamping her jaw tight, she resisted the urge to cry out or even whimper. Neither would get her anywhere. Who would hear her so far from the city? She could not seem to staunch her tears though.

When the man released her chin and looked at her hair and face, he seemed to notice the tears, falling in silence. He frowned.

The other riders neared. Hoofbeats thundered within her body, causing her teeth to vibrate.

And then, they stopped.

She watched as a handful of men dropped from their mounts. The fear that had gripped her before seemed pale in comparison to the growing flood that overtook her now.

The men came around the one in front of her. What would they do? What could *she* do?

"Please..." she tried. "I'm not—"

"We know who you are," one of the men said in broken English.

She didn't know if she was relieved to be able to communicate, or more afraid at his words.

"Wh-What?" she stuttered.

"We want the one called Kuruk." His features were hard, the lines plain. She could not read anything from them.

"I...I don't know who you're talking about." Her words came out trembling. What would they do to her now?

"Liar," another said, stepping forward, anger naked on his face.

The first man put a hand to the angered man's chest and urged him back. Then he turned to Lily. "This is not good."

Somewhere, deep in her mind, the image of the boy in the jail cell came to mind. "Is he in Wharton City? In jail?"

A change on the man's face—acknowledgement. "You do know, then."

She nodded. "I saw him. Today."

The angry man's features formed a snarl, and he leaned forward. He seemed to have a rather intense reaction. Was he more connected to Kuruk somehow? The lines in his face betrayed his advanced age, perhaps the boy's uncle...or *father*?

"For the first time," she rushed to say. "Just today."

"We need him released," the other, calmer man said. Was he though? Or was it a ruse? There was something almost eerie about his demeanor.

"But I have no authority. No power to do so. Or even to tell someone to do it." She widened her eyes. Why must she speak so truthful? If she hoped to survive, she needed to think faster.

"But you are daughter of sheriff."

"Yes." She dropped her face. Her father would not trade. Dare she say so? Or wait, and let them find out? When she lifted her gaze, the man's glare bored into her.

"There is more?" He narrowed his eyes.

"No." She shook her head for emphasis.

The man took out his knife.

"Please!" She stepped away.

Two men grabbed her from behind, one on either side.

She fought against them as they brought her forward, to the one who wielded the large blade. "You don't understand!"

The man to the left held her left side still while the man to the right jerked her to his chest, pinning her arm and then gripping her hair at the scalp. Her head was now immobilized.

Why? What did they intend to do?

Then the man who had spoken with her, whose eyes were now hollow, aimed the blade for her throat. And swiped.

Dan was fast at work, saddling his horse. He couldn't shake the feeling that something terrible had happened. Emptiness filled him. A deep pit of nothingness.

Straps were secure, everything looked good. But as he went to put his foot in the stirrup, something stopped him. Did he have the heart to go looking? To perhaps find her already...already...

He set his head against the side of the saddle. *Oh, God.*

What if she was? What if she had done something to herself? Could he forgive himself?

He didn't know. But he *did* know that he couldn't continue with doubt.

The previous evening, he had searched the stream near her parents' house. For whatever reason, it seemed the first place to look. The place he had found her when he had to tell her about Joseph. Something in her eyes that day made him think she'd had thoughts of...ending it.

He had been out searching until he couldn't keep his eyes open. Now that he'd had a couple hours restless sleep, he would push on.

"Where do you think you're going?"

Dan spun.

It was Brandon.

"Don't try to stop me." He glared at his boss with a hardness he hoped was recognized. There was nothing Brandon could do that would keep him from going.

"You can't leave. We have a trial in an hour," Brandon said, crossing his arms.

"It'll have to go on without me." Dan turned back to his mount, double checking straps that he had already thoroughly secured.

"You are not only the star witness," Brandon said, his voice firm, not raised, not pleading, but level, calm. "You're the *only* witness."

Dan paused.

"Can you let Joseph's killer go? Be released without consequence?"

Dan looked over his shoulder. "Can they not delay my part?"

Brandon shook his head. "You know it doesn't work that way. Judge Anders heads back to Tucson on the noon stage and back to San Francisco in the morning."

Dan closed his eyes. He had to think. There had to be some other way.

"I know it's difficult. But let Slim and Eli search for her after they deliver the brave for the trial. You are needed elsewhere."

Brandon was right, and Dan hated that he was. Releasing the saddle, he nodded.

Clapping his shoulder, Brandon said, "Let's get my horse saddled and we can head out."

Again, Dan relented.

Within the quarter hour, they were joined by Slim, prepping his horse.

Dan couldn't help but eye him. He trusted Slim, but he didn't know Eli very well at all. What if Eli or Slim found Lily? What if she needed help? The kind that required risk? Would either of them risk themselves for her? He prayed they would.

Brandon pulled Slim to the side and spoke to him briefly before dismissing him to his mare. And he was off.

"Are we not to go along?" Dan questioned Brandon, perhaps more belligerently than he should.

"I sent Slim on to relieve Eli. It'll be time to change shifts before trial. Judge Anders wants to see you before we bring the brave."

Dan didn't have to like it. And he didn't. Still, he mounted alongside his boss and they made their way to Wharton City.

After tying off their horses outside the café, Brandon and Dan waited for Judge Anders to join them. The case was to be heard in the church just down the way from the café.

It wasn't long before the judge came out of the café, chatting with Sheriff McAllen.

The hairs on the back of Dan's neck stood up. This, too, he didn't like. Not only was the man cozying up to the judge, he didn't seem to care one bit that his daughter was out there...somewhere...missing... maybe dead.

"Steady," Brandon said under his breath.

Was that for Dan? It was so soft and subtle it couldn't have been heard by anyone else.

Dan held his place.

"Good morning, Judge Anders." Brandon stepped forward, offering a hand.

"Good morning, Mr. Miller, Mr. Hayworth." The judge shook Brandon's hand then reached for Dan's.

He complied. Reluctantly.

The judge's gaze lingered on Dan, a question in them. "Are you fellas ready to get this business behind us?"

"I always am." Sheriff McAllen spoke up. "Seeing justice done always suits me. Sorta settles my stomach."

How was Dan going to make it through this morning and not punch McAllen square in the face?

"Shall we, then?" Brandon held an arm out toward the church. Did he sense Dan's tension? Or was he just ready to shift the focus back to more pertinent things? Either way, Dan was grateful.

As they walked down the dirt-packed street, Dan spotted a flurry out of his periphery.

He turned.

Slim seemed to be making an effort not to draw attention to himself. *Nice try.*

All four men turned toward him.

"Morning, your honor." Slim took his hat off and dipped his head.

Dan rolled his eyes.

"I just needed to tell my boss something real quick. Ranch business." Slim saluted.

Good grief.

Judge Anders nodded. But McAllen narrowed his gaze. He seemed less convinced.

Anders moved on toward the church and McAllen didn't have any choice but to follow, glancing now and then over his shoulder.

Slim moved closer to Brandon and Dan.

"What is it?" Brandon asked, his irritation coming through in his tone. "Why aren't you at the jailhouse?"

"I was headed there, boss. Then some fella comes up to me and says an Indian told him Geronimo was willing to do a prisoner exchange."

Dan's heart dropped. Geronimo? Prisoner exchange? The world turned. Everything slowed. Surreal. *It can't be.*

Brandon's brows creased. "Prisoner exchange?"

Did he not understand?

Slim nodded. "Then he gave me this." He held out a lock of the most perfect red hair.

CHAPTER 14
The Trial

A weight settled in Dan's stomach, and it rose high into his chest. Would there be room for him to take a breath? He didn't care. "We...we have to go," he exclaimed. "Now!"

Brandon's features were set and grim. Did he consider his options? What was there to think about? They *had* to save Lily. No matter what.

"Boss—" Dan's voice was hard, demanding.

Brandon held up a hand. "Just...give me a second."

Dan sealed his mouth, but not easily. He clamped his teeth together. Hard. Would he lose his mind waiting for Brandon to come up with his words? There could be no other choice, could there?

Brandon looked at Slim. "Do you know the man who brought this to you?"

Slim shook his head. "But he seemed clueless. Maybe even afraid."

"Hmmm..." Brandon's brows furrowed.

Dan shifted his feet. He would go out of his skin if this took two minutes more.

"Can you track him down?" Brandon kept his gaze on Slim, refusing to look at Dan.

Slim gave Dan a sideways glance, which Brandon seemed to ignore. "I think so, boss."

Brandon nodded. "Do it."

"But—" Dan ground out.

Brandon's hard gaze cut him off. "We need all the information we can get. There is no sense in running off half-cocked."

He had heard this speech before. With Cutie...wanting to run off after Mariena when she was in trouble. It seemed reasonable to him at the time. But it didn't now. Maybe Cutie didn't think it so sensible then. Not when his heart had been so involved.

Should Dan take a step back and listen?

Just the thought made him dizzy. It wasn't possible. He had to— *needed* to—get to Lily. Now. All the things that could be happening to her flew through his mind. And his urgency to see her safe compounded.

He would find a way. *Had* to find a way.

Slim walked farther off in the direction he had come.

Brandon eyed Dan. "Let's get you to the church. The judge won't take too kindly to being put off."

What could Dan say that would distract Brandon? Something that his boss wouldn't expect? Dan was daft if he didn't think Brandon would be on his guard against such a tactic. No, for certain, he saw right through Dan.

But how would he extricate himself?

Could he?

They moved on toward the church. Each step seemed heavier than the last. Carrying him farther and farther from Lily, from what he should be doing.

This was torture.

As they approached the short set of stairs that went into the building, Brandon indicated that Dan should precede him. His gaze was stony, but there was a tell in the way the corner of his mouth twitched. Did he regret his position?

Dan had not thought of how to slip away. Perhaps he need not deal in subterfuge.

"Boss, I..." Dan put a hand on the railing. "I know it's not easy to see what the right thing is."

Brandon swallowed and looked at the door to the church.

"And I get it," Dan said, hoping against hope that Brandon would hear him out. "But Joseph is gone." His voice broke when he said the man's name. Why did he feel so guilty all of a sudden? "We can't bring him back no matter what we do."

Brandon's gaze fell on Dan. The man's mouth twisted. And Dan knew—the man felt responsible for Joseph. Just as Dan did. And Dan understood that burden. But Dan carried another, heavier burden—for Lily. So, he pressed on.

"But there's a chance for Lily...if we'll act now. If we wait, if we don't..." Dan let his words trail. "We could lose her, too."

Brandon's gaze hardened. "Don't you think I know that? You think this is easy?"

Dan couldn't look at his boss as the harsh words crossed the space. The man wasn't going to relent. And it burned Dan. Heated him. It took all his restraint to remember who this was and not use rather base methods to eliminate this barrier.

"But we can't forget what happened. Nothing about this erases that Joseph died and justice must be done. The truth must be spoken."

Dan met Brandon's gaze. A plan began to form. "What if I don't remember anything? They'll have to let the brave go."

Brandon shook his head, his top lip curled back, and his next breaths were somewhat seething. "You wouldn't do that. Not the man I know. He wouldn't bury the truth. Not for anything. The Dan I know is a good man, a man who cares about what's right. No matter what."

Dan looked down at his boots. As much as he hated it, Brandon was right. He did care. But he *loved* Lily. He would gladly sacrifice himself for her. But what of this? It was an impossible choice. How could he make it?

Peering up at Brandon, Dan said, "You can't ask this of me."

Something passed over Brandon's features in that moment. Sympathy? Concern? What was he thinking?

Lily woke to the rumble of voices. Where was she? Opening her eyes, bright light assaulted her senses. Was it yet day?

She remained silent and attempted to take in what information she could. Her life may depend on it. Male voices and the snorting of horses were all she heard.

What could she remember? Closing her eyes, she worked through the haze of memory.

Dan's rejection. It still stung.

Then she had taken the horse and run off. Toward Mr. Owen and Cook's. But she hadn't made it. No, she got lost.

The horse led her to a stream. And next...

Apache. Took her. The knife.

Her hands flew to her neck. Bound. Wrists protested against the burn of the rope.

But the tender skin under her ear was well. There were no cuts, no breaks in the skin. How was that possible?

As she pressed against her throat at various places and at different angles, she swept across a mass of blunt-ended tresses. Had they cut a section of her hair? For what purpose?

Proof of life.

Would they hold her for ransom? As a negotiation piece to get the brave that sat in prison?

Her heart fell. Who would care enough to wager anything for her? To sacrifice on her behalf?

It wasn't like her father would give up the brave. Or that anyone she could think of would risk themselves.

Dropping back, she winced. It seemed that only a thin blanket kept her off the ground. And the earth beneath was rather firm.

Was there hope? Was there anything to hold on to? Anything to live for?

She could hear her grandmother's words, chiding her. "With faith, with God—there is always hope."

Faith? She'd given up on that years ago. Where had it gotten her? The blunt receiving end of an empty bottle. Faith, indeed. Who needed a God that punished children in such a way? At the hand of their own mother! If he wouldn't—or couldn't—protect her then, what would make her think He could now?

Glaring at the sky, she dared Him to prove her wrong.

Interesting. It wasn't that she didn't believe He existed. Just that He cared. Perhaps His only consideration was to toy with His creations. Move them about. Amuse Himself.

Prove me wrong.

She rolled back to her side, curling into herself. How long would it be until these men decided no one was coming for her? What would they do with her then? Just kill her? Or would there be more?

What did it matter?

Her fingers sifted around her neckline to find the locket. Something about it always brought some level of comfort. Maybe all she was due in this world anymore.

It wasn't in the folds of her dress.

She reached around her neck, feeling for the chain.

Nothing.

Stricken with panic, she started to breathe heavily. Had it fallen off? Been pulled off when they moved her? Or when they had cut her hair?

Maybe...

Her heart dropped.

Did one of the Apache take the token from her when they spotted it? Think it something of value? Something earned for their part in her capture?

Moisture welled in her eyes. It was certain, then. Nothing had been left to her in this world. Nothing to cling to. Nothing to assuage her fears. Nothing to let her be at peace.

She glanced back into the sky.

You win.

Dan kept his head down as he made his way to the jail house. Why, he wasn't sure. Who would know what had happened? What he had planned?

But it seemed his guilt must be written all over his features, so he continued to move forward with his face turned to the ground. Best keep his presence as much a subtlety as possible. The less people noticed him, the better.

He neared the jail house, and no one had yet stopped him. Not even to comment on the weather. Letting out a breath, he thanked the Lord for his fortune.

Only that filled him with more remorse. What would God think of his actions? Of his choices? He skirted the line. Rather closely. And, from what the preacher often said, the Lord did not deal in technicalities, but with the heart of a person.

Then God must see that his intentions were right and good. His aim only to save Lily. How could that be wrong? Where was that balance between mercy and justice with the Almighty?

Pushing that question to the side, Dan steadied himself. He didn't have time for it now. This is what he had to do. For Lily.

He took a quick breath and pressed into the door. And then he was inside.

Eli and the deputy on duty both looked up from their stations. The brave sat in the corner of the cell, his head down between his propped-up knees and his chest, face dropped into his folded posture.

"What do you want?" Deputy Barnes was quick onto his feet. An accusation in his eyes.

Could he blame the man? Dan's appearance had not been anticipated. Who they would have expected, he didn't know. But it wasn't Dan.

Eli seemed curious but prudently withheld any opinion he might have. Maybe Dan had been too hard on the lad. Would he prove helpful?

"I'm here to get the prisoner to Judge Anders." Dan eased his posture. Nothing would be gained by bristling. He needed to exude confidence. As if there were nothing amiss about his behavior.

"Now that don't seem right," Barnes crossed his arms. "Ain't you s'pose to be telling your piece to the judge?" The deputy glanced at Eli and back at Dan.

Again, Eli betrayed nothing in his stance or features. He was good.

Dan rolled his eyes. "I'm not about to answer *your* questions."

Barnes narrowed his gaze.

"I've got a job to do. And I intend to do it." Dan meant every word of that statement. He stepped across the room toward the cell, snatching at the keys on the sheriff's desk.

The deputy grabbed the arm that reached out. "Lest you forget, ranch hand, I got a job to do, too."

Dan jerked away, still gripping the keys.

Barnes puffed out his chest. "You ain't taking that Indian nowhere."

Eli stepped between the men. "What's going to happen when Sheriff McAllen and Judge Anders wonder why Dan hasn't returned with the boy?"

The deputy looked back and forth between Dan and Eli. There was no sign of give in him.

Would this work? Dan hated that Eli had stepped in. It might save Dan's skin from taking more drastic measures, but now he had involved the younger man in a way he hadn't wanted to.

"What say we *both* walk the Indian over to the church?" Barnes said, a sneer on his face.

Not what Dan wanted to hear. But something he had anticipated. "Very well. Let's. We'd best get going. Judge Anders doesn't like to be kept waiting."

Barnes watched Dan, staying close behind him as Dan opened the cell, secured the Apache's wrists with handcuffs, and led the youngster out of the enclosure.

"Shall we?" Dan raised his brows.

The deputy moved to the front door.

Dan followed, tugging the boy along. He nodded to Eli as they left.

Once outside, Barnes glanced at Dan and moved in the direction of the church.

"What are you thinking?" Dan did his best to put disgust in his voice. It wasn't difficult.

Barnes turned. "What?"

"We can't walk this Indian through the middle of town. What are you trying to do? Cause a riot? Wouldn't Sheriff McAllen like that?"

The deputy winced. "Yeah. Let's take the long way."

Dan slipped behind the jailhouse and they walked toward the side yard. He did not relish what he must do. But it must be done. His time was already running short.

Stumbling, Dan pushed the brave into Barnes. Thrown off balance, the deputy lost his footing. He struggled with the boy while trying to remain upright. Landing on his backside, the deputy was pinned as the Apache fell on top of him.

Dan rushed forward as he drew his pistol. He made it into position just in time.

When Barnes looked up, he was staring into the barrel of Dan's gun.

"What the—?" Barnes pushed against the brave.

Dan cocked the hammer. "Don't move."

The deputy widened his eyes. "You...you can't be serious!"

As much as Dan wanted to explain, to defend his actions, there wasn't time. So, he swallowed and watched as Barnes shifted so his hands were visible.

"I never took you for a traitor," Barnes said, his words thick with disdain.

Dan pushed down any response. What right did he have to defend himself after all? He reached down and pulled the Apache off the deputy.

He relieved Barnes of the gun on his belt and put it in his holster. Then Dan pulled out Barnes's handcuffs.

Moments later, Dan had cuffed Barnes to a post behind the jailhouse and gagged him with his bandana.

Dan hesitated for a moment, wanting to apologize at the very least. But doubted that would do any good.

So, he took the Apache brave's elbow and picked up step again toward his horse.

They moved with ease around the backs of the buildings. In a few minutes they would be mounted and on their way. How he could get away with this, he never knew. Perhaps God was with him?

"Freeze!" a voice called from several feet back. "Or I'll give you another hole in your head."

Dan stopped. Had they been spotted? Keeping the brave close, he turned.

Sheriff McAllen had a rifle, aimed at Dan's heart.

CHAPTER 15

The Escape

"Sheriff—" Dan started.

"Don't." McAllen moved closer.

Dan swallowed. Hard. How could he have failed? He was sick inside.

"I can't imagine how you *thought* you'd get away with this." McAllen had shortened the gap between them.

"I had to try."

McAllen scoffed. "Had to try. It was doomed to fail."

Dan would've asked how the sheriff knew. But he didn't have to. He hadn't asked Brandon to lie.

When McAllen and Judge Anders got suspicious, all they had to do was step outside, find Brandon tied to the nearby tree, and ask him.

So much for his heroics. But what of Lily? She didn't deserve this. After so much pain in her life...

Dan met McAllen's gaze. "You don't care that they will kill Lily?"

McAllen frowned. "That's what you say." He seemed uncomfortable with that.

Could it be? Did he care more than he showed?

Dan remembered how the sheriff looked at Lily and how he'd

spoken to her the day they'd sought McAllen's blessing. And Dan well remembered how angry he had been at the man's words.

But just now the sheriff's hard exterior had slipped. If only for a moment. And there, underneath, was a father.

"Are you willing to risk it?" Dan glanced at the gun, still pointed at his chest. But it didn't, in truth, concern him as much as the reality that Lily might be left to Geronimo's band of raiding Apache.

McAllen's gaze didn't waver, but his features did. There was something there...a shift around the nose and eyes that hinted all was not well.

"I don't think you are, sir." Dan stepped forward, into the barrel.

"You don't know. You can't know." The man's voice shook on the last word.

"What? To love? To lose? To hurt?"

"To lose a child." McAllen's mouth became a thin line. And the hands holding his rifle were no longer steady. The weapon had a slight tremor to it. "To bury your son."

Dan's chest tightened. He didn't know. Nor could he imagine. The searing pain at the thought of losing Lily tore at him. And he doubted he would ever be whole again.

But a child...

How was that? To lay a child in the ground to eternal rest?

Still...Lily was his daughter.

"You have this chance to save one. So that you won't bury both." Dan squared his shoulders. Though he ached inside, he needed to be firm, to prove he could do this. "Help me. Trust me to bring her back. I *need* to bring her back."

Sheriff McAllen stared at Dan for a few seconds. Then he nodded and lowered his gun.

Was this happening? Would the man let him leave?

"Go." McAllen seemed to deflate in that moment. "Save my girl. Bring her home."

Dan nodded. Time was not on his side. So, he resisted the urge to speak further. He just grabbed the brave and ran the rest of the way to his waiting horse.

After putting the brave up first into the saddle, he mounted behind the boy and pressed his heels to the mare's flanks.

And they were off.

Lily lay, her eyes red and raw. The tears had come, though the emotion within her seemed so much deeper than sadness. So much more than grief. To the point she almost felt nothing. Numb.

Still, the tears came.

Strange.

Was it possible to be cried out? She believed she had reached it many times. Hadn't she passed it now? Overcome, overspent, denied by God, and with finality, she accepted that the end was near.

Would it be painful? Or would she just slip away? What awaited her? More pain and suffering? Or a release into nothingness?

That did not sound so bad. To rest, to no longer fear, to no longer hurt...it did not seem terrible. Rather, she may welcome it.

Footfalls neared.

How long had it been since she had interacted with another living soul?

The Apache had left her to herself for some time. She had relished it. And resented it. For she wondered how long until they might tire of the wait and come.

That question would want for an answer no more. The steps came close.

Still, she made no move. Instead, she closed her eyes. Would they do it here? Now?

She held her breath.

Hands gripped her shoulders and jerked her upright.

Stumbling, she worked to balance. She opened her eyes and focused.

Only one Apache stood before her—the one who had been so angry. He was no less in this moment. His dark eyes examined her face, which had to be swollen.

She opened her mouth but shut it again. There was nothing she could say...or wanted to say.

His brows came together. "Kuruk. You see my son?"

His son! Dare she answer? What would come of it?

He shook her.

The violent back and forth pulled at her head and neck muscles. And the next thing she knew, she was flung across the space. She couldn't catch her step and new she would fall. Then suddenly, her body slammed against something solid with her side.

She cried out and fell to the ground. Pain coursed through her from the left side of her torso. And her arm. Was it broken? It throbbed, and she couldn't move her hand without an intense ache shooting through it.

"Speak," the man commanded.

Deflating, her body lay lax against the ground. Could she stand if she wished? There was so much pain. Would angering him more make him end this sooner?

He came alongside her and squatted.

She didn't look. Couldn't bring herself to.

He grabbed a fistful of hair near her scalp and jerked her head up.

Another loud gasp escaped her lips as her head seared with heat.

"Speak!" he yelled in her face. The words loud and demanding.

"I..." she started weakly. Could she even form a cogent thought?

"What?" He angled her head to the side, pulling up, dangling her upper body even more by her hair. Would it not rip from her head?

"I...did..." She said as she gasped for air. Her eyes watered, moisture coursed down her face.

"I listen." He moved his face closer. Heat seemed to radiate off him.

She panted. "All I...know...is that...he was...in the...jail."

He let out a disgusted sound and released her.

She dropped as if a rag doll. It did not help her already injured side and arm.

"You white eyes no nothing but lies." He stood and stepped away a couple of paces, crossing his arms.

Did he consider how to proceed? She prayed he would do her the kindness of—

A man shouted in another language from farther away.

She peered up but could not raise her head or face. Her vision was hazy. The pain made her dizzy. But she thought it was the man from the stream. From behind the bush...who had better English and had made the decision to trade. Was he the leader?

Would he decide it was time to end her misery? Or was he here to stop the abuse?

The men spoke back and forth in what she supposed was their tongue. She did not know what they said. But one word stood out to her—Goyahkla. Why? What was this word?

Rustling around her increased. The sounds of the men's discourse must have drawn others. But they did not add to the discussion.

The word 'Goyahkla' circulated a few more times. But was it a word? Perhaps a name...

Her brain was foggy...and tired.

No...it *was* a name. That was Geronimo's actual name. Among the Apache.

Was this man Geronimo?

She worked to concentrate once more on the interchange. The man she believed to be Geronimo was not pleased with Kuruk's father. Why? Geronimo couldn't possibly have a care for her wellbeing. After all the raids and attacks he had led, killing hundreds...thousands of innocent men, women, and children. No, he didn't care for her. Only what her continued existence might do for him.

Little did he know, that was nothing. No one would bargain with him for her. She had no value.

Yes, she was lost. And hopeless.

Perhaps Kuruk's father knew this. Maybe he even thought that if someone did come, they could overtake them...that they didn't actually need her beyond the proof of life they had sent.

Was he wrong? In this case, it hardly seemed so.

The more Kuruk's father spoke, the more Geronimo listened.

But the former Medicine Man pointed to her and then to his eyes. And spread his arms wide. What was that? Some manner of strange speak? It almost seemed as if he shared a superstition related to her. Or a vision. Geronimo was, after all, a shaman. And his band believed all manner of supernatural things about him. Many white people had started to wonder if he did, indeed, have powers beyond what they could see.

Another man yelled from farther away.

The group stirred with excitement. Loud calls sounded as they pulled out weapons.

Did they prepare for her demise? Would they have some sort of ceremony?

Geronimo spoke to one of the men beside him and pointed at Lily. The man, younger than both Geronimo and Kuruk's father, stepped toward her and lifted her to her feet. While he wasn't gentle, he didn't jerk her either.

Then she was face-to-face with Geronimo. Had he not moved on with the others rushing toward the man who had made the earlier announcement?

His gaze stole her breath. His eyes were the darkest, deepest black. Ominous. What was he thinking? There was a hardness about him. Would she even call it...*death*...within his stare? No fear, no life...just hollowness and emptiness.

He cared not for anything. And he would not hesitate to snuff out her life. Indeed, it was likely his plan. All along.

Dan heard shouting as he approached. Kuruk had helped guide him through the wilderness to this place. Did the boy know what was happening? It seemed he did. For they had arrived.

Every muscle in his body tightened. And his heart raced. All would come to a head soon. Things would be settled. Lily would be free or dead. He prayed for the best.

The sounds increased as he urged the horse onward. What was he riding into? He'd best prepare himself for anything. Pulling his pistol out, he trained it on Kuruk.

Maybe that made him a cad. But he was doing this for one reason— to see Lily safely home. And he would do whatever he must to make that happen.

He jerked on the reins, slowing the mare. Then the Apache seemed to come from everywhere. How had they hidden? Where had they been? The greenery was sparse here. Yet, they had not been visible before. And they surrounded him now.

The horse halted, rearing slightly. Dan held to the pommel, steadying himself and Kuruk, whose hands remained cuffed.

Arrows were notched and trained on him. Would they ignore their fellow brave? The one they had hoped to welcome back into their tribe? Or did they only seek to assert their position?

Either way, Dan raised his arm holding the pistol, making a greater show of the fact that he had the brave at gunpoint.

Shuffles and grunts sounded throughout the gathering. But no one made a move toward him.

Dan turned the horse so he could survey the group. Where was Lily? He saw no sign of her. Had they only taken what they needed to prove they held her and then discarded her?

His heart dropped, but he kept a firm stance and stoic features. He could not let his fear or trepidation show.

"The girl," Dan said to no one in particular. But his words were short and clear. "Bring me the girl."

Kuruk cried out in his own language.

The men stirred.

One called off toward the south.

Then all stilled. Except Dan's mare. She continued to shift, restless. Did she sense Dan's uneasiness? Would it affect her ability to cooperate with him?

Hoofbeats tromped against the dirt. Then, from that southern direction, a cloud of dust preceded a painted horse bearing a rider.

Who could it be? It was not Lily.

As the man neared, Dan's heart stopped. The features, though roughened and worn, fit those of the sketched renderings of Geronimo.

It was true.

His and Lily's chances of survival just diminished.

Geronimo approached, sitting tall upon his mount. And why wouldn't he? Had he anything to worry about? There was no threat against him in this place. He and he alone would make the decisions.

Any power Dan had was a loosely held illusion, and he knew it. For whatever reason, Geronimo had a care for this boy, and he wished the boy returned. That was the only reason Dan still breathed. And it may be Dan's only hope of walking away. But it did not, in truth, protect him.

If the Apache Medicine Man tired of this, Dan was certain he would just have them both killed. It did not suit the man to trouble himself over confrontations such as this. Not when two more deaths would do nothing to disturb him.

The painted horse slowed to a stop several feet short of Dan's dark brown mare. Men had parted as water cutting before a canoe when Geronimo maneuvered his horse through them.

Geronimo stared at Dan. As if he sized the ranch hand for their interaction.

"I have brought the boy as requested. Bring me the girl."

One of the dark brows on the weathered face rose. An odd expression on such a hard face. Was he...amused?

With no response forthcoming, the silence thickened.

Dan narrowed his gaze. He wasn't prepared to play games, no matter who this was. "We had a deal. I only ask you to honor it."

"Honor." Geronimo grunted. "What does that mean to white eyes?"

Dan paused. How to respond? But what had happened at the hand of other men to the Apache did not mean Dan, or Lily, had to pay the price. "It means a lot to me."

Two figures topped the rise behind Geronimo. A man and a woman. Lily? Could it be? She was alive? But she leaned heavily on the man and her cries were audible even from this distance. What had they done to her? Bile rose in his throat, but it was nothing compared to the heat filling him.

Dan heard footsteps approaching from behind. He shifted the horse and called out. But as he did so, something solid landed on the back of his head.

And all was black.

The call that went out from the small crowd was familiar. How was that possible?

Lily looked up from her concentrated efforts to focus on the happenings several feet ahead. A man...a cowboy...fell from his horse, dropping to the ground.

Who? A cowboy? Had someone done the unthinkable?

Yes, there was the Apache brave, struggling to remain aloft on the animal. Within a few seconds, a larger man came forward and helped the young brave down.

Shouts lifted from around the group. And several of the men descended on the fallen cowboy.

That voice, the glimpse she'd had for that moment...

She closed her eyes and pushed through the cloudiness that was her thoughts. Dare she hope it was Dan?

Her heart thumped harder. If it was, he was in danger. What would these Apache do to him?

"No!" she screamed. "No!"

The man who'd been assisting her held her back.

She attempted to pull away from him, but she hadn't the strength to stand on her own.

Geronimo waved a hand over the cowboy and spoke in their language.

The men moved away from him.

Lily angled and turned as much as she dared, but she couldn't get a clear view to make out any details. *Please, let him be all right.*

The young man gripped her again and led her forward once more. With great pain, she pressed on. Might he take her to the wounded man? Was there anything she could do to help?

Several rather pained moments later, they neared the man's collapsed body. But he started to stir. Was he coming around?

The brave all but deposited her next to him.

She fell to her knees with a gasp, clutching her wounded side with her good arm and letting her injured arm fall.

Raising gingerly to his hands and knees, the cowboy put a hand to his head.

Now, with his hat no longer leaning against his head, his hair shone in the sunlight. The black waves brought tears to her eyes. Dan.

He came for her.

He did care.

There was someone in the world that valued her...even might love her enough to risk so much. Indeed, they may meet their end... together...here.

Dan lifted his head and met her gaze.

"Lily," he breathed. He reached out an arm and winced at the movement.

"Don't." Her voice shook. Was she so emotional? "You're hurt."

"I don't care." He scooted forward and took her hands.

She whimpered but bit her lip to keep from making more of it.

His brow creased.

Shaking her head, she glanced at Geronimo, who still watched them.

Only then did Dan seem to realize they were still surrounded. He got on his knees, drawing closer still. But the shift upward seemed to play with his ability to balance.

Lily gripped his arm with her good hand and tugged at him, encouraging him to lower once more.

Geronimo stared, his gaze just as hollow and empty as she knew it to be. Death certainly awaited them.

She wanted to lean into Dan, to tell him so many things, to melt into him and let him know that after everything, she still loved him.

The Medicine Man spoke to one of his men and they retrieved Dan's fallen pistol.

It was then brought forth and handed to Kuruk's father, who scowled—just as angry as ever. Did he blame them for his son's plight? That didn't make sense. What did it matter? No explanation would be allowed, nor would it suffice. Not in her estimation.

She curled closer to Dan. He wrapped his arms around her, turning so his back was to the gun, such that he would protect her as much and for as long as he could.

The hammer cocked. It was the loudest sound she had ever heard.

"Lily, I..." He pressed a kiss into her hair.

"Oh, Dan!" She closed her eyes.

"No!" A commotion broke out.

The shot that seemed imminent was not fired.

Dan eased his grip on her, and they turned to find Kuruk standing between them and his father.

The boy spoke in fast, indiscernible words to his father.

Anger deepened the lines on the man's face. And he did not lower the pistol.

Kuruk stepped closer to his father, closer to the gun.

His father ground out a few words.

Kuruk shook his head. Then he shifted his focus to Geronimo, his tone pleading.

Geronimo muttered something.

Was the boy requesting these men let Dan and Lily live? Why?

Dan's gaze remained intent on what transpired, all the while maintaining a hold on Lily.

She leaned into him. Her head started to swim.

Geronimo made a motion toward Kuruk's father.

Kuruk looked to his father.

Nothing happened. The man's menacing glare and aim remained on Dan and Lily.

Geronimo spoke again, this time more firmly.

Kuruk's father un-cocked the gun and lowered it. Then tossed it to the side. He said something, his features displaying his disdain, and then walked off.

Lily looked between Kuruk and Geronimo. What would happen now?

"Kuruk say he owes you life debt," Geronimo spoke at last. "That he will trade his life for yours."

What? Why would the boy do that? They had put him in jail. Kept him from his family. Was it because Dan freed him?

She nodded to Kuruk.

He turned his face away. As if he were shamed by her attention.

Shamed? He just restored her and Dan's lives.

"You have reprieve. *This* time." Geronimo let his gaze linger on her and then on Dan. It made a shiver go down her spine. For certain, the man was to be feared.

He let out a sharp cry, and the men around them rushed off. In the next moments, she heard the many horses thundering off into the distance.

Then she fell into Dan, her strength depleted.

Lily came in and out of consciousness. She knew terrible pain. And Dan's arms. When she would stir, his words soothed.

But he sounded desperate. Himself distressed. What had him in such a state?

Her hold on consciousness would only last for a few seconds, though, before the pull to darkness dragged her back into its depths.

Then there were hands. She murmured. Were these Dan's hands? No, they were not tender and gentle, they were probing, testing.

She pressed into the thicket that kept her from awareness. Could she fight it? The effort took much of her reserves. And the pain that the hands wrought was not inviting.

Her struggle snuffed, as if her fingers slipped from a hold on a ledge, and she fell back into the black of unconsciousness.

Shifting her body made it ache. Did that mean she moved? Her chest vibrated. Had she made a sound?

A voice spoke soft words over her.

Where was she?

She opened her eyes; the lids weighed more than she ever remembered. And the brightness that greeted her stung.

A blurred figure leaned over her. And spoke in a comforting tone.

Focusing on that, she blinked. Why was her mind still so hazy? How long had she lain here?

With every close and open of her eyes, things cleared. Somewhat. The person took better shape, but the features remained a mystery.

Could that be Cook? Was she at Cook's cabin?

But she seemed to be abed. Had she been placed in Cook and Mr. Owen's bed? That wasn't right.

Her head ached to think so many thoughts.

"How do you feel?" Cook said.

The words seemed as if spoken from far away, and they wavered. But Lily made them out. What was wrong here?

"Y-yes." Lily's simple answer came out croaked. Her throat scratched to provide it.

"It's fine if you can't talk, darlin'," Cook said. Now her voice wavered in another way. Was she sad? "You've been through a lot."

"W-where...?" Lily couldn't push out more than that. Her mouth was dry. So dry.

Cook looked to the side. Did she not wish to say? Either way, she continued, "We're at the Miller ranch."

That comforted Lily more than she'd thought it would. But she knew why—Dan must be nearby. Somewhere. Was he waiting to see her?

"Please, don't stress yourself." Cook fussed over Lily's blanket. "The doctor said you need not be excitable. And he gave you some medicine to help you rest."

Ah. Medicine to help her rest. There was the source of some of her difficulty. With any luck, it would fade soon.

"Water." Lily wished so much for the coolness on her parched throat.

Cook nodded. "Of course." The woman patted Lily's hand and slipped from the room.

Lily scanned the area, as much as she could from where she lay. This must be one of the rooms she'd spotted down the hall by the great room. Was she in one of the children's beds? Or in the room that had been locked? The one she had been forbidden to enter? What was the secret of this room, if so?

Pushing those thoughts to the side, she turned her mind to more pressing things—Dan. Where was he? Why hadn't he been here?

Footsteps in the hall alerted her that someone approached. They weren't the hurried *clip-clip* of Cook's footfalls. It was the clomping of boots. Could it be...?

A tall frame stepped through the slender opening in the door. And her heart soared. Dan had come.

She was overcome. Her emotions welled within, building so great that tears threatened. But she fought them. There was so much she wanted to say. But her voice would not allow it. So, she chose one word.

"Dan."

It came out ragged and raspy. But it was the best she could do.

He halted at the sound of his name, and his gaze sought hers.

She couldn't see that detail clearly enough to make out what he might be thinking. Curse these tendrils of medicine that lingered!

Dan recovered and came to her side. He carried a cup of water. Two things for her to be thankful for.

"Don't let me hurt you," he said as he sat on the bed, scooped an arm under her upper body, and cradled her to himself.

She couldn't help the whimper that escaped.

He froze.

"It's...okay. I'm...fine." She attempted to reassure him. Being this close to him, the scent of him filling her senses, the touch of his body, strong and firm against hers, was enough to steal all thoughts. Never mind the momentary discomfort, she would be here forever if she could.

As he met her eyes from this distance, his features were clearer. Their depths displayed just how far his concern went. How extensive his regard for her. Was it, indeed, love? No matter what his words had been.

It took her breath away.

He tore his gaze away and lifted the glass. "Water?"

She nodded.

Raising the rim to her lips, he watched intently as she sipped.

He was so careful—letting her sip a little at a time but tilting the cup upright at regular intervals. When she'd had several sips, he pulled the glass away and set it to the side.

But his eyes remained fixed on her lips. For concern of her condition? Or for a desire to kiss them?

How she wanted to close the distance between them and show him with such a gesture that she still cared. But there were too many things that needed to be said. Too much to be resolved between them. Could he just hold her for a little while though?

He did not seem to be in a hurry to let her down. Continuing to cradle her to his chest, he asked, "Are you well?"

"I think so." Her voice was better. Stronger.

His gaze scanned her features, her hair...everywhere he could look. "I was so..." He took in a breath.

"I know." She tried to lift the hand that wasn't pinned against him, wanted to touch his face. But she found it to be wrapped and encumbered. And pained by her efforts.

He put a gentle hand on her injured arm to still her efforts. "Be careful. Your arm is broken."

She widened her eyes. "Broken?"

He nodded, his expression sad. "The doctor has been here and tended you."

Meeting his gaze once more, she wondered how she could turn this conversation. How would she broach the matters she wanted to speak of? Or would he?

Perhaps she should just sit in this moment of peace.

He let out a long breath. "I was so worried."

The words, soft and tender, fed her. They alluded to his consideration for her.

"I don't know what I would've done if you had been killed." His mouth twisted.

"But I wasn't," she said, her voice insistent.

He nodded. The emotions on his features were difficult to read.

"Because of you," she reminded him. "Because you came for me." Her heart swelled. He *must* love her. For certain he thought she was worth the risk. Worth the chance.

And that meant everything to her.

She closed her eyes.

The long fingers of darkness reached through to the edges of her consciousness.

Opening her eyes, she furrowed her brows. "What?"

Dan now appeared guilty.

The darkness thickened, strengthened.

"What did you—?" She strained to make the words.

The water. He had put something in the water.

"Why?" She put more effort into that one word than all the others. Thinking became difficult.

"The doctor said you needed to rest. To heal," Dan said. Why was his voice sad? Or was that her imagination?

What was real? What was haze?

But he still held her. If anything, it seemed he cradled her closer.

She fought to keep her eyes open. Was she angry at him? Shouldn't she be?

He pressed a kiss to her forehead. "Sorry, my sweet Lily. But it's best."

His words came from a great distance. And they were the last thing she heard before a wave from the depth crashed over her.

Dan shuffled into the kitchen. He set the glass down. Why did he have to deceive her? It didn't endear him to her for sure. And it went against everything in him. To his core.

But it had to be done. She needed her rest.

And she'd refused the last time. That had been a mess. Poor Cook didn't have it in her to try that again.

"Did she take it?" Cook reached for the glass, staring at the liquid. The amount gone was rather difficult to measure.

"Yeah," Dan murmured.

Cook paused. "What's that mean?"

Dan met her gaze. "Nothing. I gave it to her."

Cook quirked a brow at him.

"You asked me to get it in her, and I did," Dan said, leaning on the counter.

Cook tilted her head. "You didn't twist her arm or anything like that, did you?"

Dan offered her what he hoped was an exasperated look. "Twist her arm? You know I have my ways." He waggled his brows up and down.

Cook turned to the sink bucket. "Oh, fie, you old charmer. Save that for your lady."

Dan relaxed his shoulders and leaned back again. If only Lily were that easy to convince. Was she? For a moment, she *did* seem at peace in his arms. But did she relish it as he did? Could she forgive him his earlier thoughtless rejection?

And even if so, had he just made it worse?

Would he ever get this thing right?

"Now get on with ya," Cook swatted at him. "Outta my kitchen."

Dan offered her a put-on smile and ducked into the dining room. But as he made his way to the front door, he slowed. He wanted to go to Lily's room, to keep vigil over her as he had done for hours these past couple of days.

Though at this point, it was probably best she get good rest. He had been satisfied that she would be well and recover.

Then what? How would he make right what had gone wrong?

He shook his head and moved out the front door and off toward the barn.

This was just one thing he would need to make right. Would Judge Anders want a pound of his flesh before all was said and done?

Dan had only seen Brandon in passing the last couple of days. The man had spent much time in town, working things out with the judge and sheriff. What had Sheriff McAllen had to say? For certain, the man would not incriminate himself. Nor would Dan implicate him in any way.

But what would become of Dan's efforts in aiding Lily was unknown. Freeing a man on trial for murder was not something folks out here took lightly. If it weren't for the sake of the woman he loved, would he?

Dan wandered amongst the stalls. What could he do that might be productive? Muck the stalls? Clean saddles? Check the fences?

Eli and Slim were tending the herd. So, there wasn't a need for him there.

As he moved back to the barn's opening for the shovel and bucket, he heard a horse nearing. Had Brandon come back?

The animal halted just outside, and the rider dropped down.

Dan stepped beyond the wide door and spotted Eli patting down his horse. Great. Another uncomfortable situation.

Eli spotted him.

Dan tipped his hat.

And Eli nodded.

"Need any help?" Dan asked. Might as well offer. Pleasantries were always a good place to start.

"Nah." Eli shook his head. "I'm just headed in to muck."

"I'm about to do that myself." Dan lifted the bucket he had grabbed.

Eli paused.

"Guess you'll have to find something else to keep you busy." Dan shrugged.

"Or we could both get after it and be done in half the time." Eli smiled. He led his horse into the paddock to the right side of the barn.

Dan considered that. Seemed about right. He waved the younger man in and grabbed another bucket.

Eli accepted it. They each took a shovel and headed farther back. Then got to work.

They shoveled and cleaned in silence for a time. Dan wondered if he needed to say anything. Did the younger man hold Dan's deception against him? Would Dan, were the situations reversed?

The truth was, he'd appreciate the acknowledgement if it were him.

"Hey," Dan paused, standing upright and looking at Eli a couple stalls away.

Eli did likewise. "Yeah?" He wiped at his forehead with his bandana.

"About what happened at the jailhouse—"

Eli waved a dismissive hand. "No need. I understand. I'd have done the same."

Dan's brows rose. "Truly?"

"You bet. If someone I loved was being held like that. You better believe I would do everything I could to see them safe."

Dan let out a breath. He definitely had not given Eli the time he deserved or the credit. Perhaps he should get to know the man better. "All the same, I didn't like lying."

Eli shrugged. "I know."

Dan nodded. Then turned back to his work.

The younger man did the same.

They continued to work for some time, only passing random conversation and quips along the way. All in all, in was rather amiable.

Yes, Dan was going to like getting to know Eli.

The younger man finished before Dan was halfway through his last stall.

"I'll see you outside." Eli grabbed his bucket and shovel as he moved off.

Dan went back to work. But a disruption just outside drew his attention. Had something happened to Eli?

He set his shovel against a post and moved toward the sound.

Even from inside the barn, he was able to spot the wagon through the wide door. Had Brandon come home? But something about the wagon didn't seem right. Though it did look familiar.

The flash of a woman's long dark hair and a very distinctive male voice carrying on the wind gave him the answer he needed—his pal Cutie had arrived, along with his wife and Dan's friend, Mariena.

Lily woke. Again.

The fog cleared easily this time.

And the room took shape and form. It was familiar. Only...

She wasn't alone. Cook? Dan?

No. The presence was not familiar.

Dare she stir and alert the person that she had awakened? How long could she delay?

Whoever had joined her must be here with Dan or Cook's permission. Perhaps even at their behest. Right? It gave her reason to trust.

She turned her head toward where she sensed the presence.

The silhouette of a woman with long straight hair sat, reading. But at Lily's movement, she set the book to the side and leaned forward. Her every gesture flowed as if a dance. So graceful.

"How do you feel?" The words were melodic and spoken in a deeper tone.

Who was this woman? With the window behind her, it was difficult to make out her features. But Lily had the suspicion that she *did* know her. Somehow.

Rising, the woman's soundless steps carried her to a table near the door. She poured water from a pitcher.

Lily pushed up slightly with her uninjured arm. Goodness, she was sore. But she did her best to ignore the pain.

Then she could make out the woman's profile. She was Indian! Though her dress was the same as one Lily or Amanda would wear, this woman was Indian. There was no denying that.

Lily gasped.

The woman turned.

And Lily's breath caught in her throat. It wasn't just any Indian. It was Mariena...the maiden Cutie had married.

There were no words. Would Mariena recognize her? Or had she already known before she set foot in this room?

Could Lily curl up and disappear? She had thought her humiliation complete when Dan pulled her out of the saloon. Or when her father had spoken those horrible words in front of Dan. No, this was it.

Unless...

Did this mean Cutie was here, too?

She settled back onto the bed not even noticing the throbbing that ensued. Closing her eyes, she laid her good hand over her face.

"What is it?" Mariena asked. The swish of her skirt let on that she drew nearer to the head of Lily's bed.

Lily made a small opening between two fingers so she could peer through with an eye.

Mariena appeared concerned. Worried even. Did she not consider that she cared for the woman who had all but thrown herself at Cutie? Would have done anything to win him back? In *those* days.

But Lily wasn't that woman anymore. Was she?

A hand lay on her elbow, light and gentle. "Shall I call for Cook?"

"No." Lily slid her hand down her face. She maneuvered, with care and slow movements, to sit up. It was only somewhat successful.

As she relented and collapsed into the pillow, she noticed that Mariena had set down the glass and stuffed another pillow behind her while arranging the one already there so Lily could recline more easily.

"Thank you." Lily looked down as Mariena stepped away.

She retrieved the glass and returned. "It is good for you to drink."

The sleeping medicine. Lily held up a hand. "No, I thank you."

Mariena's forehead creased. "But you must. You need your strength."

Should she share with Mariena what they were putting in the water? Did Mariena know? The two of them had to start somewhere. And that may as well start with Lily trusting the woman.

"Cook and Dan have been putting stuff to make me sleep in the water. A trick so I will take it." Lily's voice wavered on the last words. She hadn't realized how much it bothered her.

Mariena also seemed troubled by this. "But I got this water. Myself. At the pump."

Lily arched a brow.

"I put nothing in it. Only water." Mariena put the glass forth again, offering. As if her assurance would be accepted without question.

Shouldn't it? After all, Lily had no reason to not trust *her*. Lily looked at the liquid. It did make her throat sting all the more, wanting for its quenching coolness.

At length, she nodded, reaching for the cup.

Mariena released it to Lily and it almost toppled. Warm hands soon surrounded Lily's one fine, shaky hand again. And Mariena helped Lily drink.

It was as good as hoped. Maybe better.

Lily took in several sips and smiled at Mariena, pressing the glass back into her waiting hands. "Thank you."

Mariena returned the glass to its spot beside the pitcher.

"Do you think..." Lily began, but let her words trailed. Should she focus on such menial things?

"Yes?" Mariena turned, sweeping her long hair behind her shoulder.

"Would it be possible for me to get something to eat?"

Mariena smiled. "I will ask Cook."

Lily watched as she moved toward the door. But in her gut, Lily felt something solid settle. And she had an urgency. She wanted to...*had* to say something to Mariena. The longer things went, the more awkward it would become. And the harder.

"Mariena," she called.

The lovely woman shifted, returning her focus to Lily, taking a step back toward the bed.

"I..." Lily bit at her lip and looked out the window. Maybe she should have thought about what she would say before she started.

Mariena smiled. "Do not worry. I think all is not as once it seemed."

Lily's gaze jerked to Mariena's.

"And even more it is different now," Mariena continued. Then she went from the room.

Leaving Lily to wonder after the things she said. About what she might have meant. And more than that...

What did she know?

Dinner had been rather uncomfortable. Dan counted down the minutes until he would be called out. For Brandon had returned just as they were sitting down. But his boss never asked to speak with him. Not even as dinner finished.

As everyone handed their plates to Cook, Brandon was the first to rise with his wife then he escorted her to their room. He did seem rather tired. Even next to her. Amanda still had not delivered. And she was weary.

'Any day now,' the doctor said.

That didn't seem to comfort the boss's wife.

Cook rounded up the children next and sent them off to their evening things.

Dan couldn't help but smile as Nisto, though growing into that awkward adolescent stage, hugged his sister and Cutie. He had missed them. As had Dan.

Nisto paused then, making cooing sounds and offering his fingers to the active young one on Mariena's lap. They had all been introduced to the new addition to Cutie's little family. The dark-eyed, chubby-fisted girl reached for Nisto's hand, securing her hold.

His smile widened.

"Nisto," Cook warned.

The look she shot across the room dared him to defy her. Even if Nisto believed it, Dan knew well enough that the tiny girl had captured Cook's heart as well. And the older woman could no more fault Nisto his delay than excuse her own tardiness with getting dinner ready this evening.

Still, Nisto shook his fingers free and followed the others.

Cook watched them go before creeping over and gathering the bundle up herself.

Cutie stood and came around the table. Would he now leave with his wife for an evening stroll? Or something more?

Instead he stopped behind Dan. Clapping him on the shoulder, he coughed and said, "How about you and I give that old fishin' hole a once over?"

What would they do that for? It was late. Not the best time for fishing. Then Dan realized—it was not for catching. Maybe not even for fishing. Cutie wanted to talk. Must they?

The only saving grace was that Cutie seemed a little unsure of the prospect himself. Perhaps it would be less talking and more riding then —something Dan *would* appreciate—silent companionship.

So, he nodded and rose, setting his hat on his head. He tipped the brim to Mariena, but she had eyes only for her husband.

Dan made an effort to look away as they exchanged whatever glances or gestures they wished to.

And his heart ached for Lily. Would they ever reconcile? Ever have this comfortable, secret communication between them?

He hoped so. But doubt gnawed at him.

Cutie joined Dan at the front door, and they headed to the barn.

In a few moments, they had saddled a couple of mares and were off.

They stopped at Uncle Owen's fishing hole and let the horse's refresh themselves. Dusk had fallen. It would behoove them to return sooner rather than later. Before the wild animals of the evening came out.

Cutie left his horse to graze and settled himself on a thin patch of grass.

Dan considered him. Dare he join his friend? It would certainly lead to *talking*. Was he ready for that? Would he welcome it even? Maybe Cutie wished only to become more informed about the state of things.

As long as they didn't talk about *feelings*.

Dan settled a couple arms' lengths away.

"I miss this sometimes." Cutie exhaled.

"Yeah?" Dan looked at him.

Cutie nodded, watching the horizon. "Sometimes. Don't get me wrong. I love my life with Mariena. And the work we are doing. Will do. But there's something so simple and peaceful about this life."

Dan nodded. Simple. Peaceful. Yeah...that's not how he would describe the last couple of months.

They sat in silence for a moment.

"So, you want to tell me about it?" Cutie challenged.

Dan took in a breath and stared ahead. This was awkward. "Not much to tell."

"Try me anyway." Cutie's tone encouraged. Made it seem like it wasn't such a big deal.

Dan looked to the ground between his boots. "I let a man die. Right in front of my eyes."

Cutie was silent.

"Then I found his sister, Lily, had nowhere to go. So, I—"

"—felt responsible and offered to take care of her," Cutie finished for him.

Dan nodded. The man knew him well. "Figured we would need to get married."

"Huh..." Cutie mumbled.

Dan jerked back. Was Cutie questioning him? Then again...

Why did it sound so absurd when laid out like this? Did he truly have to propose to Lily? Or had the heat of the moment produced the urge?

"Go on," Cutie prompted.

Dan shook his head. He wasn't sure he wanted to.

"I don't want you to be upset with Cook, but she told me about the misunderstandings between you and Lily and—"

"Lying," Dan corrected.

Cutie picked up as if Dan hadn't spoken. "And the whole encounter with Geronimo's band."

Dan looked opposite Cutie, to where their horses had wandered in their grazing. One of them should be keeping an eye on the mares.

"So, I'm piecing this together...knowing what I do about your...pa... and, even so, I find myself wondering something," Cutie continued as if Dan had invited further discussion.

Indeed, he did not. Nor did he want it.

"Why would you put her off like that if you loved her?"

"What?" Dan jerked his focus toward Cutie. Who did he think he was? "What makes you think I love her? It was an arrangement made to—"

"Don't give me that, Dan." Cutie glared at him. "Not me. I know better."

Dan met Cutie's hard stare. It made him uncomfortable. Was Cutie right?

Relaxing his shoulders, Dan relented. "There are times when I know it. Times I feel certain. And times when I don't think I know my own mind at all."

Cutie smirked. "Ain't love great?"

Dan frowned.

The half-smile fell. "It gets better."

Dan looked away. "But I've rejected her. Just like..." He started to say 'you,' but caught himself.

"Say it—me—and every other man she ever trusted."

Dan nodded but wouldn't look at Cutie.

"You're right. I was a cad. And a coward. Are you?" Cutie's voice rose.

"Seems so." Dan shrugged.

"I don't believe that. Not for a minute," Cutie said. "Not you."

Dan nodded and grumbled. "I'm not perfect."

"I know. But you've always been honorable."

Closing his eyes, Dan hated how an anchor weighed in his stomach in that moment. If only Cutie truly knew him.

"But that's all right." Cutie clapped his shoulder. "God takes all kinds. And has plans to use us all."

"I don't know." Dan stared off into the distance. Cutie's understanding of God was more like Brandon's. More personal.

"How else can you explain someone as messed up as me getting turned around and ending up with a prize like Mariena?" Cutie elbowed Dan.

"I can't. Never could." A chuckled slipped from Dan's lips. "You're right. God must care."

"All joking aside, I do believe God had a plan for me. It included Mariena. And He has a plan for you. Does it involve Lily?"

"How would I know that?" Dan bristled. "Even if I believe what you're saying about God. How would I know His thoughts about me and Lily?"

"Do you love her?"

Dan paused, looking deep within. To his heart. It swelled with affection at every mention of her name. And he couldn't shake her. No matter how he tried. She seemed to be forever etched into his mind. Could he escape?

"But..." he said before he could stop himself.

"'But' what?" Cutie challenged, his features showing kindness and patience with Dan's questions.

"I..." Dare he speak of it? Cutie may know a bit about Dan's past. But Dan hadn't shared everything. No, there was something he held close...he'd never told anyone about that night...

Cutie watched him.

Perhaps if Dan were to share, Cutie would be the one with which to do so.

"I once failed someone I loved. And it cost them...and me...a great price. I'm not sure I have it in me to let that happen again."

Cutie's brows furrowed. "What are you talking about?"

Dan sighed. "It happened many years ago. When I went to my first Sweetheart's Dance. I'll never forget it. I had been excited 'cause I asked Bessie Parnell to the dance.

"I kissed her that night. And stayed out later than usual. But I made curfew."

"Of course, you did," Cutie said, a smile forming.

"When I got home, my ma...she was in a bad way." With his statement, the mood between them had changed. Everything was solemn, and grim. "Pa had encouraged me to go but begged me to be back soon. He said Ma was not well. But I didn't listen. I was too eager for that kiss."

"Any boy that age would—" Cutie inserted.

But Dan cut him off. "By the time I got home, the doctor was with Ma and they wouldn't let me see her."

All was quiet between them.

"I never got to say good-bye." Dan let his head drop, his gaze to the ground.

Cutie sat for several seconds, letting the moment sink before he spoke. "That was so long ago."

"It mattered."

"Of course, it did. But do you think your ma wanted you to stop living? To not find lasting love?"

Dan looked away again. "We should get back. It's getting dark. Coyotes'll be out soon." He stood.

Cutie stood as well, though he didn't move toward the horses as Dan did.

It didn't bother Dan. He would return without Cutie if he had to.

"Dan," Cutie called.

He wanted to ignore his friend. But they had been through too much together. Cutie deserved better. So, Dan looked at him.

"Don't let this be your story. Or *her* story."

Dan forced out a breath. He should never have let Cutie start this conversation.

Cutie stepped toward him, and Dan grabbed for the reins. The former ranch hand came upon him, and Dan handed off the horse Cutie had ridden.

But Cutie paused at the hand-off. "If you don't care for her enough to fight through this. Then you don't deserve her."

Cutie then walked a few steps away and mounted.

Dan stared after him, stung. Why would Cutie say that? His friend? Say that he didn't deserve Lily? Was it true?

Cutie turned the horse before stilling it. He watched Dan. Was he bothered by his friend's expression? "But hear this—in Christ, you deserve every good thing. Because of forgiveness. Maybe you just need to forgive yourself."

Dan squared his shoulders. A part of him wanted to let Cutie's words soak in, wanted to mull over them. Another part didn't want Cutie schooling him. Perhaps he should think on it later.

But if he were ever to move forward with his life, he would need to pay his father a visit. They'd have to have a real conversation. Perhaps for the first time ever.

He ground his teeth and mounted his steed.

Something urged him to go at that moment.

Now? In the darkness?

But he knew...there would be no sleep, no peace for him as long as this hung over his head.

"I'll catch up to you," he called to Cutie as he turned his horse in a southerly direction.

"Where do you think you're—?" Cutie started.

Dan nodded to Cutie and with no further comment, urged his horse forward. He didn't look back to see what Cutie did, only kept his eyes on where he was headed.

What would he say? How would he go about this conversation? So many years had passed; so much had been long buried.

Not anymore. It had resurfaced.

He pushed the mare until he spotted the dim light within his father's cabin. The lone lantern could only be the bedside light, soon to be extinguished. It must mean his father was still awake.

After sliding off the horse, he then moved toward the porch. He couldn't have taken slower steps if he were walking to his own execution. Would part of him die here tonight? Or would he leave a bit more whole than he came?

Now at the door, he knocked.

Nothing.

But he knew his raps had been too light. On purpose?

So, he knocked louder.

Movement within warned that his father came. It would be a minute.

The man mumbled and grumbled all the way to the door. The first words Dan could pick up were, "What in tarnation?"

"Pa, it's Dan."

"Dan?" The door opened. His father leaned heavily on the door-frame, worry etched on his features. "Everything all right?"

"Yeah." Dan pulled his hat off.

"Then what the devil are you doing here? Scaring old folk out of bed like this?"

Dan swallowed. How could it be that after all this time, even after what he had lived through with this man, Dan still felt like that small, intimidated boy who just wanted the man to care about him enough to take him fishing, just once?

"I need to talk."

"What?" The older man's voice rose. "Talk? Now?"

"Yes, sir," Dan said, squaring his shoulders. This was his due. After all he'd been through, he had more than earned the right for a say-so about a simple conversation.

Pa glared at him for a moment. Then his gaze softened. "Well, come on in, then."

Moving to the side, the man allowed Dan to pass.

So, he walked into the family home. It transported him back to those days of hurt and want. The days when Ma was all he had. And then she was gone.

Pa had done the best he could to fill the gap, but Dan's heart had been so ravaged by the abandonment and lies, then by his Ma's death, that there was little hope of recovering any semblance of a relationship. No matter that Pa gave up the games. No matter that he went straight. No matter.

He would forever be the man of lies. The man that let Dan's ma die.

And it was time for them to face each other and each say their piece.

Dan turned as his father closed the door. He watched as the feeble, shaking body, attacked by age and an illness the doctors couldn't identify claimed his body a bit more each day.

Then the man faced him. "What do ya' need, son?"

Son. Did he care that the man used the word so casually? As if it meant nothing more than their biological relationship to each other?

"I want to know..." Dan swallowed.

"Yes?" The older man squinted in the dimness.

Dan's eyes stung a bit. He needed to get control over these warring emotions.

Silence lengthened between them.

"It's late, Dan. Are you sure you don't want to talk in the morning?"

Dan shook his head.

"Then spill it, boy. Say what you need to say." Pa's voice had an edge to it. Almost as if he knew. And wanted to get it over with.

"Why?" Dan shot the word at his father. No pretense. No qualifications. Nothing.

"Why what?" There was such fatigue in the man's tone. From age? From the day? From his ailment? Or from this issue?

Dan didn't know. But he wouldn't let the man off without answers. "Why weren't *we* enough for you?"

The man blinked. "That's what you thought? You thought you weren't enough?"

Dan looked to the side. Would his father dodge the question now? What was the use?

"You, your brother and sister, and your Ma were *everything* to me."

"Then why...?" Emotion choked off the rest of Dan's question.

"I thought I needed to provide a better life. I *knew* I could. If I could just..." And the man's voice trailed. His eyes, which had lit for a second, dimmed.

"What? Leave us? With handfuls of broken promises? Struggling? With Ma, who could barely keep her head up, not to mention fight, to make ends meet?" A flare of anger shot through Dan.

"I'm not saying I was right." Pa's words were quiet. "You didn't ask me that. You asked me why."

Could it be that Pa's honesty was not enough for Dan? What did he expect? He had known it wouldn't be pretty.

"I wanted to do better, son. I did. I just...didn't know how." Pa hung his head and deflated into a dining chair.

Dan stepped toward him. Then paused. Would he accept the man for who he was and try to move on? Or allow this bitterness to continue growing deeper roots?

Closing the distance to his father again, he laid a hand on his shoulder. "We only *needed* you."

CHAPTER 17
The Decision

Dan did not sleep. Not that he slept fitfully. He didn't sleep. At all.

Cutie's words plagued him. His interaction with his father had both soothed and stirred his emotions. And his actions in so many ways—with Lily, with the brave—haunted him. They convicted him, admonished him for his wrongdoing. He could neither deny nor escape them.

So, he found himself on the porch of the homestead, settled into a chair, watching the sunrise.

Truth be told, he felt guilty taking in such beauty knowing the wretchedness within himself. Would there ever be enough retribution for what he had done? The hurt he had dealt? Notwithstanding the crime he had committed in freeing Joseph's killer?

He hung his head. What he needed was forgiveness and mercy.

Was Cutie right? Would God forgive him? The Bible spoke often of forgiveness. His own mother had said it plenty. And the preacher sure did tell of it enough.

But was it real? How could a person be responsible for such sin one second and free from it the next? All because they said some words to God? It seemed like hogwash.

He got the sense, though, that his efforts to absolve his own guilt in his mind would not be successful until he received God's forgiveness.

So, what did he have to do? Just ask? Talk to God? How?

He closed his eyes. And thought about what he should say.

Brandon and Uncle Owen often talked about prayer as nothing more than telling God what you think. As if you were sharing with a friend.

God?

This seemed pointless. But wasn't that what faith was all about?

You there?

There was that doubt. He must believe.

I don't know what I'm doing. But I trust that You are listening. And that You understand. I've been trying to do right. It's not been working out so well.

Was he being too casual? But everyone insisted God understood. That the words weren't as important as the fact that he prayed or the meaning behind what he prayed.

That whole 'trying' didn't pan out when I was younger, and I'm only making a mess now. Do You really have a plan for me? That's difficult for me to swallow.

I've always been the one people overlook. I guess You know that, though.

What I need to say is...I have done some wrong things. I have committed some 'sin' as the preacher calls it. And I know that sin is bad.

I kept secrets from Lily, I rejected her, I hurt my Ma and Pa, and I took the Apache brave when he was on trial—I guess that's like stealing and lying at the same time.

Please forgive me, God. And help me forgive myself.

Dan opened his eyes. And looked around. He could swear he wasn't alone anymore, but he didn't see anyone. Could it be...God?

It did seem that the things weighing on him were somewhat lighter. Was that his imagination?

But he chose to believe it was God. That was his part—to trust God was at work though he couldn't see it.

Dan leaned back in the chair and continued watching the sun make its appearance.

After some time, the front door opened. He turned just as Brandon stepped out.

His boss offered him a small smile. "Good morning."

Dan nodded at him. "Morning. How's Mrs. Miller?"

"As good as she can be. She's ready for this baby to make an appearance. I suppose we both are—eager to meet the little one." Brandon strolled across the porch, in front of Dan, and sat at the other end.

Dan smiled. What would it be like to anticipate a child of his own? Wonderful? Exciting? Scary? All of it? He shifted his focus back to his boss. "It's gotta be soon, though, right?"

Brandon tilted his head as he, too, watched the sky turning colors. "I'd think so. Doctor expected so by now."

Dan frowned.

They sat in silence for several, stretched out minutes. Each one was worse than the last.

When he could stand it no longer, Dan broke the spell. "Are we, um, going to talk about what you've been doing in town?"

Brandon glanced at him. And slowly nodded. "We best."

Dan drew in a deep breath. It was time.

Brandon launched into it. "I met with Judge Anders and Sheriff McAllen. As you can imagine, neither were happy with our little charade."

"You..." Dan stopped him. "You didn't tell them you had anything to do with it, did you?" That wasn't what they had planned.

Brandon's smile seemed tired. "You know I couldn't lie."

Dan lowered his head. He did.

"I don't know if Judge Anders was more upset about the fact the whole thing made his trip wasted time or that it is delaying him getting to San Francisco and pushing back his whole docket."

Looking back toward his boss, Dan furrowed his brows. Of all the things that would be troublesome about this, the inconvenience to the judge's docket was not top of his list.

"I know," Brandon huffed. "Perspective."

It gave Dan only more reason to worry after the consequences.

"We had several long conversations," Brandon explained.

Dan did feel for the man. Politics and law were not his strong suit, nor did they interest him.

"Either way," Brandon said on an exhale, "Judge Anders will see you this afternoon. He plans to make a final decision about what needs to happen to you."

"No!" a voice sounded from the other side of the front door.

It opened, and Lily stumbled out.

"Lily!" Dan was on his feet in a second and next to her in another moment. "You shouldn't be out of bed."

She looked up at him, her eyes glazed and pleading. "I couldn't stay cooped up one minute more."

Dan grimaced.

"Besides," she said, looking at Brandon. "There's nothing wrong with my legs. Just this left side and bum arm."

Though Dan wasn't happy about it, he couldn't make himself send her back into the house.

Brandon seemed to feel otherwise. "Let me fetch Mariena. She can attend to—"

"No," Lily said, her words biting. "I need to say my piece."

His boss's eyes widened. Had he not anticipated Lily's sassier side? Dan bit back a smile.

She looked between Dan and Brandon, not settling on either. "I insist that I stand next to Dan on any crimes committed in regards to freeing that brave."

Lily breathed heavily. Was it just her or were her breaths audible? A bit too audible?

"I won't have it," Dan said.

So, he would tell her what she would do? "Won't have it?" she challenged. "The brave was taken for my freedom. I *will* stand beside you."

Dan looked at Brandon. But Brandon's gaze was on Lily. Was he trying to decide something?

"Lily." Dan set a hand on her uninjured arm. "I knew what I was doing. And I'd do it again. You did nothing wrong. It was all my doing. And I deserve whatever comes my way."

"No." Her voice softened as she set her eyes on him. "You only tried to save me. I won't let you be punished for that."

Lily's heart ached as Dan's eyes met hers. His raw emotions were bared before her. He did care for her. He *did*.

Brandon cleared his throat.

She had quite forgotten Brandon was there. Dropping her head, she broke eye contact with Dan.

"I'll...um...stir Mariena," Brandon said as he passed them and moved into the house.

She opened her mouth to protest, but Dan tugged her toward a chair. As she sat, he took her right hand in both of his.

"I must tell you, Lily. Something good has come from all this."

She arched a brow. "Oh?"

Would he speak now of how wrong he had been? Or of how sorry he was? Of how he truly loved her?

"I have asked God for forgiveness."

Asked *God* for forgiveness? *God?* Why God? Did he not need *her* forgiveness?

"And He has done something wonderful. Inside me." Dan pulled a hand away to make a motion in front of his chest. "There is such mercy for me."

Still skeptical, she was leery of his words.

"I only hope you can forgive me. For so many things I said to you, for hurting you, for letting your brother's killer go free—"

"For what?" She waved a hand in front of her face. What did he say? Her brother's killer what?

He furrowed his brows. "The Apache brave. Kuruk."

"Kuruk? What about him?" She narrowed her eyes. A sense of dread filled her chest like a bubble. Would it burst? What then?

Dan swallowed. "He's the one."

"The one who...what?" How could she be so afraid of an answer and so sure of it?

Closing his eyes, Dan drew in a deep breath before expelling it. Then he met her eyes again. "The one who killed Joseph."

She pushed Dan's hands away, and her good hand flew to her mouth to keep from crying out.

He reached for her arms with tentative hands.

She couldn't let him soothe her. She wouldn't. Jerking away, she shook her head. "No. It can't be."

His hands dropped. "I...yes, it is."

"And you...chose to set him free? Rather than have him pay for his crime?" Tears seeped from her eyes.

"For *you*. Only for you," he said, his voice quiet and broken.

"How can I...?" The tears would not stop. Nor would the waves of sadness and grief. She needed to get away. Now. "I have to go."

"Please, Lily. Let me—" He leaned toward her.

"No!" She rose, pulling back. "Let me alone."

Moving away, she threw the front door open and stormed in. How could this ever be right?

Dan sat in the furnished chair at the front of the church. The dais had been set with a small table and chair for Judge Anders. And additional small tables had been set up on either side of the main area for him and Sheriff McAllen, each with two chairs.

Here, his fate would be determined. He would either be sentenced to prison time or some other such consequence. It seemed doubtful he would be hanged. The judge couldn't be that angry or have any such law to stand on.

A few of the townsfolk had come to see the spectacle. Was it more a testament of what little excitement there was in Wharton City? Or were they truly interested in what occurred? Did any of them have a stake in the happenings here?

Deputy Travers glared at Dan, a sneer on his face.

Dan ignored him. Best not give the man anything to encourage him.

The chair beside Dan sat empty. He imagined if Lily were there, as she had so vehemently declared she would be. Would that have made him worried?

Yes, it was probably best she was not.

Would anyone sit with him? Stand with him? He hoped not.

But as he stared at the seat, Brandon Miller slid into it.

"What are you doing?" Dan muttered under his breath.

"I'm your cohort," he said.

Dan rolled his eyes. "Not in the least."

"Either way, we stand together."

Deputy Barnes stepped to the center of the dais and called the room to order. Everyone stood and then he announced Judge Anders.

As the judge took his place, there was movement to Dan's right. He turned and could only see Brandon's back. His boss was having a harried discussion with someone. At some point, the man conceded.

The congregants were called to sit.

As they did so, Brandon moved off and Lily lowered herself into the seat with great care.

What? Why had she come? He didn't want her here.

As he opened his mouth to say so, Judge Anders started speaking, "Would the accused please stand?"

Dan stood.

Lily struggled to her feet.

And Dan prayed she would step away. Somehow, someway...come to her senses and move back. He couldn't bear it if she were thrown in prison, too.

The judge looked at the defendant's stand. "What is this?" he demanded. "There seem to be *two* defendants. I expected only one. Mr. Hayworth, you best explain yourself."

"Your Honor, it was not my intention to—"

"Your Honor," Lily interjected. "If I may, I would like to speak for myself."

There was a collective gasp in the audience. Even the judge pulled back a bit from her request. The judge glanced at Sheriff McAllen, who stared at his daughter, mouth agape.

When Judge Anders found his voice, he said, "You may, Mrs..."

"It's Miss. Miss Lily McAllen," she supplied.

Judge Anders jerked his head back toward the sheriff so fast Dan feared he would injure himself. But Sheriff McAllen would not remove his gaze from Lily.

"Your Honor?" Lily prompted.

"Yes, yes." Judge Anders shifted his focus. "You may speak, Miss McAllen."

Lily leaned on the table with her right arm and came around it, stepping out in front of the dais.

"Your Honor, I have come to stand in *my* rightful place with the defense because all actions taken by this man, Mr. Daniel Hayworth, were on my behalf. He took the Apache brave, Kuruk, to make an exchange and end my captivity to Kuruk's tribe."

If Judge Anders was surprised, he didn't show it. Of course, he wasn't. Brandon must have shared all of this. But that didn't mean the judge anticipated Lily's arrival. Or for her to stand with Dan. Nor did Dan. Not after this morning.

If it were possible, watching her, with all her poise, confidence, and courage, Dan fell in love with her all over again. He fought the urge to pull her into his arms and kiss her breathless.

The judge's words broke into Dan's thoughts. "Thank you, Miss McAllen. Please resume your seat with Mr. Hayworth."

She did her best to make her movements smooth and free of any limp. Again, Dan admired her strength.

"Your Honor." Sheriff McAllen spoke up. "You can't let my daughter stand there and accept punishment for what this ranch hand has—"

Judge Anders hit the table with his gavel. "I can and I will."

The people murmured.

Another hit with the gavel. "Order!" he called.

A hush fell in the church.

"Now, it is my duty to uphold the law. And to see justice is carried out—the guilty are punished and the innocent are not."

Silence.

"And this creates a problem in this situation."

No one spoke.

"Is the Apache brave, Kuruk as you call him, guilty? Perhaps, maybe, likely...but we cannot know with certainty under the law. Testimony was not collected, he was not given proper trial, nor given opportunity to be cross-examined and face his accuser.

"This was denied because he was aided and abetted by the defendant which, if he was convicted, would itself be a crime."

Dan was getting confused.

"However, since Kuruk was not convicted or sentenced, such is not the case. So, I have no choice other than to do the following."

This was hurting Dan's head. He looked at Lily.

She stared at the judge.

A quick glance at Sheriff McAllen, though, told that the lawman was not as satisfied...or perhaps he was just as confused.

"Would the defendants please rise?" Judge Anders's voice boomed.

Dan stood and shifted to offer Lily an arm, but she was already almost to her feet. So, he faced the judge.

"Mr. Daniel Hayworth, Miss Lily McAllen, it is the decision of this court that all charges are dismissed. You are free to go."

Dan was certain his knees would give out. He leaned on the table for support.

"But," the judge said, his voice loud over the crowd, "You are hereby warned that you are under careful watch—a probation of sorts. Keep your noses clean. I don't want to see either of you again."

"Yes, Your Honor," Dan said.

"Yes. Thank you, Your Honor," Lily said at the same time.

Brandon came around and took Dan's hand, pulling him into a quick hug.

Dan slapped his boss on the upper arm.

When Brandon moved on, Dan turned to speak with Lily.

Only...she was gone.

CHAPTER 18
The Value

Lily pressed breaths out of her lungs as she rushed into the churchyard. She paused and let the rhythm of her breathing even out.

What had happened in there? Had Judge Anders truly declared them free?

Then why wasn't she happy? Celebrating?

Her chin dropped as her heart fell—because it marked the end. For her and Dan. For any remaining semblance of a relationship with him. Maybe even for living in the safety afforded her with Mr. Owen and Cook.

She scanned the small town front before her. Where would she go? What would she do? Returning to her parents' house was not an option. There was the saloon...

But it didn't seem viable either. Somewhere along the way...she came to think...*more* of herself. Believe she was worth more.

She wasn't making any sense.

Yet, it was true. She couldn't make herself truly consider a life in a brothel or a saloon. Why? No one else cared what happened to her.

That did not seem honest though.

When she had been in trouble, Dan had come. Even so, she doubted he would have her now. Would she have him?

She pushed onward, toward the town's livery. It would not do to be standing here when Dan came out, in all his celebratory fineness. Would she be happy for him? Or ache?

As she neared the livery, she felt along the neckline of her dress. First, to ensure the cloth covered her birthmark as usual, then to seek out the comfort of the locket.

It wasn't there! She startled for a moment. Then remembered what had happened to it. And was sad once more for her loss. But as she closed her eyes, she could remember her grandmother's face. The woman would speak words from the Bible over Lily.

And, in times such as these, Lily could not escape it.

"The darkness cannot hide us from God; but to Him, the night shines as bright as the day."

This was grandmother sharing about her favorite Psalm. What number? One hundred and thirty-something.

Lily shook her head. It was nothing of consequence. God did not consider her more than any other animal to be used. Why should she consider Him?

Now at the livery, she requested her horse. The man nodded and moved off.

"God knew all about you before you were born, Lily. He covered you in your mother's womb."

What? Covered me in my mother's womb? As if God would have even noticed anything within that woman. Or did he have a care for Lily's mother? That would be something—God loving Ma and not caring one bit about Lily's abuse.

Maybe she wasn't worth much, then. Not even to her Creator.

"Here she is, Miss McAllen," the man said a bit loudly as he pressed the reins into her hand.

Turning her attention to the man, Lily's face warmed. Had he been speaking to her while she'd been so deep in thought?

"I thank you." Then, shifting, she moved off. As she continued to dwell in the memory, more words came, all in the voice of her grandmother.

"The Bible says, 'I will praise Thee; for I am fearfully and wonderfully made...'"

She did remember how her little girl heart marveled at God and how He must have made her like she made things from mud after it rained. But what He had crafted was so delicate, so fine...and so wondrous!

"Thine eyes did see my substance, yet being unperfect..."

Such truth. She was unperfect...in so many ways. And everyone knew it. Everything she did...and even things she didn't do...were on display for the whole of Wharton City to mull over and gossip about. How would she ever get a fair shake in this town? Or anywhere?

Maybe God was right...she was unperfect and did not merit His attention or care.

She put a foot in the stirrup and the stable keeper assisted her as she mounted the horse. After an awkward and somewhat uncomfortable ordeal, she was settled into the saddle.

Then her grandmother's voice came to her even more clearly.

"God has a special book. Where He has written down all your days. How long you will live, what great things you will do...what kinds of things will happen to you...for the rest of your life."

The mare stirred and shifted, but Lily was caught. God knew all her days? Planned out her life? Could that be true?

"Miss? You all right?"

She turned. It was the keeper. His gaze on her was rather curious.

Offering him a smile she hoped was reassuring, she said, "I'm fine. Just distracted."

He moved back toward the livery but glanced in her direction once or twice, shaking his head.

It did not stop Grandmother's voice from coming again, *"The Psalm says that God is with you when you go to sleep and when you awake..."*

Did God stay with her? Then why? Why the abuse? Why the years of pain? No...it couldn't be. She wouldn't have it.

Kicking her heels into the horse's flank, she prodded the animal into action. The mare seemed ready to comply—all but leaping forth and into a gallop. Lily gripped the reins tight and leaned over the muscled neck, letting wind rush over her.

Even the speed and rush of the wind could not drown out those words coming from within.

"I know the thoughts that I think toward you, says the Lord, thoughts of peace, and not of evil, to give you an expected end."

Expected? Nothing about her life was expected. Except, maybe, the pain.

"Then shall you call upon Me, and you will pray to Me, and I will listen to you. And you shall seek Me, and find Me, when you search for Me with all your heart."

A growl rumbled in her throat, rising, climbing, until it found its release. As it did, she jerked hard on the reins. The horse jolted to a stop, kicking up dust and dirt clumps.

"No!" she cried up at the sky. "No! You cannot say that!"

Silence.

"You can't turn this on me!"

But she knew. That's not what this was. It was an offer—she could cling to her pain and let it eat at her or surrender it into His plan.

What would she do? What would happen if she *did* let go of her bitterness?

A gentle voice whispered on the wind, *And I will be found by you.*

Getting out of the church was more difficult than Dan expected. But his mind was on one thing—getting to Lily. Where could she be?

Perhaps gone to the café? Back to the Miller ranch? Or possibly to Uncle Owen and Cook's?

Where? He couldn't spend the rest of the day searching. Time was critical. To his heart. To hers. Yes, he sensed this was the case.

He needed to find her. Soon.

Who could he ask? Who would know?

Turning this way and that in the church yard, he struggled.

But he stopped. There was no one. Or rather, no one else. Except...

Lord, show me. Help me.

And he knew.

He just knew. There was no real way to explain how. But he did.

Running, he raced for the post in town where he had tied his horse. It wasn't long before he was in the saddle and on his way.

Uncle Owen and Cook's cabin appeared in the distance. It stirred his heart, already beating hard. Would it not explode from his chest?

He didn't bother to secure the horse when he came close to the small house. Hopping down, he rushed to the door. Could he restrain himself to knock?

But he did. Pounding more than anything else on the solid door, the moments stretched into eternity before it opened.

And she was there.

Lily.

Standing there in the opening.

His chest heaved. And he wanted to pull her against himself. The image of him ripping off his hat, grabbing her, and kissing her moved like a stage show in his mind. It took all he had not to make it reality.

His breaths came too fast.

"Dan...?" Her words were weak.

Was she truly so surprised?

"I...I had to find you." His breathing evened.

"Why?" She dipped her chin and peered up at him. Then she turned and moved back into the great room.

Deflated, he watched her cross and ease into a chair. The scene from earlier in his mind vanished and gave way to this surreal picture before him.

He closed the door. And glanced around. "Where is Uncle Owen?"

She shrugged. "Went off to look in on a friend."

My father, Dan mused. He lifted his gaze and stared at Lily across the space.

She soon averted her eyes. Was his gaze so intense?

He couldn't form words.

"What do you want, Dan?"

Did her lip tremble when she spoke his name? Why was he so fixated on her mouth?

He gripped his hat, looking down as he shifted his feet.

"There are a few things I think you should know." With slow steps, he moved toward her.

"What?" She folded her uninjured arm over her midsection.

"I wanted to tell you that your father helped me that day. He caught me taking Kuruk. Could've stopped me. But he didn't. No, he let me come for you. Even asked me to bring you home."

Dan was just short of where she sat.

"My father?" She turned her gaze from him. The tears were now evident in her eyes.

"Yes," he said as he knelt in front of her, placing a hand on either arm of the chair.

"What are you doing? Why are you telling me this?" She looked at him once more.

"Because I want no more secrets between us."

There was confusion in her eyes.

"Because I love you." He leaned forward and pressed his lips to hers. Letting the connection fill him anew, strengthen him, and bring that thing deep within back to life.

Lily gave way to his kiss, melting to him as she had before. She wanted more...more of him. All of him. And this connection with him.

But she could not pay the price. Not anymore.

As she came back to herself, she pressed against his chest with her unwrapped arm.

He pulled back. "Lily?"

She looked down at the rather small space between them. "I can't."

His lips brushed against her forehead. "Can't?"

"No." She had to clear her head. Her body longed to fall into his. If she didn't put more distance between them, she would lose herself. "I can't."

She pushed harder.

He leaned away, his gaze on her.

How could she stop the tears? They were the least of her concern. And the last place to expend her strength.

"I can't do this anymore." She closed her eyes, wanting to shut out the evidence of his pain written all over his features.

"Lily, I—" he started, reaching for her.

"No." She jerked away. "How can you not see? We've been here before. This same place. And it did not end well."

"No, we haven't." His mouth was set. He seemed serious. Did he not understand what she said?

"What is different?" she challenged.

He dropped his head for a moment. Then lifted it so his eyes caught hers. "I have a confession."

Her brows furrowed. "Yes?"

"I have been so wrong."

She bit her lower lip. How she had longed to hear these words.

"I was a coward."

She closed her eyes.

"And you deserve so much more." He reached out and grazed her cheek. Then let his hand fall.

It was difficult to not lean into his touch. And even more so not to seek it again now. How could he know what these words would mean to her? What a balm to her weary heart they would be?

"I..." he started, but seemed to struggle to find his words, "...have been afraid."

She creased her forehead as her brows rose. Afraid? Dan?

"I blamed myself for failing my ma. For not being there for her when she died. And..." His words caught. "I couldn't bear the thought of failing you."

Pieces fell into place. She began to see things in a new way. From his perspective...one of a wounded heart. One that she knew all too well.

One that needed mercy...and grace.

"If you still can't forgive me, I understand. I hurt you. More than once." Dan pulled back even more, as if preparing to stand.

She gripped his sleeve.

He paused, meeting her gaze.

"Maybe you're right," she said, measuring her words, choosing them carefully. "I did deserve better. You did, too."

His countenance fell.

"But..." She reached forth and tipped his chin up, so he faced her. "I know I want you. With all your rough edges. With all the places you need extra love."

He gripped her elbow, pulling her toward himself.

"Because you already see my shortcomings. And cover them with your love." She let her gaze wander over his features, taking them in, memorizing them. "We can trust that God's grace will fill in the gaps."

Pausing, Dan's eyes searched hers.

"I have found a newness and peace in surrender. And faith. It's a start, and I am learning."

Dan moved toward her, his face a breath from hers. "Lily McAllen," he said, his voice raspy. "Will you be my wife?"

She touched the side of his face with tenderness. "I—"

He held up a finger and touched her chin. "Just so you know. There won't be any getting out this time."

She smiled, and her eyes watered. Could she ever have dreamed of being so happy? "With all my heart, I will."

His mouth pressed to hers. And they were lost to the world.

Until the door creaked opened.

And they pulled apart.

Mr. Owen and a man that seemed to be an older version of Dan stood in the doorway.

"Well, Eugene, seems we'll need that church on Saturday after all," Mr. Owen announced with a wink.

Dan laughed, the sound rumbling in his chest and vibrating through her as he held her close.

One look in Dan's direction, and she wagered that to be his intent. She hugged him as well as she could with one arm, relishing the reality that she wouldn't be parted from him again come Saturday.

Dan kissed the top of her head and murmured, "Saturday."

Dan stood beside Cutie. How much longer would it be? He would go out of his skin!

Cutie poked him. "Don't be so antsy."

Couldn't Dan just kick him and be done with it? He shot Brandon and Slim a look. They sat in the front row with Uncle Owen and his Pa.

This day had been long in coming. Yet, it had only been two days ago he and Lily had reconciled.

Still, it had been too long to wait. He wanted to know that Lily was his and his alone. And that they would never be parted.

The back door to the church opened, drawing his attention. A few other heads turned, and the pianist sat up, alert.

But it was Amanda and Cook, coming to find their seats. They maneuvered, not so gracefully with Amanda's larger girth, through the filled church to their husbands.

Wait...if they had arrived, that must mean Lily was ready. Deep breaths in and out. Dan was certain he would lose his ability to breathe if she didn't appear soon.

Mere moments later, however, the door opened and Mariena entered. She wore a simple pink dress and had pulled her hair back. Just lovely.

Smiling, she passed down the center between the two sections of pews. Once she got to the front, she made eye contact with her husband, winked at him, and moved off to the other side of the pulpit.

Then the congregation stood, and the pianist banged out bold chords.

Dan's gaze flew to the back of the church. But the door sat behind the left section of the pews. So, until she came around those standing congregants, he wouldn't be able to see her.

So, he waited. And took steady breaths.

Then she came around that corner and became visible. Dan's every thought was gone. Including his remembering to breathe.

She had worn her blue dress. The one he liked so much. With the tiny flowers. It pleased him that she thought about his preference this day.

It wasn't this that made her so beautiful though, she was radiant—her smile, her eyes. Everything about her shone when she looked at him.

And she came down the aisle toward him. Only then did he remember to breathe. He wanted to fill his senses with her, with this moment, this day, with all it meant.

After all they had been through, their attempts to escape trouble and trials, they had found the answer lay in running toward each other. And today, they would seal it with a kiss. For as long as they both should live.

Epilogue

L ily woke comfortable and at peace in the arms of the man she loved.

Bliss.

Would every morning greet her like this?

Her husband shifted beside her.

Her husband.

Was it true? Was life so good?

"Morning," he said, pressing a kiss to the side of her face, to her hair, to her neck.

"Morning." She turned onto her back. "Husband."

He leaned over her, smiling. "I like the sound of that."

"Then I will say it again." Lily threaded her fingers through his hair. "Husband."

He kissed her lips.

"Husband," she said it again.

He smiled. "I think you are doing that just to steal kisses."

"And what if I am?" She brought her hand around to rest on the side of his face. "Does that bother you? Husband."

"Not one bit." He pressed his lips to hers again, letting the kiss linger.

She tilted her head, giving him better access for a deeper kiss.

A knock sounded on the door.

Dan growled.

"Who could that be?" Lily asked, pulling the sheet over herself.

"Well, I don't know," Dan bemoaned, grabbing for his clothes. "But I'm certain they'll get an earful for disturbing my *wife* on the morning after her wedding night." He winked at her.

Overcome with awareness of her lack of decorum, she slid further under the covers.

Once decent, Dan opened the door only far enough for him to peer out.

"Slim!" Dan ground out. He did not sound happy. "This best be important."

She couldn't see Slim, thank the Lord, as Dan kept the door mostly closed. But she heard him stumbling over his words. Was he as embarrassed to have disturbed them as she was that he was here?

"Spit it out. I haven't got all day," Dan pressed.

Was it just her, or did she hear a hint of a smile under his words? Did Dan find the tiniest bit of amusement torturing Slim?

More rumblings of Slim stuttering were audible.

"What?" Any pretense of Dan's joviality was gone. "Now?"

Dan turned, shutting the door.

Lily sat up, bringing the sheet with her. "Did you just slam the door on Slim?"

"What? Uh..." He looked back at the door. "Maybe."

What was going on?

Dan seemed to forget about Slim and moved back to the bed. "Amanda is having the baby. Today. Now."

Lily widened her eyes. "What?"

"Yeah." Dan ran a hand through his hair. He looked down and to the side. Why was he not so thrilled?

Because they'd have to get dressed and join the merrymaking.

"I understand," she said, taking his hand, "That having a baby can take a long time."

He glanced at her. "Yeah?"

"Maybe hours," she said, smiling.

Leaning her over, he wrapped his arms around her. "I see, Mrs. Hayworth. Well, if that's the case. We'd best get started on ours."

She giggled as his mouth found hers.

In that moment, she prayed that from all their hardship, new life would bring an abundance of hope and joy into their lives. And soon.

Keep reading for a preview of the next book in the Convenient Risk Series!

Thank you, dear reader, for for reading along with me! If you enjoyed this story, I would sincerely appreciate if you would submit a review. It would mean so much to me!

To read more about these characters, follow along with the Convenient Risk Series. Find it at:

https://saraturnquist.com/convenient-risk-series/

Author's Note

Hello! Writing clean Historical Romance is quite the adventure...in creativity and in research. I love the marriage between fact and fiction that I must weave to make these stories a reality. And I appreciate that you come along on the journey.

For *A Convenient Escape*, I researched the historical happenings in Southeastern Arizona during the late 1800s and was pleased to rediscover Geronimo. Not that I am at all pleased with the happenings surrounding him and his band of renegades, but this piece of history is fascinating.

So, what is truth here? The facts? Geronimo, as named by the Mexican and United States soldiers, was known to his people as 'Goyahkla' or 'One Who Yawns.' He was a Medicine Man in the smallest of the Chiricahua Apache tribes, the Bedonkohe. But he was never a chief, though he led his band of Chiricahua Apache in raids against the Mexicans and Americans living in the region of the border (in Southern Arizona and Northern Mexico).

His consideration for a captured Apache brave named Kuruk is pure fiction. The character Kuruk is of my own making, as is his father. My imaginings of the person of Geronimo are, as well, my own. Though pictures of the Apache leader exist and can be found online.

In the end, Geronimo surrendered, lived in confinement from his surrender in September 1886 until he died in custody in February 1909. Before dying, he did dictate his autobiography to S. S. Barrett.

The research into Geronimo's life was intriguing, disheartening, and just sad. It was difficult to fathom how many lives he took throughout the course of his tiraid across the west. But the reality of the missteps, halftruths, and out-right lies he encountered in his life from the governments of Mexico and the United States was also hard to wrap my mind around. Does the end justify the means? Is there a real hero here? That may be up for debate. It doesn't seem as if anyone's hands were clean.

A train platform was a terrible place to catch your breath. Much less one as busy as this.

Ada Clara Miller had been knocked and bumped too many times to count. What a way to treat a lady!

She shifted, attempting to move out of the direct path of travelers. But that didn't seem to help. No matter which way she looked, people bustled about, hurried and harried.

Where was *her* train car? What time would the train leave? How much time did she have to linger? For certain, she made no progress as it was.

Reaching for her timepiece, pinned near the neckline of her dress, she checked for the hour. Had it truly been twenty minutes since she had stepped off the last train?

And all that time, she had been floundering about? Some grand adventure-seeker she had turned out to be...couldn't even manage her way through the train station. What would her brother think of her now?

She frowned. Brandon would likely send her, trunks and all, back to Richmond and make her promise never to leave again.

No. She could do this. She would.

Another bump from the side found her fighting for balance.

"Excuse me," she all but screeched. Who would be so thoughtless?

She released her timepiece and grabbed for her carrying case. But encountered resistance.

Glancing up, she met the glare of a scraggly, rough-looking man who had taken hold of her bag and pulled at it.

Had he run into her on purpose? As a ruse to distract her?

What a fiend!

Gritting her teeth, she jerked on the handle of her bag and kicked at the man. Her foot flung wild, but connected.

The man hollered as she fell, holding naught but the handle. She looked up and pushed her torso off the ground. Now in a sitting position, she could only watch the back of the man as he moved off.

"Stop that man! He stole my bag!" she yelled.

A few heads turned and looked after him, but no one moved to pursue. Nice town.

Ada pulled out a handkerchief and blotted at her eyes. How could she ever have thought she'd make it out here?

Swallowing against the lump in her throat, she worked to pull herself together. She must be a sight—sitting here, on the platform, fighting tears. But she needed the moment.

Not that anyone cared.

She took in two deep breaths. It was time. No more of this.

Two pairs of boots came to a halt just in front of her.

What did this mean? What could they want? Was she in trouble?

She looked up and saw the man who had taken her bag. He was held in place by another man—with kind eyes and a strong jaw. The would-be rescuer seemed none to happy as he held on to the ruffian's collar.

The more confident man who seemed to have the situation well under control watched her. "Ma'am, I'm afraid this miscreant has something to say to you."

She sniffled, her breath catching. Really? Right now? Would she lose all control of her emotions? Eyeing the sturdier man in the cowboy hat, who was rather handsome, she felt her face warm.

He gave the robber a good jerk.

"I'm sorry, miss," the thief said, though his heart definitely wasn't in it.

But her gaze remained fastened on her rescuer.

He turned and spoke to the man who had accosted her. He ground out, "Drop it."

The rough man hesitated.

A jabbing movement from the man who had come to her aid brought about a hiss from the other.

Her bag fell to the ground.

"Now don't cause anymore trouble," the handsome man said. He then released the rather uncomfortable-looking scoundrel who then stumbled and rushed off.

Ada's gaze was torn between her bag and the retreating figure.

Though her attention was elsewhere, she sensed more than saw the kind man move closer.

Turning toward him, she watched as he extended his hand.

"My apologies, miss. I hate that you've received such a poor reception into Arizona."

She waited for a breath, staring at his hand.

"Please, let me try to remedy that." His voice was soothing and his presence calmed her frayed nerves. Where had he been this whole trip?

Ada slid her gloved hand into his calloused palm.

He lifted her with ease.

And she was on her feet quicker than she would have thought. So much so, that she found herself closer to him than she'd expected.

He braced her arms. "Whoa, there. You all right?"

Her face heated even more. From damsel in distress to fainting flower. My, my... she was a storybook cliche.

"Yes." She took a step back, removing her hands and arms from his. "That is, I'm just fine. A little shaken is all."

She groaned inwardly. Why must she share that? As if things weren't awkward enough.

Clear blue eyes examined her features. He did seem so pleasant. And caring.

Wait. What was she thinking? She didn't know him any more than the man who'd attempted to steal her bag. Fine independent woman she'd make. Indeed.

She ran a hand down her skirt, smoothing over wrinkles that would have to be pressed out.

"I...thank you for your concern, sir. And for your assistance in retrieving my things. But I—ah—have a train to catch."

And, as a fact, she did. How soon?

Her worry must have been evident on her face as the man's brows furrowed.

"Can I help you find your train car? Get aboard?"

As if the one mishap made her completely useless! She straightened, tugging on her traveling jacket.

"No, I thank you. I am quite capable. I just need to gather my..." She crouched down and picked up her carrying case. "Bag."

It was rather awkward, picking up without the handle attached. However, after tipping it this way and that for some moments, she managed to maintain her hold on it.

"All right then, miss. I guess I'll be on my way." He tipped his hat to her and turned.

She wanted to stomp her foot. How childish her behavior! He had only wanted to help. He *had* helped. And this was how she repaid him—with her girlish, stubborn attempt to prove something.

"I..." she called after him.

He looked over his shoulder.

"Thank you." She looked at the ground as her face burned. "For your assistance."

He nodded and shot her a smile before continuing on his way.

She was thankful he did turn away when he did as her knees had weakened.

What an adventurer indeed!

To read more, find *An Inconvenient Acquaintance* here:

https://saraturnquist.com/an-inconvenient-acquaintance/

Acknowledgments

So, here I am writing Acknowledgements again...there are so many people who have influenced and touched my life while pouring into this book. They are just too numerous to count.

To everyone who asked about the process, let me talk about it or share my characters and story in development, I thank you. It is true you are part of the creation of this work in a unique way.

I can't forget my Word Weavers Page 13, who listen and read my work each month and give me valuable feedback that hone me as a writer and allow me to sharpen my skills to present better work for the world.

My Advanced Reader Team, you all are more appreciated than you know. You make my writer heart so happy!

Hannah Conway, my writing mentor, who is part of every book through advice and letting me bounce ideas off her. You are so inspiring...and I hope I can be one millionth the assistance for you one day.

Mary Wood, who really does hound me for another chapter, your feedback has been incredibly valuable. Thanks for trouble-shooting and plotting with me.

My editor extraordinaire, Julie Sherwood, I don't know how I would be where I am as a writer without you kicking my butt and keeping me honest each and every novel. Keep it real. Every. Time.

Cora Graphics, you turn out a cover that amazes me each time. And I adore your talent and love for what you do.

VerBull Photography, thanks for getting my "good side" :-)

My husband and number one fan, Greg Turnquist, this quarantine has been nuts, but you still made time for this book to happen. You are it, babe. We're doing it.

For my sister, you make me want to be better. For my dad, you make me feel so good to have achieved this dream of writing. For my mom, I will love you forever. And for my kids, you give me every reason to smile.

Last, but certainly not least, my readers, you give me a reason to keep writing.

A Less Convenient Path (Book 3)

She is in a hopeless situation. He doesn't have a chance.

Mariena's native nation has been ordered to a Reservation but her tribe was attacked en route. She and her young brother wander in a wilderness filled with dangerous animals. Until...

Cutie happens upon them as he flees his own demons. Can Mariena awaken something he never expected? Even bring him to believe in himself once more?

A story of two people without peace. Will they find in each other the very things they are missing?

A Convenient Escape (Book 4)

She has nowhere to go. He has nothing to lose.

Lily has known hardship and rejection. Her brother takes a job at the Miller ranch. Now with no ally, she becomes desperate to get away...by any means necessary.

Dan is prepared to do whatever it takes to ensure Lily is cared for... even if that means proposing marriage.

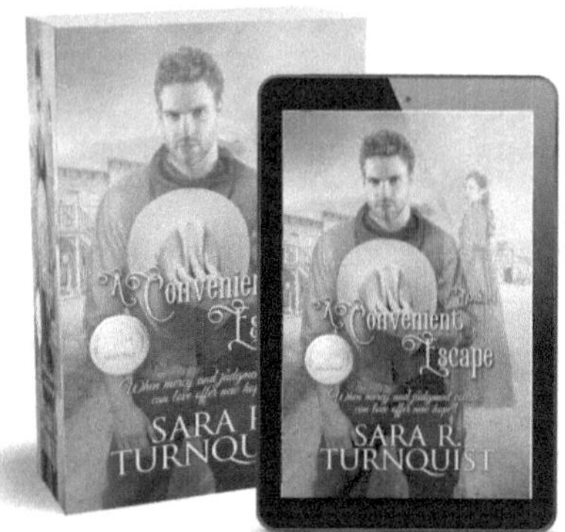

Will they make it to the church? Or find themselves victims of lies, disillusionment, or the ire of an Apache rebel?

An Inconvenient Acquaintance (Book 5)

She wants adventure. He needs a place to belong.

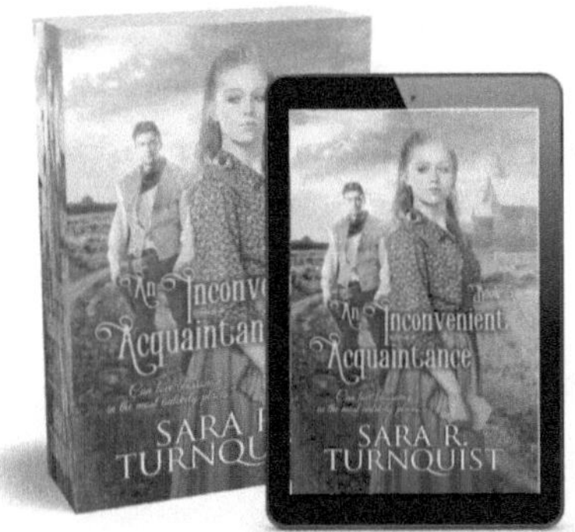

Ada the new schoolteacher in Tombstone. Her desire for independence stems from tales of the west. But she never expected to find herself torn between two men—one who promises safety and security, the other's future is uncertain and offers excitement.

Slim is determined that he will not become involved with a woman of privilege, Ada's fiery personality intrigues him. And soon he is vying for her heart with a man he'd rather not trifle with.

Will they find what they seek in each other? Or will they become caught up in a shootout at the O.K. Corral?

These Golden Years (Book 6)

A collection of short stories through the year.

Dorothy "Cook" Miller and "Uncle" Owen Miller are living their best life and marriage. Though it is not without bumps along the way. Join them as they walk through the year together with its measure of mishaps and laughs. This collection of short stories shows that marriage can be fraught with misunderstanding. But also has its share of lighter moments.

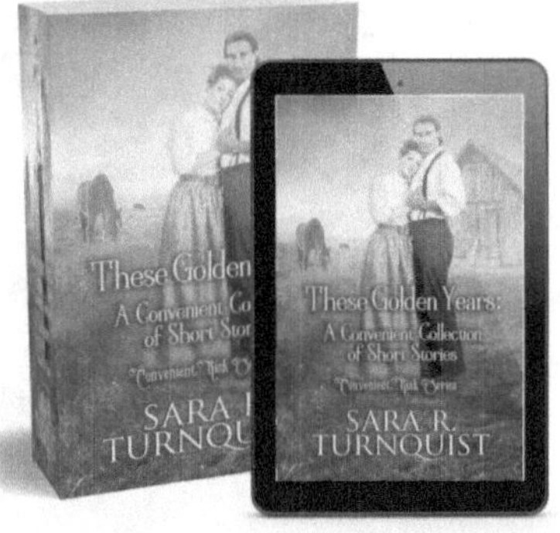

An Less Convenient Arrangement (Book 7)

She has lost all hope. He has little desire to stay by her side.

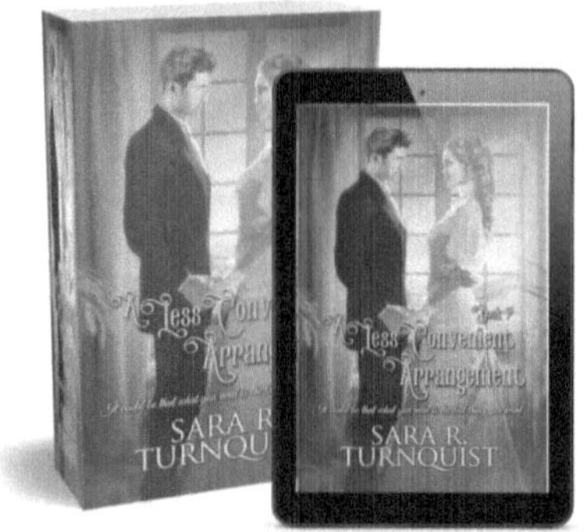

Sadie finds herself in dire straits after her father absconds with everyone's money. Her mother's failing mental stability also becomes a trial she is not certain she can overcome. Is there anywhere she can turn?

Though his one goal is to return to Richmond and a partnership in his father's law firm, David is drawn to Sadie and softens to her plight. He offers what help he can, but resists being pulled into the mess that has become her life. Until he starts to care beyond that initial attraction.

Can she stand strong against the challenges facing her?
Will David risk following his heart regardless of the cost?
Or take the first out offered to him?

Ranch Hands Collection

Four Stories from the Miller Ranch

About the Author

Sara is a coffee lovin', word slinging, Historical Romance author whose super power is converting caffeine into novels. She loves those odd little tidbits of history that are stranger than fiction. That's what inspires her. Well, that and a good love story.

But of all the love stories she knows, hers is her favorite. She lives happily with her own Prince Charming and their gaggle of minions. Three to be exact. They sure know how to distract a writer! But, alas, the stories must be written, even if it must happen in the wee hours of the morning.

Sara is an avid reader and enjoys reading and writing clean Historical Romance when she's not traveling.

Please follow along with her journey through her newsletter at: http://
saraturnquist.com/list

Happy Reading!

facebook.com/AuthorSaraRTurnquist

instagram.com/sararturnquist

x.com/sararturnquist

youtube.com/@SaraRTurnquist

pinterest.com/sararturnquist